BEYOND THE STARS AND SHADOWS

BEYOND THE STARS AND SHADOWS

KRISTEN MARTIN

BLACK FALCON PRESS

For information contact:

Black Falcon Press, LLC

https://www.blackfalcon.press.com

Library of Congress Control Number: 2021907245

ISBN: 978-1-7361585-4-8 (hardback)

Cover Illustration by Damonza © 2021

10 9 8 7 6 5 4 3 2 1

For those who believe in things unseen...
and all of the mysteries that lie in between.

1

WHO WOULD HAVE thought it possible to have a mid-life crisis at twenty-eight?

Such youth. Such zest. So much life yet to be lived.

Until I heard the one word that changed everything.

Pregnant.

I hadn't given much thought to this happening. I, unlike most of the female species, did not have dreams of "the perfect marriage" or starting a family of my own. Hell, I wasn't even sure what was happening when my soon-to-be-fiancé got down on one knee. It was sweet, I suppose. And unexpected. And downright terrifying.

But *kids*? I didn't know I had a line to be drawn, but it turns out I did. It was quite a big one, too.

I know what it is I'm "supposed" to say. Something along the lines of . . . *I may not have wanted kids, but I'd do it for him. For us. For our family.* Or . . . *I never considered becoming a mother, but now that I'm about to be one, I couldn't imagine things happening any other way.*

But I'm not going to say any of that. Why? Because it's the furthest thing from the truth.

Before you go on and judge me (*yeah, I see you*), I want to preface this by saying that I had a less than traditional upbringing.

My mother? Hardly remember her.

My father? Incarcerated when I was eleven.

Why, you might ask? Because of the sudden disappearance of my mother—in which *he* was the primary suspect. So much so, they locked him up for it.

He's been behind bars ever since.

When you grow up in a dysfunctional home setting like that, it really makes you question everything. I remember hearing the girls at school talk about their "dream man" and their "dream weddings", and I honestly wanted nothing more than to punch them in the face.

I was twelve.

I was also living with my recently divorced—thrice over—harebrained aunt, whom I ran away from on a regular basis. *I mean, wouldn't you?* Between the disappearance of her sister; her brother-in-law being a total sociopath; and inheriting *me*, the irony of "coming home" was too much for me to wrap my head around, seeing as I never got to know what a "home" was in the first place. And so, the thought of providing *that*—something so foreign, so unknown—for our soon-to-be family of three scared the living shit out of me.

To make matters worse, my fiancé and I hadn't exactly had the whole "kids" discussion. After peeing on an ungodly amount of pregnancy tests, I knew it wasn't a fluke. I also knew I had to tell him.

The first words that came out of my mouth?

"I'm sorry."

How's that for a pregnancy announcement?

We're equal parts responsible, buddy, and yet here I am, apologizing for something I'm not even sure I wanted in the first place.

His response?

"How far along? Will you be showing at the wedding?"

Shallow fuck.

With all the hormones coursing through my body, I'm surprised I didn't clock him in the face right then and there. I'm also surprised that I didn't leave him. But if you've ever been engaged before—if you've ever planned a *wedding* before—then you know that once you're in, it's nearly impossible to claw your way out . . . no matter how badly you might want to.

After a tearful, hormonal, wreck-of-a-week later, I went in for an ultrasound. Alone. I was staring at that stupid ring on my finger, wondering how I'd ended up here—engaged to a man (ahem, *boy*) I couldn't stand, about to face the reality of becoming a mother when I never had the full experience of having one myself. All thanks to the one person who *vowed*, swore up and down, to protect her. Who's now rotting in jail like the prick he is.

What a fucking joke.

If I sound bitter, it's because I am. While other kids were having birthday parties and celebrating the holidays, I was in a fucking courtroom. Testifying.

Let me reiterate: I was twelve.

No kid should ever be subjected to that.

No kid should ever be subjected to *me*.

I mean, look at what I've become. You're probably thinking . . . *she's the protagonist of this story?* Damn right, I am. Don't act like you don't have shadows and baggage, too. We all do. Welcome to being human.

I digress. Where were we?

Oh, right. The doctor's office.

So I'm miserably engaged, unwillingly pregnant, and utterly alone, waiting for the doctor to return with the results of my ultrasound. I should have guessed by his abrupt exit that when he re-entered, he'd be wearing anything but a smile. I'll never forget the way his mouth pressed into a grim line. The way he spoke the words that, once again, altered my entire reality.

"There's no heartbeat."

Oh.

Based on the information I had given him, I'd only been about seven or eight weeks along, so yes, quite early for an ultrasound; but it was the blood test that sealed my fate. Urine tests are only so reliable—but blood? There's no denying the story *it* tells. And this story?

No longer pregnant.

"Most likely a miscarriage. One in eight women have them, many occurring *before* the woman is even aware she's pregnant."

Hmm.

As much as I'd like to describe the tidal wave of emotions that washed over me in that moment, I can't. To this day, they still confuse me. There was relief, yes. But there was also a lingering sense of failure. Betrayal. And *sadness.* It's strange how even when it's something you thought you didn't want, the feeling of *loss* is right there to remind you of what *could have been* . . . how things *might* have played out differently had life's circumstances been different.

It's cruel. Palpable. Unrelenting.

I wouldn't wish that feeling upon anybody.

That was in October. I'll never forget it—the changing of the leaves as I pushed the hospital doors open, a paper bag in one hand with a free month of birth control (ha!), a prescription in the other, and tears streaming down my face from behind my sunglasses.

If you're assuming my fiancé and I are no longer together, you would be correct. That was the first thing I did when I got home. Threw the birth control in his face and told him to give it to his next girlfriend. Left the ring on the counter. Stormed into the bedroom and started packing a bag . . . when I realized that it's *my* house. So I grabbed *his* suitcase instead and told him to pack his shit and get out of my life. He didn't say anything. Didn't so much as flinch. Didn't yell. Didn't cry. Didn't even fucking apologize. His silence spoke volumes as he rolled his suitcase out the door, started up his truck, and drove off.

I haven't heard from him since.

And I wouldn't hear from him ever again after the news reported a tragic accident involving him flipping his truck into a ditch, just four months after we'd split. Two unexpected losses within one year, both involving what could have been my potential "future". *Chaos theory at its finest,* my mother would have said.

It was brutal in the most incomprehensible way.

Because I'd felt truly and completely . . . alone.

With my dysfunctional family situation, I'd had no one to tell the engagement was off. No one to tell that my ex-fiancé had *died.* No one to give a damn about my life except for me. Call me cruel and heartless, but at that point, as far as I was concerned, it'd never even happened. None of it. Best to just forget and move on.

Believe me, I've tried.

It wasn't until later that next year, after I'd rid myself of everything that reminded me of him—including that house—that I was (apparently) due for a reminder. I had just slid into a relaxing bubble bath after a long day of working at the university library, when the strangest sensation came over me. I remember clenching my jaw as the entire lower half of my body contracted . . . and released. I figured it was just due to cramping—I've been known to have severe cycles a time or two—but my diagnosis changed *real* quick when it happened again.

And again.

5

Shorter bursts.

Immense pain.

Accelerated breathing.

I sound like I'm about to go into labor.

Sharp stabbing. Squeezing. Tension.

Wanting to hold my breath but realizing it's too painful.

Unusual breathing patterns.

*I **feel** like I'm about to go into labor.*

I reached across the ledge of the tub for my phone. Checked the date. July 17, 2029. Did a quick count on my fingers. And lo and behold, it had been nine months.

Another contraction, this one *brutal.*

I made a sound that I've never made before.

It sounded—and felt—like a *push.*

How? Why? This is impossible.

Jaw clenched, I gripped the edges of the porcelain tub, my knuckles turning white. A grunt.

Another push.

And another.

Zero possibility of it being menstrual cramps.

And on and on it went.

Until the water turned lukewarm.

Until it lost its heat entirely.

Sweating. Shaking, Stuck between hot and cold.

Confused at the impossibility of this moment.

It felt like *hours* had passed until my gut-wrenching cry.

And then, *finally* . . . sweet, sweet release.

Misty-eyed, I looked down at the water, at the crystal-clear surface. Just as it'd been before. As if nothing had even happened.

And that's when I knew . . .

That there are far more realities that exist beyond this one.

2

THE MOON IS especially bright tonight. As I lay on the roof of my apartment complex, splayed out like a starfish with one foot jammed between the door and its frame, a feeling of ease washes over me. I've always had an affinity for the sky, the stars, the moon—the immensity of it all, the endless expanse that is space. How we got here. Where we came from. Why we're here.

Even with my shitty childhood, I've always liked to pretend that each star is a clue of some sort, each constellation a gateway to another realm, one that holds a certain set of answers for each stage of our evolution . . .

A way to escape.

I often wonder where that escape was four years ago.

I really could have used it then . . .

My thoughts scatter as the metal bar running along the middle of the door begins to beep. *Already?*

With a sigh, I take one more mental snapshot of the sky above me—the focal point being the Majesty herself, the Moon—before sitting upright and using the doorframe to slide into the dank stairwell. The hair on the back of my neck stands, and I can't help but do a double take. I don't know what it is I expect to see, but the shadows up here, the ones that dance and sway against the brick walls, can be quite deceiving. It's almost as if they want company—like I've been chosen. Selected. The perfect companion for loneliness.

Indeed, misery loves company.

Oftentimes there's such a pull, I almost feel bound. Like it's pulling and I'm pushing. Two resisting forces. Like I *can't* leave, even if I wanted to. Like something is determined to keep me here . . .

But not tonight.

Lights flickering, I grab onto the paint-chipped railing and hoist myself to my feet. I can hear the pressure gauge on the door release as it shuts behind me. I take the steps two at a time, counting the floors as I reach the landing of each one. *Eight. Seven. Six. Five.* Fourth floor.

I grab the handle and yank the door open, knowing full well that with too little force, it'll stick. I smile as it glides open, catching a glimpse of my reflection in the narrow glass pane. To say I'm overdue for a haircut is an understatement. Blonde waves meet scraggly navy ends at my shoulders, my messy fringe now completely covering my chestnut eyebrows (thanks, mom), even going so far as to tickle the tops of my eyelids.

First order of business: find a pair of scissors.

One glance at my watch indicates that time's gotten away from me . . . *yet again.* Judging from the silence in the hall and the lack of light underneath the long line of doors, everyone's asleep. Seeing as it's three o'clock in the morning, I don't blame them.

When I finally reach the end of the hall, I slip into my studio-size apartment and remove my coat. The chill from outside remains, sending shivers down my spine the moment my fingers make contact. I secure it onto the hook behind the door, walk past the kitchen (which is a single island with a sink and a stovetop), then make my way to the living room, which happens to double as my bedroom. Definitely a downgrade from my former house, but eh, what can ya do?

I situate myself on top of the bed, but not before grabbing my laptop from the nightstand. An array of fingerprints graces the illuminated screen. I sigh, using the back of my shirt sleeve to try to get rid of them, but it only smears the unwanted collection, making the whole situation even worse than before.

I log in to my email, immediately feeling overwhelmed by the number of bolded items on the screen. I start the process of sorting through each of them, paying close attention to the ones from my boss, Professor Haven.

Hmm. More than I'd anticipated—a whopping twelve compared to his usual four or five.

Reading them in full, I tag the ones I need to review once more or follow up on for clarification. Only then do I realize what day it is. *Shit.*

Shit shit shit.

I scroll all the way down to the end of the list, opening the starred email that contains the application to renew my position as "Professor's Assistant" for the next semester. The timestamp haunts me.

Due at midnight tonight.

Now technically yesterday since it's past 3 A.M.

I groan, hitting my hand against the keyboard. Once again, my stargazing has severely interrupted my responsibilities in the waking world. As I often do, I start running through multiple scenarios in my mind. I've been Professor Haven's assistant for three full semesters now. He's a bit on the eccentric side, but he seems to like me nonetheless—we get along, I turn in my work *mostly* on time—in my opinion, we've got a good thing going. Surely he'd consider my application, even if it *is* just a few hours late? To make matters worse, it's Friday night (now Saturday morning), meaning I won't have an answer from him for two whole days.

I glance up from my computer, my gaze traveling from one wall to the other. The state of my apartment is much like the state of my life—cramped, messy, and rapidly unraveling. Trying not to feel like my livelihood hangs in the balance (*when doesn't it, though?*), I open the application and begin filling it out.

Name: Elara Friis
Date of Birth: May 11, 2000
Residence: 1762 N. Pine Grove Lane Apt #4144
Denver, CO 80204

My fingers unwillingly stop their typing. *Don't go there, don't go there* . . . My eyes travel back up the screen before focusing on my birth date—the one I also happen to share with my mother. Different year, of course, but May eleventh. It should be a happy day, a celebratory day—a mother and daughter sharing the moment they each entered this world . . . but now it just reminds me that she's gone.

Unsolved.

Forgotten by everyone except for me.

I shake the thought away as I force myself to answer the remaining questions. Luckily, I've done this before, my fingers flying across the keyboard as I answer each question in the exact same way as all applications prior to this one. Even with my emotional detour, I manage to finish it in record time and hit submit. The confirmation email pings in my inbox and, much to my surprise, a chat window appears at the same time.

Professor Haven: *I was starting to wonder if you'd finally quit on me.*

I smirk before typing back, *Me? Quit? Never. But hey, thanks for the reminder.* I pause before adding, *You're up late.*

Professor Haven: *Late? It's early. And who said anything about reminders? Might I remind you who the assistant is in this scenario? I knew you'd remember to submit it . . . eventually.*

I let out a sigh of relief. *So we're good for another semester?*

His answer sends me right back into a tailspin. *I know this is asking a lot for a Saturday, but I need you to come in. Can you be at my office by noon?*

His request gives me pause. *Is everything okay?*

Professor Haven: *Noon, Elara.*

I watch with trepidation as his online indicator fades from view and the chat box disappears. In an effort to keep my feelings of unease at bay, I begin to scroll through the emails he'd sent earlier, looking for some reference point, something to hint at what this meeting might be about, but there's just a bunch of midterm essays in need of scoring.

My eyes travel to the upper right corner of my screen. 3:55 A.M. There's no point in trying to sleep. I may as well get a head start on these papers, seeing as they're due on Monday anyway.

I load the first document, once again catching my reflection in the screen. I can't help but revert to my original train of thought. *First things first: find some damn scissors.*

3

RAINDROPS SPLATTER ACROSS the windshield of my Jeep Wrangler as I make a left out of the apartment complex onto the main road. Much to my surprise, I actually *had* fallen asleep in the middle of grading papers and had awoken with just enough time to take a quick shower, throw my hair into two messy braids, top my ensemble off with a beanie, and grab my completely drained laptop before hitting the road. As it always does, the clock taunts me. 11:53 A.M.

I don't live far from campus, but seven minutes?

Even for me, that's pushing it.

The stoplight ahead shifts from yellow to red. I come to a screeching halt while simultaneously digging in my center console for something to eat. My fingers graze a small plastic tub of trail mix with dried cranberries and peanuts. *Ah, breakfast of champions.*

Between stuffing my face and hitting every red light, I finally pull into my designated parking space at the University of

Colorado Boulder. The tree towering above me releases one of its leaves, fresh dew still dotted along a canvas of red and orange. It floats onto the hood of my car, only to be picked up by a gust of wind from the impending storm. I swing my car door open, the sound of more fallen leaves crunching underneath my boots. A shiver creeps down my spine as the wind picks up again. I love the fall here, but I'll be damned if it isn't chillier than usual.

I reach back into my car, leaning over the driver's seat to grab my laptop and my cell phone, searching far and wide for my bag, only to realize that I'd left it at home. With a sigh, I secure my phone in my back pocket and tuck my laptop underneath my arm before climbing out of the Jeep. Raindrops hit my face as I rush toward the Astronomy Sciences building. I don't bother to look at the clock on the wall because I already know what it says: LATE.

The elevator doors open and I round one corner, then another, before booking it as fast as I can—slippery boots and all—down the hall. The door to Professor Haven's office is slightly ajar. I don't bother knocking as I poke my head inside, but he's nowhere in sight. My gaze lands on his desk, searching until I see a sticky note smack dab in the middle of the desktop computer.

Elara: Room 108B.

That's at the other end of the building.

Gritting my teeth, I step into the office and hastily pull the note from the monitor before heading back the way I came. First corner, second corner, elevator down. I pick up the pace as I jog to the end of the hall, the numbers growing larger as I whizz past them. When I finally reach Room 108B, I'm panting and a bit frazzled, but I don't so much as bother to pause and collect myself. I burst through the doors, immediately spotting Professor Haven hunched over a desk at the front of the lecture hall. Papers are strewn everywhere and only when I'm halfway down the steps does he look up from whatever has him so preoccupied.

He doesn't greet me, which is odd—he just gestures with one hand to come closer while adjusting his glasses with the other. As I draw nearer, something gives me pause. Perhaps it's the disheveled state of his graying hair or the crinkles at his eyes that seem to have spread since I last saw him, but something's *off.* A spritely man, there's something noticeably different about him in this moment—something that goes beyond just being "tired" or "not getting a good night's sleep". He looks . . . *troubled.*

I drop my laptop onto the desk, wincing as it *thunks* against the hard surface. My eyes rove the piles of essays before me, realizing that about half of them are ones currently sitting in my inbox, awaiting their lettered fate. I shift my attention to Professor Haven, who's still hunched over on the other side of the desk, rifling through one of the drawers.

"I see you went old school," I say, hoping to break the silence. "I haven't seen this much *paper* in decades. Is there something I can help you find?"

The frown on his face seems to indicate that my question's landed wrong, but he doesn't respond right away. A few moments later he says, "How can something be found when it doesn't even exist in the first place?"

Ah, yes. Haven and his riddles. I've grown quite accustomed to them, although I can't say I'm necessarily fond of them. "What do you have there?" I ask, pointing to the folder in his hands.

"*This* is a record of every student I've ever taught. First and last name. Student ID number." He flips through the pages for emphasis. "I've searched far and wide and *he* doesn't exist."

I angle my head, confused. "Come again?"

"This paper . . ." His voice trails off as he continues his search, scattering the many piles sitting atop his desk. "Have you read this one?"

Before I've even had the chance to register his question, he flings a thick stapled packet right at my face. I manage to catch it, thanks to my catlike reflexes, but not without some mild effort. I skim through the pages, vaguely recognizing the text, noticing that some of the sentences jump out more than others. "Axel Volaris," I say, the name sliding off my tongue like butter. "Perhaps he's a new student?"

"I have no record of him. I wasn't notified either. I spent all day yesterday checking with the other professors, even going so far as to check with University Administration."

"And?"

"He isn't in the system."

"Maybe it's a mistake," I offer with a shrug. "Or maybe he's a transfer?" Even as I say the words, I have a hard time believing them. Universities are like prisons. They know exactly who's in and who's out at all times, as well as how much you owe—and they'll be damned if they don't squeeze you for every cent you're worth. Sometimes I think the alumni have it worse than the students who are currently enrolled.

"There's always a paper trail," he mumbles.

I stand there in silence, watching as he continues to talk to himself. Suddenly, it feels like I'm intruding on a very private conversation. I turn to leave, but he stops me. "You really don't recognize it, Elara?"

His tone is so off-putting, so *unlike* him, that I begin to read the paper, line by line. I can feel him watching me, his eyes searing into the side of my skull like coals in a burning fire. I'm halfway through the first page when it hits me right between the eyes. This is *my* paper—one I'd written for this very class . . . *twelve years ago.*

Professor Haven swivels his desktop monitor toward me. "Ran a check for plagiarism. It's a 98% match."

My throat catches before I even speak. "How is that even possible? I've never uploaded *any* of my previous classwork or essays, unless it was to the university's servers when I was enrolled here—*twelve years ago.*"

"Servers which, as an assistant, you've had full access to."

I gape at him, baffled. "Are you saying that you think I . . . helped a student *plagiarize*?"

"I don't know how else this *Axel* character could have gotten your paper—unless you willingly gave it to him or he's some cyber-hacker who got past the servers' firewall." He shakes his head. "Unfortunately, that isn't all. It seems more students have caught on, directly quoting entire sections of your original paper—almost half the class. And after what's happened in years prior, I simply cannot ignore it. There's a reason Dean Lawrence put strict policies into place with regard to hiring past students as Professors' Assistants—plagiarism being at the top of the list."

"Professor Haven," I say, my panic rising, "I had no part in this. I can't even begin to guess *how* the students got access to my paper, but they certainly didn't get it from me."

"Regardless, this doesn't look good because once *I* submit these to the server . . ."

"But, Professor, you said it yourself—this *Axel* person doesn't even exist! There's no paper trail."

"I'm afraid there's no way around it, Elara. I can't report half the class for suspension or expulsion, not when the common denominator is a paper that *you* wrote."

"Twelve years ago!" I nearly shout. "A paper that I don't even *have* anymore! This is a mistake, a misunderstanding." I can feel my bottom lip begin to quiver, so I quickly bite down on it, nearly drawing blood.

"As much as I want to believe that, what this looks like is a former student with an A paper who slapped a fake name on it and willingly distributed it to current students to help with their midterm essays."

The false accusation causes my head to spin.

"It's happened before, Elara. Not with you, but with previous assistants in other departments." His voice drops to just above a whisper. "I'm a tenured professor. This cannot—*will not*—happen in my department. I will do whatever is necessary to ensure that. And seeing as assistant applications were due yesterday and yours was submitted after the deadline . . ." He exhales a loud sigh before setting his hand on the edge of the desk. His remorse is palpable. "I need your badge, Elara."

The realization of what he's just said hits me like a ton of bricks. "Professor . . ."

"Despite this unfortunate turn of events," he says, gesturing to the plagiarized papers littering his desk, "it has been a pleasure these past three semesters. Truly."

I stare at him, dumbfounded, unable to blink, move, or breathe. *This isn't happening.* I wait for him to apologize, to crack a joke, to change his mind, to *believe* me . . . but his expression holds firm. I unwillingly drop the badge onto the desk, even though what I really feel like doing is flinging it at his face. "I'll say it one more time, Professor. For the record. I have *never* heard the name Axel Volaris, and I have *never* been an accessory to plagiarism."

He keeps his eyes trained on the desk as he says, "You are dismissed, Elara. I thank you immensely for your time. You have been a great help to me over the years. You will not be easy to replace."

There's an undeniable finality to his voice, and it takes everything in me to fight back the tears piercing my eyes. I know better than to beg—his mind is made up. I may have just lost my job, but I'll be damned if I lose my dignity, too.

"The pleasure was all mine, Professor." The words feel foreign as they leave my mouth, like some robotic presence has taken over. I gather my belongings, then head toward the lecture hall doors for the very last time.

4

THIS SHIT DAY definitely calls for a pick-me-up. Even though I'm now officially unemployed—and beyond broke, I might add—the first place I head to is my favorite café. Situated just off campus on the corner of University Boulevard and Reicher Street, I've drank more coffee and graded more papers here than I can count.

The warmth envelopes me as I step foot inside the establishment, the scent of freshly ground coffee beans floating around me. A welcome reprieve from the biting cold, I pull my beanie off, hair matted against my head. I undo my braids, quickly running my fingers through the slightly tangled strands, before waving to Kensie, my favorite barista, who also happens to be my closest friend. I signal to him to make me the usual—a chai tea latte—before snagging my favorite spot in the joint: a worn-in oversize leather chair next to a faux fireplace, complete with a matching ottoman *and* an end table.

Many a day I've spent in this very spot, happily cooped up, surrounded by papers and books, high on one too many caffeinated beverages. Kensie's even joked (although I wish he were serious) about getting a plaque inscribed just for me—one that would hang on the wall, right above my chair. Of course, I think it's a *brilliant* idea, and I'm always a bit disappointed when I walk in and see that there's still no plaque . . . *yet.*

Just as I'm getting situated, Kensie approaches me with a steaming white cup and saucer. I gently take it from him, admiring the beautiful flower he's so artfully crafted into the foam before taking a long, delicious sip. I can't help but let out a long sigh, momentarily feeling like all is right in the world . . .

But then reality hits.

Kensie seems to notice this sudden shift because he asks, "Too much foam?"

The look in those amber eyes is so earnest that I quickly shake my head before shooting him a small smile. "This," I say, holding up the cup, "is absolutely perfect."

He grins, pressing his palms together in a prayer-life fashion before bowing his head, his dreadlocks bouncing with the movement. "Happy to hear it. Let me know if you need anything else."

I'm about to spill my soul to him when a group of five students walks through the door. I force another smile. "Looks like you've got your hands full."

"Mallory had the audacity to bail today, on a *Saturday* of all days, so it's just me. Can't say I'm surprised." He rolls his eyes. "Talk later?"

"Wait," I say, shuffling around in my pockets for my wallet— but before I can pay for my drink, he's already turned away from me.

"It's on the house," he says from over his shoulder as he hurries back to the counter.

Smiling, I set my drink on the end table before sinking into the plush leather chair. I kick my feet up onto the ottoman before setting my computer on my lap. I open it, the screen flashing briefly, before remembering I'd drained it last night— and, because I'd woken up late, I hadn't had the chance to charge it. I look down to my left, smiling at the charger that's already plugged into the wall. Kensie really does think of everything.

I sip on my coffee until the battery has just enough juice for me to log in. I'm about to open my inbox when it dawns on me that I don't need to check emails nor grade any papers. *Because I no longer have a job.* Not only that, but I was fired for something I *didn't* do.

Feeling disheartened—and slightly infuriated—I'm about to close my laptop when I get an idea. I click on the web browser and, without hesitation, type in the name *Axel Volaris.* I don't know what it is I expect to find, but one thing's obvious: it isn't exactly a commonplace name. I scan the first page of results before scrolling to the bottom. Nothing of interest. I click to the next page and the next until my eyes burn. *Seems my search has yielded absolutely nothing.* Annoyed, I slam the screen shut, then hastily reach for my latte.

I'm mid-sip when my gaze wanders to the front of the café, just outside the window. I blink, then blink again when I realize there's someone standing there . . . a man. A man who seems to be staring *right at me.*

The world around me seems to stop in place.

There's that strange pull again.

Because it's dreary out, I only catch a glimpse of him before he disappears. My brain tries to rationalize what I've just seen . . . before making the connection with the rooftop last night.

Not surprisingly, my curiosity gets the better of me.

I slide out of my seat, using my laptop to reserve my spot (not that I really need to), then rush over to the door. I do my best not to cause too much of a scene, but I can immediately sense Kensie's distress. As much as I don't want to tear my eyes away from the rain-spotted window, I glance at my friend with the most reassuring half-smile I can muster, even adding a little wave to let him know everything's fine.

I push the door open, then turn right. I walk a few paces, but I don't spot anyone up ahead. I stop in my tracks, squinting as I look across the street, then behind me. No sign of him. I decide to jog to the stop sign at the end, puddles splashing around me as I go. I turn the corner, but the intersection is empty.

A chill sweeps across the back of my neck.

With my hands in my pockets, hair now drenched, I powerwalk back to the café. I rack my brain for an image, a memory, of what he looked like. *What was he wearing? What color was his hair? Was he tall?*

Yes, I *think* he was tall, but that's all I've got.

Or perhaps I'm just seeing things. *Jobless and delusional. We've got ourselves a real winner here.*

I'm sopping wet when Kensie greets me at the door, eyes alight with concern. "Everything okay?" He hands me a small towel.

"I thought I saw . . ." He waits for me to finish, but I think better of it. I squeeze the water from my hair before handing the towel back to him. "Never mind. It's been a strange day."

"Would it be better with a cranberry almond scone?"

I can't help but grin. "Why, yes. Yes, it would."

"Hey, you're coming to open mic night, right?" he says as he turns to head back to the counter.

I follow behind him, suddenly feeling like the worst friend ever. "Oh . . . that's tonight, isn't it?"

He plucks a scone from the glass case and tucks it into a brown paper sleeve. "Don't tell me you forgot. And don't you dare bail on me. Mallory's already filled that quota for the day."

I grimace as I take the bag from him. "If I'm being honest, I did forget. And after a day like today . . ."

"Stop right there. You are not leaving me to deal with a bunch of college freshmen *alone*. I can hardly stand them sober."

I chuckle at that. Over the years, open mic night has turned into a bit of a free-for-all. Students, especially those underage, have made it a habit of sneaking in booze to spike their coffees while listening to the meta ramblings of their peers. The owner had cared at first and had almost banned it altogether, but after learning what kind of trouble kids were actually getting into nowadays, he'd decided to let them enjoy their art with a little bit of alcohol. He'd even gone so far as to hire buses to pick them up *and* take them home. Better to give them an alternative to the usual weekend "rager". It's been a hit ever since.

"Come on," Kensie coos, wiping the counter with a touch of flair. "There'll be our usual provisions. And, from the sound of it, *'after a day like today'*, it's the perfect excuse. I'm not taking no for an answer."

I glance at him, my eyes drifting to the stock room in the back. It *has* been a while since I've had a good ol' Bailey's and coffee. "Fine," I sigh. "Nine o'clock, right?"

He beams at his victory. "See you there, E."

I give him a cheeky grin before popping the rest of the scone into my mouth and heading out the door.

That night, I'm dressed in black leggings and an oversize charcoal sweater, hair thrown up in a messy bun with the largest-framed glasses I can find. Might as well look the part if

I'm going to suffer through this. Okay, so it's normally not *that* bad, but some nights . . . some nights it's downright atrocious.

As I pass by the café windows, I can already see the crowd that's gathered—hence another reason why I have my designated "spot". Even though Kensie's technically working tonight, he's sitting in my chair with his feet propped up, clearly waiting for me to arrive. I grab the handle of the door and pull it open, rolling my eyes as he frantically beckons me over with an insane flourish of his hand. "I was starting to think you'd bailed."

I glance at the time on my phone, then show it to him. "It's five after."

"Might as well be an hour." He angles his head near the makeshift stage. "Just look at the line they've formed already."

"Eager, aren't they?" I notice the clipboard in his lap. "Stage duty?"

He makes a gagging sound. "It seems Mallory decided to show up after all. *Somehow,* she got here before me, so she called dibs on counter duty." He pouts. "So yes, I get to deal with the little artists-to-be."

"You know they're only like, ten years younger than us, right?"

"Try fifteen," he scoffs, getting up from the chair. He starts to head toward the counter, but not before slipping two miniature bottles of Bailey's into my hand. "I'll have your drink right out, Miss," he says at an obnoxious volume as he weaves through the budding crowd.

I smile, shaking my head as I take a seat. Within seconds, the lights begin to dim, and I can only hope that Kensie shows up with that coffee stat. The first presenter walks toward the stage, unfolding a crumpled piece of paper from his pocket. Hands shaking, he grabs the mic.

"This poem is called Fleet Charm."

I tilt my head, amused. Surely two words I've *never* heard together, but hey, that's what open mic night is all about. He clears his throat, but I hardly hear the beginning, or any part of it, really, as Kensie stalks toward me, two steaming mugs in hand.

He sets them down on the table and pulls up a folded chair he'd hidden behind mine. "Your coffee, Madame."

I frown at him. "I thought these were for me," I say, clinking the two mini liquor bottles together.

"Share much?" he swipes one of them from my hand with a grin. "If we're starting off with a winner like *Fleet Charm*, you *know* I'm gonna need all the help I can get."

"Here, here," I say, dumping a good portion of the creamy alcohol into my coffee. We clink our spoons before swirling and sipping.

"My, if that doesn't remind me of my youth."

I nearly spit out my drink. "Oh, shut up. Just because we're in our thirties doesn't mean we're old. And in the eyes of the Universe—"

He holds up a hand, then whispers, "No need to go on. You know my brain glazes over at that sort of talk."

"Indeed, it does. Your loss," I tease.

The Fleet Charm poet rattles off his last line, replacing the mic on the stand with gusto. Confidence restored. Kensie and I join the others in clapping, even though we hadn't heard a word of it. The next presenter steps onto the stage, a guitar slung over her shoulder. Her copper hair gleams in the spotlight as she pulls the stool closer to the mic. "I'd like to play y'all a song tonight, if that's all right." Her southern accent blares across the speakers. "This one's called Golden Waves."

"Definitely more promising than Fleet Charm," Kensie whispers as he nudges me.

I snort. "No doubt about it." I glance at his clipboard at all forty-three names. "Holy shit, we're going to be here for hours."

He catches my drift. "That's kind of the point. And you better stay—for the *whole* thing."

"I'm gonna need a few more of these, then." I shake the empty Bailey's bottle.

"On it," he says, scooting his chair back. "I've got to *confer* with the next five victims," he nods his head toward the stage, "but I shall return with all of the necessary provisions."

"And an oatmeal chocolate chip cookie."

He taps his fingers against the table. "It's like you *want* to get me fired. But I'll risk it, because I love you."

"I know," I say with a wink, trying to hide the guilt I feel for not telling him about what had happened earlier that day. "I'll be here, waiting."

He claws his hand before rolling his tongue against the roof of his mouth. "You're feisty, tonight. I like it."

I smirk at him, then shoo him away so that he *doesn't* get fired. He skitters off, disappearing from view within moments. I bring my attention back to the stage, lifting the ceramic mug to my lips as the last strum of *Golden Waves* is played. With a smile plastered onto her freckled face, the girl bows her head and hops off the stool. From the back of the café, a few people shout and cheer, and I make sure to clap for her, *loudly*, praying that the remaining line-up is just as decent. Because if they aren't, well . . . I'll be in for one hell of a long night.

We're halfway through the acts as artist twenty-something takes the stage. By this point, I'm in dire need of some fresh air and, from the looks of it, there's only a few other people outside. I prop up the little *Reserved* sign on our table, motioning to Kensie that I'm going to step out for a minute. Pen in hand, he salutes me from the side of the stage.

Just as I'm walking out the door, the few people I'd seen lingering push their way back inside. I huff as I nearly stumble past them into the crisp night air. My clumsiness may be due to them *or* the alcohol—probably a little bit of both.

"Well, that was rude of them."

A deep voice from the far corner of the patio startles me. The lighting is so dim, I can barely see him, but I can see the halo of smoke that's rising from his cigarette. Like me, he's wearing all black, and his face is mostly covered by the hood of his jacket.

"Yeah, well, open mic night. You know how it goes."

"No," he says, taking a long drag. "I don't."

I cross my arms over my chest. "Not from around here?"

"You're a sharp one."

He's quick, I'll give him that.

"Want a drag?" he offers.

I hold up a hand. "Nah, I'm good."

He chuckles, the sound low and deep. "Trying to prove something?"

I narrow my eyes. "I just stepped out for some fresh air."

"Seems I'm making it less so." He flicks the cigarette to the ground and snuffs it out with his boot. "My apologies."

For reasons I can't explain, discomfort settles into my bones. "I was just heading back inside, but . . . have a good night." I turn to grab the door when what he says has me freezing in place.

"Wells, right? Elara Wells? I half expected to see you up there—"

I whirl around, almost feeling brave enough to approach him even though I can hardly see him. How he knows my real name—*my birth name*—is beyond my comprehension at the moment. "I think it's best you leave."

He kicks off from the patio gate so that he's no longer leaning against it, his hands raising in surrender. "If that's what you really want."

I swallow the lump that's formed in my throat. "I do."

26

He hops over the gate, but not before saying, "There is light to be seen here yet. Carry that with you. Without form. Without regret." As if he's suddenly transformed into one of the slam poets I'd witnessed earlier.

"Goodnight, Elara."

Before I can utter another word, he quite literally vanishes into the night, blending amongst the inky shadows themselves.

5

THE LOCK CLICKS, but when I go to push the door to my apartment open, it sticks. Normally, I would blame the apartment building's infrastructure, but it's probably more due to the insane amount of Bailey's that's currently coursing through my veins. Open mic night had been a success—well, minus the chilling interaction I'd had with the brooding stranger outside the café. I try not to think about that as I try, once again, to open the door.

With my left foot forward, I lean against it, shifting most of my weight to that side. I hit my shoulder against the wood— once, twice. It doesn't budge. On the third try, it moves a little; and by the fourth, I must have knocked a hinge loose because suddenly, I'm flying into my apartment, head and arms leading the way. I nearly land face first. Luckily, the small island jutting out from the kitchen catches me.

I begin undressing as I go—sweater first, leggings second— then kick my shoes off as I make for the bed. I fall onto it, in just my bra and underwear, starfish-style. Knees dangling off the edge, I bring my hands up behind my head. I know I should get some water, rehydrate and all, but instead, I find myself staring at the ceiling.

"There's light to be seen here, yet." I repeat what the stranger had said to me, whispering the words into the nothingness above. It's kind of beautiful in a way. Also kind of sad. Do I have any idea what it means? No.

I tear my gaze from the ceiling to look at the clock on my nightstand. It's past midnight. It dawns on me just how much has happened today. I'd gotten fired. I'd spotted something unusual outside of the café and then *talked* to someone unusual outside of the café later that evening. It had to have been him, from earlier. The thought alone is almost enough to sober me up entirely.

Suddenly feeling very exposed, I pull on some pajamas and double check the door, just to make sure it is indeed locked. I check all the windows as well before shutting all of the blinds and pulling the curtains over them. "No one's getting in here tonight," I say in a drunken slur.

My mind screams at me to eat some food and drink some water. Before I can fully process that thought, my phone dings. I squint at the too-bright screen, realizing I haven't turned on any lights.

Make it home okay?

I text Kensie back. *Yes, making food. Night night,* with a string of incomprehensible emojis.

Don't forget to turn the oven off after you make your pizza. Night, E.

"Pizza?" I drop my phone onto the counter and open up the freezer. I bow my head against the cool surface, silently thanking responsible-Elara for going grocery shopping earlier that week. "Tonight," I announce to no one, "I shall eat like a *queen*." And

29

then, "There is light to be seen here yet!" I nearly double over at my stupidity.

Oh, alcohol. This is going to hurt in the morning . . .

I jolt awake, feeling as though I've been hit by a freight train. My temples are pounding at the TV I'd left on, and my throat is drier than the Sahara Desert. Thankfully, I'd been smart enough to close all of the blinds *and* curtains before passing out on the couch, but it's still so damn bright. I nearly have to peel my eyelids open, trying to survey the damage around me. There are two glasses of water, one that's completely full and one that's been knocked over. Seeing as I'd turned into a complete savage and decided *not* to use a plate last night, there's dried cheese and a mess of crumbs on my coffee table. But I'm happy to see there isn't a wine bottle or wine glass in sight. Sometimes open mic night turns into a real bender. Last night hadn't been one of those nights.

Thank my lucky stars.

Even though I've just "slept", if you can even call it that, I'm still *exhausted*. Just the perks of drinking alcohol in your thirties. Enjoy it while you're young, kids.

I groan as I click off the television, then bring the two glasses to the kitchen sink. I snatch a paper towel from the holder and drag the trash bin into the living room. I scrape the cheese off the surface with my fingernail (oh so appetizing), the sight of anything even *remotely* disgusting making me want to hurl. I return everything back to the kitchen, happy to see that I *had* turned off the oven last night, per Kensie's reminder, and fill up a fresh glass of water before setting it on my bedside table. I stare at my unmade bed, desperately wanting to crawl under the sheets and never come back out, but I know better.

Shower first. Then sleep.

Thankfully, it's Sunday, so I have nowhere to be. As I'm turning on the water, it hits me that *regardless* of the day, I no longer have anywhere to be. I try to avoid looking in the mirror because I know exactly how depressing that image would be. Combine that with a hangover and we've got a recipe for an existential crisis, coming right up.

I take my time basking in the hot water, even going so far as to sit on the floor of the bathtub. Feeling the water beat down on me, watching it swirl down the drain—I secretly wish it would take all of my problems along with it. And that when I emerge again, I'd emerge *clean*.

Of everything. And everyone.

I wrap a towel around myself and brush my teeth, then run a wide-tooth comb through my hair. I pat some lotion on my face and change into a fresh set of PJs. It's amazing how something as simple as a shower can make you feel brand new again.

I sit on the edge of my bed, forcing myself to drink the entire glass of water I'd set there. I scribble a few things in my journal, mostly about last night, before tucking myself into the blankets and covers. The curtains can only keep so much of the impending daylight out, so I find myself staring at the ceiling again. I will myself to sleep, but my brain seems to have other plans.

How am I going to pay next month's rent?

This month's bills?

When am I going to tell Kensie I'd gotten fired?

Where will I work next?

Who was that guy at open mic night? And how had he known my name? My real *name?*

I squeeze my eyes shut, wishing my anxiety away. I start to count my breaths, slow and deep. Feel the rise and fall of my chest. The panic gremlins begin to creep in again, but I continue to breathe, keeping my eyes closed.

Sleep, Elara. Float away into the abyss that is unconsciousness.

I soften into the bed even more, noticing the feel of the pillow as it cradles the back of my skull. My eyes flutter as I take a deep breath in. I relax fully, sinking into the comforter, feeling like, for the first time in the past twenty-four hours, things just might be okay.

I've played "pretend" before falling asleep ever since I was a kid, envisioning a life with circumstances the exact opposite of mine. It started off pretty normal, with dreams of two present, adoring parents. A sister; maybe a brother. A childhood filled with laughter and birthday parties and family vacations. Straight As in school. Being the golden child. Dating all spokes of the wheel—jocks, musicians, artists, dancers, the brainy types. Getting a car for my sixteenth birthday. Being sent off to college with my tuition paid in full. Studying something I actually enjoyed and making a success story out of the privileged childhood I'd been blessed with . . .

But over time, my "pretend world" has shifted to a place that isn't anything like Earth or human society. No rules, restrictions, or limitations. No money. No work. No expectations or obligations. No crime or corruption. No greed. No poverty. No worry or fear. Just a place of pure bliss. A place where I could just *be* without interruption, distraction, or judgment. I've done this for so long, *imagined* this for so many years, that it almost feels real to me . . . this "other" life. The knowledge that, perhaps, in another timeline, another existence, another *reality*, such a possibility exists *should* be enough to keep me up at night. But I find it rather comforting—hopeful, even.

That maybe this existence isn't all there is.

As if I wasn't already sure the first time around . . .

I can't tell if what happens next is actually occurring *in* the room or just in my mind, but a low, soothing hum starts to fill the space around me. My eyes begin to shutter until I feel them

32

roll into the back of my head. A new sensation, one I haven't felt before, washes over me as I float even deeper into a state somewhere between dreaming and waking life. Oddly enough, how I feel now is how I usually feel right before I fall asleep, but something's different this time.

I'm . . . *aware.*

Still completely conscious, yet I can't move.

A functioning mind in an unresponsive body.

This deep state of relaxation falters as, internally, I start to panic, willing my body to move—for my eyes to open, for anything to jolt me awake and transfer me back into my physical self. But no matter what I do, no matter what thoughts I think, my body won't respond. It crosses my mind that perhaps I've just died or I'm . . . in the process of dying?

Is this what limbo feels like?

My questions go unanswered as yet another new sensation grips me—one that makes me feel as though I'm *sliding.* It's slow and fast at the same time, like my spine has turned to Jell-O and the rest of my body has somehow liquefied for its descent down the side of the bed. Again, I will my body to move, attempting to send the neural commands to my arms, to my legs, to my lower back, but there's still no response. I am consciousness floating through an abyss, completely aware of my surroundings, yet unable to snap myself out of whatever *this* is.

Even though I'm confused and, quite frankly, terrified, something tells me that panicking isn't going to do me any good—*I mean, does it ever?*—so instead of trying to control it, or figure it out, I decide to do the most ironic thing of all.

Relax into it.

Almost immediately, it feels like I'm simultaneously floating and falling in a space so vast and an energy field so active, that they can't possibly exist on the same plane—most certainly not *here*. I also notice that the low hum has been replaced with a different sound—a slightly higher pitched whine. Almost like radio static, but not as jarring.

Even though my mind is screaming otherwise, I manage to not fight it as intrigue draws me in further. Deeper and deeper I go, the whine growing steadier, the space expanding even more. Within moments, I sense another presence, but I don't know who or *what* it is. It dawns on me, with all of my research on the cosmos, the planets, and the metaphysical, that perhaps I've tapped into an interdimensional feed. Perhaps I'm astral traveling, across space and time, without even knowing it.

But that isn't possible, is it?

And why me?

Why now?

How is it that I'm able to have all of these perfectly coherent thoughts, but not have the ability to wake my body up?

Amidst my thoughts, the blackness around me begins to lighten, but not in the way you'd expect. It doesn't get brighter— the hue just shifts from black to . . . not so black. I can see a form taking shape, although I can't tell exactly what it is. It's darker than the background, and at first it appears to be just a giant blob, but then it disperses into hundreds—no, *thousands*— of tiny wave-like particles. They move all at once, bouncing off of one another as a soft voice enters the space. I strain my ears to listen, to hear—but it's so quiet that I can't make out anything the voice is saying.

Shortly after, another voice chimes in, but this one is much lower, raspier. After a minute or so of back and forth, I realize that they're having a conversation. *Do they know I'm here? Did they somehow call me here to witness this? Or have I tapped into something completely uninvited?*

I'm about to interject—or at least *try* to anyway—when the lower-toned voice says, clear as day, "Elara."

It's weird being "removed" from my body because I feel the need to open my mouth to respond, but quickly recall that I don't *have* a body—or, at least, that I don't have use of it here, in this situation. I only have my consciousness, my *awareness*, because that's what I am.

How would consciousness respond?

I place my focus on the wave particles before me, wondering if they can somehow pick up on my thoughts telepathically. Even though there's no voice (and no mouth), I hear myself say, "I cannot hear you."

The feminine voice says, "She's not ready."

Well that I heard just fine.

Suddenly, the entity is speaking rapidly, with a great sense of urgency in her voice, and I realize that I'm able to pick up on a few things, but not everything. I hear something about the number forty-five, Professor Haven's name (surprising), something about a star system (although I don't catch which one), the number seven, and there's no mistaking the last thing she says. A name I hadn't heard until yesterday.

Axel Volaris.

If my body were functioning right now, I'm certain it'd be having a full-on panic attack. Even though I'm stunned, and still trying to process these small tidbits of information, I have the urge to ask the voice to repeat itself *and* to speak a little louder— but just as I'm about to make my request, the particles dissipate altogether. The hue shifts from not-so-black to completely black. And before I know it, I've shot upright in my bed with a giant lungful of air sitting in my chest.

Fortunately, my brain and body seem to be reconnected, so I exhale and inhale and repeat, trying not to feel too disoriented by the out-of-body experience I've just had. Even though I'm lightheaded and majorly perplexed, I can still recall what's just happened.

Determined not to forget a single thing, I reach across my bed to my nightstand and shakily pull open one of the drawers. I withdraw a notebook and a ballpoint pen, using my mouth to take the cap off. Trying to write with the current trembling in my fingers proves difficult, but I'm not exactly going for impeccable penmanship right now. I jot down everything I can remember, which doesn't feel like much—but I'm not at all surprised that my memory recall is already lapsing. It's kind of like how you remember bits and pieces of a dream right when you wake up, but if you fall back asleep or get out of bed without giving it another thought, it's as if the dream never even happened.

Except this *wasn't* a dream. This wasn't "just my imagination". Believe me, as someone who spends a lot of time in her head, I *know* when something is a figment of my imagination versus something else entirely. And this whole experience? Is definitely beyond my creative ability.

Far, *far* beyond it.

I stare at the five pieces of information that I *was* able to decipher, then quickly write down that one of the voices—the lower-toned one—had said my name.

They know who I am. Which must mean . . .

My being there was intentional.

I drop the pen before raising the notebook in front of my face, hands still shaking. *Forty-five. Professor Haven. Seven. Star System. Axel Volaris.* I stare at the words for a few minutes, willing them to make sense; wishing, more than anything, that I'd been able to hear the whole thing. I sigh, letting the notebook slip from my hands and onto the comforter. My gaze travels to the kitchen and lands on my phone. The urge to call Professor Haven, to get his take on all of this, is strong—but something in me tells me that he wouldn't know. That this wasn't meant for him.

I'm the one they'd wanted for that transmission . . .

And it'd happened for a *reason.*

6

STILL FEELING SHAKEN, I'm unable to fall back asleep. Quite honestly, I'm frightened to. I'm in the middle of chugging my fourth glass of water, but it may as well be my first. I'm so *thirsty*. I don't remember a time when I was able to drink this much liquid in one sitting.

Even as I'm hydrating, the headache reverberating deep within my skull only grows louder and more pronounced. I swig the last of the icy liquid, stumbling over to the sink for yet another refill. I turn on the tap, watching as the water swirls down the drain. Mesmerized, I nearly drop the glass as a knock sounds on the door. Trying not to feel too startled, I set the glass on the edge and call out, "Coming!"

Like the echoing in my head, the pounding is incessant. When I finally swing the door open, I'm not at all surprised to see Kensie standing on the other side—but what does give me pause is the overtly troubled expression he's wearing.

"Hey," I say with a frown as I usher him inside. "What's wrong?"

He holds his phone out to me so that it's just a few inches from my face. I take a step back before grabbing it, the words on the screen coming into focus. The headline reads: **Esteemed CU Professor of Astronomy Sciences Reported Missing.**

Without reading any further, I know exactly who the article is referring to . . . but that's not what makes my knees buckle. I blindly reach for the kitchen counter as my eyes scan the date at the top left. Once. Twice.

Wednesday, October 12, 2033.

That's four days . . . in the *future*.

As if confirming my thoughts, Kensie says, "I wanted to come check on you because I haven't seen you in the shop the past few days. Normally you're all hopped up on lattes grading papers or—wait, is fall break over? No, no, it's the middle of break, isn't it?" He continues rambling but I'm no longer listening. My eyes are glued to the small rectangular screen.

It had been Saturday the 8th. Saturday morning when I'd messaged Professor Haven. Saturday at noon when he'd fired me. Saturday afternoon when I'd gone to the café. And early Sunday morning when I'd fallen back "asleep" and had that bizarre out of body experience—the one I'd *just had*. How can it possibly be *Wednesday*? Moreover, how can I not remember the past *four* days?

Something Kensie's said catches in my mind. "You came to check on me," I say slowly. "When was the last time we saw each other?"

I know the answer before he says it. "Saturday, at open mic night, remember? And before that, at the café? When you insisted on paying for your scone which," he clears his throat before revealing a crumpled paper bag donning the café's logo, "did I mention I come bearing gifts? I figured you'd need it after *that*." His eyes travel to the phone in my hand.

As if I'd forgotten, I read the headline again, then briefly scroll through the article. About halfway down are two images of Professor Haven—one's a headshot and the other is of him standing at the front of the lecture hall. By the animated look on his face and the way his arms are outstretched, I can tell he was in the middle of one of his infamous talks when the shot was taken—probably about the relation between astrophysics and what he refers to as *cosmic beings*. Not exactly up to CU's academic code, but someone of his tenure? The administration wouldn't dare reprimand him. Plagiarism, yes. Extraterrestrial beings? No.

"So," Kensie says, pulling me from my thoughts, "what do you think happened?" He takes a bite of one of the scones, then casually kicks his feet up on the coffee table.

"To Professor Haven?" I ask, tossing his phone back to him.

"No, to Professor Snape." He gives an emphatic roll of his eyes. "*Yes*, to Professor Haven."

"I wouldn't know. The last time I saw him was Saturday around noon . . ."

The scone nearly falls from Kensie's mouth. "Then you may have been the last person to see him." He brushes his hands together, crumbs flying from his fingertips, before picking up his phone to read aloud. "Last seen leaving the CU Astronomy Building between noon and one o'clock." He angles his head, eyes narrowing. "*Elara,* what did you do?"

He emphasizes my name as if I'm some common criminal. I shake my head, furrowing my brows at him. "I didn't *do* anything. He did fire me, though."

"Oh," Kensie whispers. "Oh, I didn't know that. I'm sorry." He tosses his dreadlocks over his shoulder, his eyes growing even wider as he says, "But this isn't good. *None* of this is good. What if they come asking about him? What will you say? Do you have an alibi?"

"If *who* comes asking? What are you talking about?"

"You know," he says, his eyes darting across the room. "The *authorities.*"

"I highly doubt—"

But I'm unable to finish my sentence because the next thing I know, I hear the shouts of the Boulder County Police as they identify themselves from the other side of my apartment door.

7

BEFORE I CAN register what's happening, two uniformed officers are standing in the living room of my apartment and Kensie's hurriedly excusing himself out the door. The shock isn't enough to make me forget my manners (probably because of the whole *being four days in the future* thing), so I open up one of the cabinets and pull out two drinking glasses. Fortunately, my hands aren't shaking like they were before, thanks to the sustenance of the scone Kensie had so kindly brought over.

"That won't be necessary," the first officer says, her heather-gray eyes shifting from the glasses in my hand to my humble surroundings. From the way she's standing, with her thumbs looped in her belt and her nose turned up, you'd think she'd just smelled something rancid—or maybe her reaction is just in response to my pitiful living state.

Honestly, I don't blame her. *Welcome to capitalism.*

"Maybe not for you, Chief, but I'll take one." The second officer—a short, stout man with bulbous cheeks and a protruding stomach—gives me a polite nod and a small smile. He walks over to where I'm standing and extends his hand. "Officer Blatter," he says. "Pleasure to make your acquaintance."

What an unfortunate last name. "Elara," I say, taking his hand. "Elara Friis." I'm always grateful when I get to introduce myself. Most people say "Freese" when they see my name, but the s is silent. Elara *Free.*

"Beautiful name," he says. "What is that? Polish?"

My cheeks redden at his remark. "I'm not sure, actually. I don't know much about my family history."

"Parents?"

I bite my tongue, knowing better than to reveal that my father has spent the better part of his life behind bars, seeing as he probably had something to do with my mother's disappearance. A case, as I mentioned before, that still remains open in Boulder County to this day. At eighteen, I'd legally changed my last name. So far, I've avoided any association with the case and my so-called "father".

My thoughts scatter as the next officer introduces herself. "Chief Albeck." She doesn't bother walking over to me nor shaking my hand. I offer the full glass of water to Officer Blatter before placing the empty one back in the cabinet. His eyes glint with appreciation.

"As I'm sure you already know," Albeck goes on, "a CU professor has been reported missing—Professor Haven, of Astronomy Sciences." She removes her narrow-brimmed hat and tosses it onto the coffee table. It lands right next to my partially eaten scone. "University records indicate that you work for Professor Haven. Is that correct?"

I can't help but feel a sense of relief that not even the Chief of Police recognizes the daughter of a renowned criminal. I'm happy to answer her question. "*Worked,*" I say, doing my best not to fidget with the chipped wood on one of the drawers. This place really is a shithole.

"Worked? As in past tense?"

I bring my attention to Officer Blatter. "He recently fired me." I don't mean for my voice to go quiet, but the shame I feel is undeniable.

"On what grounds?"

Even though Albeck asked the question, I keep my eyes on Blatter. There's something oddly comforting about his presence. "There was a misunderstanding in the grading of his midterm papers." I'm tempted to continue, but when has revealing more information than necessary ever worked in anyone's favor?

"That's it?" Albeck looks less than impressed with my response. "When did he fire you?"

"Saturday. October 8th."

"Did he leave the building with you?"

"What do you think? He'd just fired me." I clamp down on my tongue, immediately regretting my tone. "What I meant to say was . . ."

My voice trails off as my gaze lands on something very unsettling just outside the window. The curtains are drawn but even so, I can clearly see a silhouette. A *man's* silhouette—which is impossible, seeing as my apartment is on the fourth floor. There's no fire escape, no platform for someone to be standing on. As crazy as it sounds, it's almost like it's floating . . .

Albeck is quick to notice the distraction and whirls around, hand flying to her holster. My focus is momentarily interrupted, but when I look at the window again, the shadow is gone.

"I hope you'll excuse the intrusion," Officer Blatter says. "We're all a little on edge today." The chief scowls at him but doesn't refute his statement. He hands me a beige-colored card that's crinkled at the edges. "You'll call us if you hear anything or notice anything unusual?"

I nod, taking the now-empty glass from his outstretched hand. "I will," I say, hating how heavy the lie feels on my tongue.

"After you, Chief," he says, opening the door. Albeck doesn't so much as look at me as she stalks through the entryway. Blatter gives me a rueful parting glance before closing the door gently behind him.

I blow out a long, shaky breath as I turn the card over in my hands. The Boulder County Police insignia stares back at me, taunting me. I swipe my phone from the counter, letting the card fall in its place. My first thought is to call Kensie, but the last thing I need right now is more questions.

What I *do* need right now is silence.

Complete and utter *silence.*

8

I CAN'T SLEEP. Not surprising, though, given the events from earlier today. I glance at the clock on my nightstand. 9:44 P.M. Earlier than I'd thought, but ideal for stargazing.

Instead of my usual trip to the rooftop, I decide on another course of action. I can't seem to shake the headline about Professor Haven from my mind, nor the visit from the police, nor the strange message I'd somehow managed to stumble upon whilst *asleep*. I can't explain it, and it may be a terrible idea, but I feel pulled to drive to the observatory that's located on campus. Perhaps Haven left something behind—a note, a clue—to indicate where he's gone.

Maybe he's not missing at all.

Even as I think it, I know it isn't true.

I glance at the counter at my phone, my car keys . . . and the lack of my university badge. *Damn.* I'd turned it in the day I'd been fired.

I rack my brain for a solution. After working at CU for a couple of years, I've gotten to know the schedules of the cleaning crews fairly well. Even though it's fall break, there's a good chance they're still there, which means the doors will likely be propped wide open. Not to mention, I *am* a familiar face—I've spent many a night in the Astronomy building's tower . . .

How would they know whether or not I'd been fired?

I don't give myself any time to doubt my less-than-fully-formed plan before swiping my phone and keys from the counter, slinging a faux fur-lined jacket around my shoulders, and bounding down the stairs to my car.

I'm only outside for a few seconds, but I'm already shivering as I slide into the driver's seat, immediately turning the seat heaters on. *Ah, the little things.* I breathe a sigh of relief as the car begins to warm, then journey onward to campus.

Just as I'd suspected, the doors to the Astronomy Sciences building are propped open. I walk inside, fumbling with my keys as I pretend to look for my nonexistent badge, then wave hello to one of my favorite staff members.

"Clear skies tonight?" Roger says warmly as he wheels an oversize trash bin down the hall.

"The clearest," I say. I pause, feeling a sharp pang of guilt as the lie leaves my mouth. "Hey, Roger, I think I may have left my badge in the lecture hall. Would you mind?" I gesture toward the door, smiling as he swipes his keycard in front of it. "Thanks," I say as I hurry inside. I descend the steps, past the tiered seats, down to the very front before veering sharply toward the desk. Nothing much has changed since I was last here—papers strewn everywhere, books open, pens scattered—but I'm not complaining. Especially since my badge is sitting exactly where I'd left it.

I grab it from the desk and stuff it into my pocket. As I do, I notice a similar card poking out from underneath a pile of papers. I gently slide it out, Professor Haven's emphatic smile staring back at me. I sigh. *Where have you gone?*

I take his badge as well, for good measure, then exit the lecture hall, waving to Roger as I press the *up* button on the elevator panel. When it dings, I swiftly step inside—lowkey feeling like I've just gotten away with murder—and press the button labeled "O" that will take me to the tower on the uppermost floor. It's eerily silent as I step off the elevator onto the navy and gray tiled floor. I briefly consider the fact that our badges track our movements before deciding to use my own to enter the observatory tower.

A draft sweeps through the room, but that's not what catches my attention. I can't remember the last time I'd been here, but I certainly don't recall it being such a . . . *mess*. Sticky notes cover almost every surface, books are flung open (some are even on the floor—*how dare they!*), and based on the dim glow of the monitors, the computers hadn't been properly shut down. As I move toward one of the desks near the center of the room, I can tell right away that the handwriting on the majority of the notes belongs to Professor Haven—not that many other staff members even use the observatory tower, but hey, you never know.

I set down my phone and keys, but keep both badges secured in my pocket. Like I have so many times before, I open the plexiglass cover and press the button to open the panels. The rectangular metal inserts slide back, then into one another, to reveal an enormous multipaned glass window. I walk backwards until I reach the telescope in the center of the room. I can't help but think back to my out-of-body experience and the strange message—more specifically, the numbers.

Forty-five and seven.

I shake one of the computers from sleep mode, praying that my username and password haven't been restricted. I silently rejoice as my login is successful, realizing that Professor Haven probably hadn't yet submitted my dismissal papers to the university before disappearing. The thought causes a knot to twist in my stomach. I push it down as I bring up a web browser and type in *Uranus coordinates.* Why? Because Uranus is the seventh planet in our solar system and, even though it may have nothing to do with anything, girl's gotta start somewhere.

I enter the coordinates into the software, patiently waiting as the telescope reads the programming and makes its necessary adjustments. When it stops moving, I look into the eyepiece, getting a perfect view of the soft blue and white planet. As much as I want to enjoy what I'm seeing, I can't seem to focus on anything but the other number in the message. *Forty-five.*

I step back from the telescope and pull one of the chairs out from under the wall-mounted desks. I grab the nearest piece of scrap paper and begin scribbling what ends up being a bunch of nonsense. Deep in my gut, I know that Uranus has nothing to do with this. As for forty-five? Not a clue.

Like I tend to do when I get frustrated, I begin to organize the many messy piles on the desk. As I'm shuffling through a stack of papers, something catches my eye. Scrawled in half-cursive, half-print—Haven's signature writing style—is the word *Aldebaran,* followed by a set of coordinates. If I remember correctly, Aldebaran is one of the brightest stars in the whole sky—and Professor Haven's favorite. His fascination with this star slowly starts to come back to me.

I enter the coordinates into the system, then look through the viewfinder. It's unnervingly bright. I zoom out some, realizing that it's just one of many stars that makes up the Taurus constellation—something I'm *very* familiar with seeing as my birthday is May 11th.

Before I can analyze what this means, I'm suddenly descended into darkness. Without warning, the power clicks off, computers whirring as they all shut down at once. I notice a reflection at the base of the telescope—a dull blue glow. I turn over my shoulder to look at the door, but there's nothing in the window next to it. I fumble in the dark for my keys and phone, then use the flashlight function to guide the way.

As quietly as I can, I push open the door and poke my head into the hallway. I look left, then right, only stepping out once I'm certain the coast is clear. The flashlight blinks, momentarily shrouding me in darkness once again.

It's then I see it. At the end of the hall.

A stream of pale blue light.

To conserve my phone battery, I turn off the flashlight and just use the light from the screen instead. I stick to the right side of the wall, moving as stealthily as possible. When I reach the end of the corridor, I'm dismayed to find . . . nothing. No footprints. No light.

As if I'd somehow imagined the whole thing.

I head back the way I came, toward the elevator, feeling both confused and frustrated that my time stargazing always seems to be interrupted. I nearly go to press the button when I remember, *duh, power's out,* and take the stairs instead. It's a long, winding way down, but when I reach the main floor, something makes the skin on the back of my neck prickle. I whirl around, pointing my dim phone light at more *nothing*.

I'm not surprised to find that the hallway is empty, seeing as it's now eleven at night. I'm sure Roger is well on his way home; however, I *do* happen to notice something a little out of the ordinary. His trash bin, the one he'd been wheeling around earlier, is sitting right in front of the lecture hall doors. Thinking back, the cleaning crew *always* returns their supplies to the janitorial closet . . .

With an uneasy feeling, I roll the bin to the side, then swipe my badge for entry. Even though my phone's barely hanging on at 8%, I tap the flashlight icon and point it around the room. I'm not sure what it is I'm expecting to see, but there's no Roger. No cleaning crew. No one.

I try to convince myself that they've all gone home— which is fairly plausible—but the power outage is a more pressing concern. I'd just been staring into a telescope, gazing at the clearest of clear skies. No storms. Certainly no inclement weather to report . . .

I jog to the far end of the lecture hall and open the door that leads to one of the university courtyards. The walkway lamps are still on. So are the lights in the building across from this one. *Hmm.*

I step back inside, letting the door click shut behind me. I march back up the stairs, debating whether or not to just call it a night and go home. The observatory is the whole reason I came here. If I can't use the telescope, there's really no point in being here. I stand in the middle of the hall, still surrounded by darkness, unable to decide. It's only when I finally make up my mind (to *leave*) that I feel an unusual urge to swing by Professor Haven's office.

Damn you, hamster brain.

I once again open the door to the emergency stairwell and begin climbing the stairs. When I make it to the third floor, I've started to think I must be hallucinating—because coming from directly inside Professor Haven's office is a silvery green glow. It reminds me so much of a serpent that I can feel my skin crawl just being in the mere vicinity of it.

Out of pure instinct, I duck down. *Why oh why does my curiosity always have to get the better of me?* Most people would think, "Hmm, that looks dangerous," and leave—but not me. Every fiber of my being *should* be screaming for me to get the hell out of there; but instead, my mind's playing out a scenario where I may be about to witness extraterrestrial life—like, from another *planet*—with my own two eyes. Perhaps *I'll* finally be the one to answer the cliché, age-old question, "Are we the only intelligent life forms out there?"

Of course we're not.

As I get closer to the metallic sheen of light, I notice a deep pulsating sensation in my ears. Not only can I hear it . . . I can *feel* it. It's indescribable—to feel your body humming and pulsing when nothing is causing it; when you're surrounded by complete and utter silence.

Gripping the ledge on the wall, I slowly bring my head just high enough so that I'm able to see into the window. The blinds are slanted at an angle, but there's no mistaking the massive, green-shadowed outlines that are hovering over the desk.

As if they've sensed my presence, the pulsating grows and grows until it's so intense, I have to physically cover my ears. I strain my eyes to see through the blinds, but it's no use. I can't seem to focus on anything except for the intense reverb that's bouncing around my skull. I press my hands even harder over my ears, squeezing my eyes shut. On the verge of passing out, I let out a slow groan. Just as I'm about to succumb, the echo halts. My eyes shoot open.

And a flash of indigo whisks me away.

9

MY EYES SHOOT open as I'm jolted awake. I sit straight up, patting my arms, my stomach, my legs. It takes a moment for my eyes to adjust to the darkness surrounding me, but there's no mistaking where I am. Palms facedown, I set my hands at my sides, pressing down on the plush down comforter. On my bed.

I'm back home . . . but how did I get here?

A migraine unlike anything I've ever experienced comes barreling through my mind. I throw the covers off my legs, hands flying to my temples as I stumble toward the kitchen. I realize I'm shaking (again) as I open the cupboard. Carefully, I remove one of the drinking glasses, my fingers reluctant to get a good grip. An alarming bout of déjà vu settles in.

Deep breath in. And exhale.

I grasp it just tightly enough and manage to set it in the sink, directly underneath the faucet. I watch as the water fills the glass. I don't even let it fill up all the way before downing its contents. As it fills a second time, my eyes wander to my legs, then my arms.

When had I changed into pajamas?

It's all so fuzzy . . .

The glass is near overflowing, but I don't bother to keep it from spilling over as I make for my bedroom. Clothes on the floor. Phone on the nightstand. Keys—I glance back at the kitchen—on the counter. At first, I can't remember what I'd been doing prior to waking, but when I see the university badges sticking out from underneath the pile of clothes, it all comes rushing back to me.

The power outage. The silvery green shadows. The flash of indigo that had brought me back . . . *here.*

I swipe my journal from my nightstand and head back into the kitchen. Leaning against the counter, I set the extremely full glass of water next to me, then fling open the notebook. In as much detail as I can remember, I write down exactly what had happened. A familiar feeling, let me assure you.

Ten minutes go by and I'm no closer to piecing together how I got from the Astronomy Sciences building back to my apartment. It's all a giant blur—as if I'd somehow unconsciously walked back across campus, got into my car, *drove* home, parked, walked up four flights of stairs, changed into my pajamas, and passed out.

Pretty sure I'd remember at least *one* of those things.

I'm tapping my pen against the page, mind whirling, when a glance at my right wrist brings everything to a grinding halt. There, on my skin, are what appear to be tiny pinpricks of silver ink—but that isn't the part that's caught my attention. What's caught my attention is the familiar shape those pinpricks are in.

The Taurus constellation.

"Where did you come from?" I whisper as I drop the pen and turn my body so that my back is to the counter. In the dim light, it appears that the ink (or whatever it is) is *glowing.* I move my left hand to my opposite wrist, hovering just above it. Heat radiates from my arm as if it's fresh ink—a fresh mark. Fascinated, but also a little afraid to touch it, I inch my index finger along the delicate patch of skin. It doesn't move or change shape—nothing worth noting happens. In all honesty, I'm a little disappointed at that.

I turn back around to face the counter, then grab the pen to record my findings. I draw the shape of the constellation as best I can, thinking back to my recent visit to the observatory. What had I been looking at right before the power had gone out? What had the sticky note with Professor Haven's handwriting said?

The word comes to me in an instant. *Aldebaran.*

As I'd discovered in the tower, Aldebaran is one of the stars that makes up the Taurus constellation. I can clearly see it depicted on my wrist because it gives off the appearance of glowing brighter than the rest of the dots.

A recollection begins to stir within me—the way my skin had crawled when I'd come across the green-shadowed figures in Professor Haven's office; the pulsating that had rendered me motionless—but that indigo light, the one that had whisked me away . . . *is it possible it'd been a cosmic being? One from that very constellation, from Aldebaran? Or, perhaps, another star like it? Could it somehow have been Professor Haven?*

Okay, whoa, Elara. Too far . . .

I run a hand through my hair, noticing that while my migraine *has* dissipated, it's been replaced by either one of two things—the notion that I'm completely delusional and on the verge of losing my damn mind; or that I've just experienced, for the *second* time this week, proof of the existence of fully conscious cosmic entities.

10

A WEEK HAS passed with no strange sightings, otherworldly transmissions, or conversations with the police—and furthermore, no news of Professor Haven's whereabouts. With the end of fall break and CU classes back in session, I haven't been back on campus since my run-in with the . . . *shadow entities*—but I have been keeping tabs on my inbox. All students enrolled in Professor Haven's classes have temporarily been reassigned to Earth Sciences.

Quite a stretch, if you ask me.

I'd thought the university had forgotten about me, seeing as I'm just a lowly assistant (again assuming the discharge paperwork hadn't been filed), so I'm pleasantly surprised when I receive an email from Professor Colter offering me a temporary position as her assistant. Seeing as she teaches Metaphysics in Early Modern Philosophy, I figure it's a better fit than any of the other sciences would be. As a formality, I open up the application and fill it out, trying to ignore the unrelenting guilt bubbling up inside of me. The incessant chatter in my mind isn't much help either. *Yes, I was fired. Yes, no one knows. Yes, it might be wrong to mislead another professor . . .*

But at this point? I'm borderline desperate. I'm currently out of work, barely able to make the rent, and my sanity might be on the verge of total collapse without rehabilitation—so yes, a distraction (like this job) is more than welcome. I send off the email, waiting for its signature *ding*, before closing my laptop and pushing it to the edge of the bed. I stare at it, drumming my fingers against my thigh.

Now what?

I could wait for a confirmation from Professor Colter; *or* I could get dressed and head to campus. Honestly, if I sit here any longer, especially in my current state, I may as well voluntarily institutionalize myself.

Decisions, decisions.

I head into the closet to change, pulling on a pair of leather leggings, knee-high boots, and an oversize plum-colored sweater. As I pull the sleeves down, I get a flash of the marking on my wrist. Even though I *never* wear my watch on my right wrist, I switch it over. The last thing I need is a reminder of how bizarre this past week has been—or, even worse, someone noticing it and asking questions . . .

Questions I clearly don't have the answers to.

I grab my laptop and toss it in my bag along with my phone, then drape one of my heavier coats over my arm, just in case. My keys jangle in my hand as I secure the front door, twisting the knob to make sure it is indeed locked. Four flights later and I'm in the parking lot, revving up my Jeep Wrangler. Another gloomy October day greets me, but I'm not put off by it. The windshield wipers swish back and forth, carrying multi-colored leaves from one side to the other.

I come to a stop at a traffic light, only then realizing that it's right around lunch time. I don't know Professor Colter's schedule, but I'm sure I'll catch at least one of her afternoon classes. I pull into my designated parking space, immediately feeling like a traitor. *You shouldn't be here. This is wrong. You're a liar.* My mind hisses and spits fire as if I'm suddenly the devil incarnate.

I pull myself together just enough to step out of my car, throw my bag over my shoulder, and walk in the direction opposite the Astronomy Sciences Building. I don't bother to glance back after I've passed by it. I adjust my watch with my left hand, pulling the sleeve of my sweater just far enough to cover it *and* the cryptic markings that lurk beneath.

As I'd suspected, the main lecture hall in the Philosophy Building is empty. Hardly any classes at CU overlap with the lunch hour. On the off chance that Professor Colter *is* eating lunch at her desk, I decide to visit her office, which is located on the second floor.

Even though I'm in a completely different building, pressing the elevator button immediately brings back unwelcome memories of the past week. Thankfully, the ride up is short, but the moment the elevator dings and the doors open again, an uneasy feeling washes over me. With caution, I step into the painstakingly quiet hall. I walk along the hallway, scanning the nameplates as I go by. Of course, her office *would* be at the very end.

I narrow my eyes, peering inside the slightly tinted windows, but there's no movement of any kind. I sigh, then look around me. To my left, there's a metal bench with a monitor hanging just above it. I immediately recognize the forms being displayed— class schedules.

I meticulously scan each line until I find what I'm looking for. *Philosophy 421. Modal Logic and Metaphysics. Professor Colter. 2:20 P.M. – 3:15 P.M.* One glance at my watch tells me that I've got a solid two hours before her next class. I eye the bench, briefly considering sitting and waiting, but that seems pointless. I review the other professors' schedules to see if the lecture hall is open until then. Indeed, it is. As a show of good faith, I decide to wait there instead.

The elevator beckons to me, but after the unsettling ride up, I decide to take the stairs. A few students linger in the hall, completely preoccupied with their phones. I slip my badge from my pocket and swipe it over the card reader, making sure that the door clicks shut once I'm inside. When I turn around, I can't help but feel slightly overwhelmed at the sheer size of the room. When I first poked my head in, I hadn't really noticed—but now, as I walk down the seemingly endless set of stairs, I realize just how massive it really is.

The lecture hall I've spent most of my time in seats a couple hundred people, but this hall? It's at least *double* the size. A jolt of dread hits me as I recall the countless hours spent grading papers for Professor Haven. I can't even begin to imagine doubling that amount. It's not like I have much of a social life anyway, but if I did, this is where I'd wave it goodbye.

I'm at the front of the hall, reconsidering my choices and how perhaps I should have gone with Earth Sciences, when the clearing of a throat grabs my attention. I scan the room in all of its maroon and gray glory. Not a single soul sits in any of the chairs. I glance from side to side, checking the entrances, of which there are many.

"Professor Colter?" I wish my voice hadn't come out so meek. There's shuffling in the far left corner of the room. My eyes focus on the spot, but it's completely shadowed. Apprehensive, I begin to move toward the exit nearest me when a tall figure emerges. Obviously, it isn't Professor Colter, but I'm intrigued just the same.

"Hello?" I call out, my voice stronger this time.

"Elara? Elara Friis?"

His voice is friendly enough, so I stay put. "Who wants to know?"

58

A figure emerges from the shadows and, even from a distance, I can see just how attractive he is. Shaggy russet hair covers most of his features, save for the thick-framed glasses he's wearing, and his five o'clock shadow does more than accentuate his angular jaw. He's wearing dark jeans and a deep burgundy sweater and, as he gets closer, I can easily read the name on his badge.

"Xero Sivalla," he says with a faint smile.

I take his hand and give it a firm shake, trying not to be too enraptured by the deep olive green of his irises. "Elara Friis. But I suppose you already knew that."

"You're the new assistant," he says, sweeping right by me to log on to the computer. "Welcome." I'm about to ask how he knows that when he pulls up my file. He opens the email containing my application—the one I'd submitted earlier that day. "I'm *also* Professor Colter's assistant. Seems she needs two from this point forward."

Suddenly feeling very confused, I ask, "Were you the one who sent me the email this morning? About the open position?"

He straightens, angling his head at me. "Would that be a problem?"

And here I thought it'd been an actual *professor* who'd done the vetting. "No," I say, hoping he won't see right through my disappointment. "I'm sure whatever authority Professor Colter's granted you is much deserved." I don't know why the words come out as bitter as they do, but there's no taking them back now.

Lucky for me, he doesn't seem to be offended in the slightest. And, much to my surprise, he laughs. "I wouldn't go that far. It's more like she's too busy to do anything other than prepare her lectures, so any irrelevant tasks get handed to me." A charming blush crawls across his cheeks before he quickly adds, "Not that you're irrelevant or anything."

Now it's my turn to laugh. "Well thanks, I guess."

His smile is warm as he turns toward me, leaning against the desk. "So, *Elara*," he says with emphasis, "what kind of a name is that?"

"I could ask you the same thing, *Xero*."

His face falls, as if realizing his faux paus. "I'm curious because it's a beautiful name—one I haven't heard before. Well, not in the usual context." Even beneath his shaggy hair and thick frames, I can see his left brow raise. "Jupiter's eighth largest moon, is it not?"

It takes all my strength to keep from blushing. If he wants to talk space with me—*especially* with the way *he* looks—then damn, we can talk about it all day long. "It seems I'm talking to a fellow space enthusiast." I can't think of anything else to say, so I leave it at that.

"In the flesh." He grins. "I'm sure you're also aware that Elara was one of Zeus's lovers in ancient Greek mythology." A shadow dances across his eyes. "It's a shame he decided to hide her deep beneath the Earth."

Being very familiar with the story of Hera and Zeus, I say, "It's a shame he felt the need to cheat on his wife." Then, with a shake of my head, "You men and your *needs*. It's a surprise we even put up with you at all."

He smirks, clearly amused. "Do I sense a feminist in my wake?"

Whatever attraction I'd felt before dissipates entirely as my ex's voice begins to ring in my ears. "If by 'feminist' you mean that I believe all people should have equal rights, *including* women, then yes. Obviously."

He quickly picks up on the fact that he's struck a chord—and a deep one at that. His smirk fades, his expression turning serious. "I'm sorry if I gave you the wrong impression. I believe that, too. Wholeheartedly."

Oh. Well now I feel like a total asshat. I'm searching for what to say next when, thankfully, my phone rings. I fish it out of my bag right as Kensie's name flashes across the screen. I hold up a finger (no, not *that* one) to Xero before turning away to answer it.

"Hey, is everything okay?" I ask. Kensie's more on the whole *text message brigade*, so getting an actual call from him is a bit worrisome.

"E, can you come by the shop?"

I go to glance at my wrist but, seeing as my watch is on my right hand, as is my phone, I pull the device away from my ear slightly. I don't know how, but an hour and a half has already gone by. "I've got class in twenty minutes. Can I swing by after?"

There's confusion in his voice as he says, "Class? Is Professor Haven back? Did they find him?"

I bring my palm to my forehead before dragging it down my face. "No, I don't think so. I mean, I haven't heard anything, so I don't know." I lower my voice. "Look, it's a long story, but I got another job at the university. I'll explain later. Class gets out at a quarter past three."

There's a bout of silence on the other end of the line. And then . . . a familiar female voice. "We'll wait."

Chief Albeck.

I get a sinking feeling in my stomach. Why the police are at the café with Kensie, I have no idea. "Hang tight," I say, trying to hide the slight tremor in my voice. "I'll be there as soon as I can."

1 1

AS MUCH AS I'd hoped to make a good impression on my first day with Professor Colter, it seems I have more pressing things to attend to—which sounds strange, even to me. I mean, what could possibly be more important than showing up for your new job? Well, cooperating with the police, for starters . . . especially when their line of questioning involves you (and your closest friend) regarding the disappearance of an esteemed teacher.

Since Xero had been the one to email me and *not* Professor Colter, I'd asked him not to tell her that I'd shown up . . . yet. He'd agreed and told me I could "officially" start next week before handing me a fresh copy of the class syllabus. I'd felt good about our last interaction, despite the misinterpreted feminism jab, so I'm not all that surprised to discover that he's on my mind the entire way to the café.

As I walk past the windows, I can't help but notice that there are no other patrons inside, nor a soul in sight out on the streets. I try to shake off the dark cloud that's hovering over me, but before I can fully collect my thoughts, the door swings open. I'm greeted by a familiar, friendly face. Officer Blatter. I glance at his badge, noticing the change in status. "*Detective* Blatter," I say with a sincere smile and a nod of my head. "I suppose congratulations are in order."

He beams at me. "Always wanted to be a detective. Ever since I was a young lad." The clearing of a throat sounds from behind him, causing him to immediately change his tone. "Do come in."

Even though I'd been made aware that she'd be here, I'm still disheartened to see Chief Albeck sitting across the table from Kensie. My spirits lift a little as Detective Blatter changes his demeanor again, winks, and leads me to where they're both sitting.

Kensie doesn't so much as look at me as I take the seat next to him. "What is this about?" I ask, knowing full well that it's regarding Professor Haven.

"We were just stopping by to grab a latte when we recognized your friend here from the other day, from our meeting in your apartment." Albeck takes a sip from her eco-friendly cup, looking entirely too satisfied. "Best chai tea latte in town, wouldn't you agree?"

I give a slight nod, feeling uncomfortable at whatever she might be insinuating, even though I have no idea what assumptions are running through her mind. I decide it's best not to say anything and let *her* do the talking.

"No need to answer," she says, as if reading my thoughts. "Kensie here has told us it's your favorite." A shadow flickers across her eyes. "He's also told us that you came *here* on Saturday, right after leaving the university, and that you seemed pretty distraught—particularly after you ran out that door." She points to the café entrance for emphasis.

I shoot Kensie a sidelong glance, but his eyes are cast down at the table. I can tell by the way he's bouncing his right knee that he's nervous. In that moment, I can't help but feel responsible for dragging him into all of this.

"Yes," I say, feeling pleased with how calm my voice sounds. "Kensie had just brought me my drink when I thought I saw someone standing outside the window."

"Who was it?"

"I don't know."

"Was it a woman? A man?"

"If I had to guess, I'd say it was a man." I glance at Detective Blatter. "But this was *before* I'd found out that Professor Haven had gone missing."

"Why did you go after him then?" The suspicion in the chief's eyes is all too apparent.

My thoughts flit to my incarcerated father. My breath nearly catches as I send a silent prayer that Albeck hasn't pieced together who I am and how we're connected. It isn't difficult to imagine what she'd ask . . .

Why would you go running after a stranger, Elara?

Who were you expecting it to be?

I choose my words carefully. "I saw someone staring at me through the window, that's all. I was curious as to who it was. I thought, perhaps, it was a student?" I shrug, hoping that it comes off as sincere. While that last part isn't true, the rest of it is.

"And you came back for open mic night?"

My mind flashes to the stranger I'd conversed with that night. *There is light to be seen here yet.* Had it been him? The stranger from earlier? If so, how am I just now piecing that together?

"Elara?" Chief Albeck presses.

"Yes," I say. "I came back for open mic night."

"Did you have further contact with Professor Haven in between?

I shake my head. "No. The last I saw him was at the university earlier that day."

The officers exchange a dubious look. I'm relieved when it's Detective Blatter who says, "Kensie also mentioned that he didn't see you for four days after the fact."

Just when I thought I'd been let off the hook for one thing, I get pulled right back under. I try not to seem too rattled, but I can feel my thoughts going a hundred miles a minute. I can't possibly tell them about the strange message I'd received, nor my encounter with potential *cosmic beings*—there's no way in hell they'd believe me . . .

And could I really blame them?

From the looks on their faces, I know I'm taking too long to respond. Truth is, I don't know what to say. Those four days are just as much a mystery to me as they are to them. I can't possibly account for that time. So how can I avoid saying something incriminating when I don't even know the truth myself?

"The reason no one saw her," a low, sultry voice says from behind me, "is because she was with me."

Even though I'd just met him, I'd know that voice anywhere. I turn around in my seat to find Xero *inside* the café, leaning against the window near the door. When had he gotten here? How had I—*we*—not heard him come in? Even more to the point, how had he known where to find me?

With unmatched confidence, he strides over to our table before pulling an empty chair in front of him. He spins it around so that the back is facing us, then takes a seat. He runs a hand through his tousled hair before addressing me, "Sorry I'm late, Elara."

Although I don't know why, it's clear he's trying to help me—and somehow has a plan to do so. Before I can overthink things, I do the one thing I've never been very good at. I improvise.

"It's okay," I say, doing my best to follow his lead. "We were just finishing up here."

Albeck shoots me a warning glance before turning her attention on the newcomer. "And you are?"

"Where are my manners?" Xero adjusts his glasses, pushing them up the bridge of his nose, before extending his arm across the table. "I'm Xero Sivalla, one of the senior assistants at CU Boulder."

She doesn't shake his hand. "For Professor Haven?"

He doesn't so much as flinch at Albeck's accusatory tone. "Professor Colter, actually. Modern Philosophy."

"And exactly where were you and Ms. Friis for *four* days without contact?"

"I own some property up in Allenspark." In one deft move, he's got his phone out and is scrolling through photos of the most gorgeous cabin I've ever seen. "Elara and I were chatting at open mic night, and she asked if she could spend a few days up there. I suppose you could say it's become a sort of . . . *refuge* for many of the assistants at CU." He sets his phone on the table so that it's perfectly within reach of the officers. "Seems we both needed to get away to enjoy the rest of our fall break."

The way he says *we* has my mind spinning in eighteen different directions—all of them oh so *good.*

Albeck narrows her eyes at him before turning her gaze on me. "Is this true?"

I nod in earnest. "Every word."

"Do you have proof of your communication regarding this trip?"

Out of the corner of my eye, I see Xero place his hand over his phone. Taking it as a cue, I pull my own phone out and, for reasons I can't explain, load my email. I tap **Sent Messages**.

What I find in my inbox is more than unusual—because these messages? Are ones I never sent.

Trying not to look totally taken aback, I slide the phone across the table to Chief Albeck. She begins to scroll through our correspondence, brows lifting in what I can only assume is complete and utter surprise.

"Well?" Blatter says, prompting her.

"All here and accounted for," the chief says, not even bothering to hide her disappointment. She firmly sets the phone in the space between us before pushing her chair all the way back from the table. "We'll be in touch."

Detective Blatter seems just as thrown off by her sudden change in demeanor as the rest of us. "Thank you for your time," he says with a tip of his hat before rushing out the door after her.

I watch as they pass by the windows, waiting until they're completely out of sight before turning toward Xero. There's no point in trying to hide the incredulous look on my face. "Thank you," I say, feeling relieved and confused at the same time. "I can't even begin to guess how you pulled that off—but thank you."

"You're most welcome."

I can feel the questions piling up, burning at the back of my throat, but Kensie interrupts before I get the chance to ask any of them.

"Glad that's over with—and E? How about the next time you go away for an idyllic weekend in the woods, you remember to invite me, will you?" He swipes a towel from a nearby table before walking off, muttering about the stresses of being a barista in a college town.

Credit where credit is due.

"Think now's a good time to ask him for a chai?"

I exchange a small smile with Xero but notice that his doesn't reach his eyes. There's something else lingering there. Something I can't quite place . . .

"It's on me," I say, not wanting him to leave just yet. After he gives a gracious nod of his head, I scoot out of my chair and signal for Kensie to get behind the counter.

"What's all this about?" he whispers, throwing his apron over his head. "And don't say Professor Haven because I already know that part. But you two? In a cabin? In the *woods*?" The way he emphasizes that last part makes my skin prickle—in a good way. "Who is he, Elara?"

I glance back at Xero, only to see an eerily serene man who didn't just lie straight to the authorities to keep a complete and total stranger safe—but something tells me that last part . . . may not be *entirely* accurate. "He's just an old friend," I murmur, unable to explain why or how the sentiment feels so true.

I watch, somewhat absentmindedly, as Kensie makes our lattes, but when I turn back around, with both of our drinks in hand, Xero is gone.

12

IT CROSSES MY mind to head back to campus, but the larger part of me says doing so would only make me look desperate. Still, I'm intrigued by Xero's behavior and what's just happened at the café. I'd been so lost in my thoughts and Kensie had been wrapped up in perfecting our drinks that neither of us had seen him leave. We hadn't heard him either.

I offer Xero's chai to Kensie, which he graciously takes, before waving goodbye and heading out the door. I know my friend deserves more inside information than I've given him, but until I know what's going on, there's not much I can say. For now, it's best he thinks I wandered off to a cabin. With a stranger. For four days.

Very un-Elara of me.

Deep in my core, I *know* that's not what happened. I would have remembered—especially since it was allegedly *Xero's* cabin. I may not be as attuned to the mundane details of life, but the things that stick out? The unusual? *Those* are the types of things I'm hardwired to remember.

Seems my thoughts have taken me all the way around the corner to the parking lot. I fish in my pockets for my keys, taking the final swig of my latte before setting it in the cupholder. I tuck the key into the ignition, swing my bag over my lap and into the passenger's seat, then gently rest my head on the steering wheel. The sleeves of my sweater are pulled up just enough to reveal the ink underneath my watchband.

I stare at the markings for a few moments, sigh, then pull the sleeve back down. I turn the ignition all the way on, immediately feeling better at the familiar rumbling of the engine—but that feeling is ruined the minute I realize that I don't know where to go. I don't want to go back to the café. I don't want to go to campus. I don't want to go home. What I want . . . is to escape. Even if it's just for a little bit. *That illusory cabin in Allenspark is sounding pretty good right about now.*

For reasons I can't explain, I suddenly feel the urge to activate my Jeep's GPS touchscreen. I only drive to and from a couple of places—my apartment to campus, campus to the café, and my apartment to the grocery store. That's it. I certainly don't need a GPS to drive within a 10-mile radius. So I'm surprised—and also not surprised at all—to discover that the last coordinates punched into my GPS read: Allenspark, CO.

What the actual fuck?

Does this mean Xero's story is . . . true?

I chew on my lower lip, debating my options. If I thought showing up on campus might look desperate, imagine driving an hour out of town to a cabin you've supposedly been to *without* an invitation.

But, since I'm likely not getting any answers from Xero, this is the only lead I've got. I know if I don't go, I'll just be sitting around wondering what *would* have happened if I had. And that settles it right there. I put the car in reverse, pull out of the parking space, and head due east before hopping on Highway 36.

The hour goes by in a flash and, before I know it, I'm pulling into the driveway of cabin number 511. It's not lost on me that 5-11, or May 11th, also happens to be my birthday—*and* my mother's birthday. I blow out a long breath, disregarding any and all feelings that tell me this isn't just a coincidence and to get the hell out of there. I've come too far, not to mention, that chai tea is running straight through me.

The gravel is damp from the recent rain, leaves scattered all over the partially paved driveway. The sun remains unseen, held captive behind a canvas of grey. I shut the door to my Jeep and click the lock button, marveling at the sight on the hill above me. It's more of a mountain than a hill, but eh, semantics. Regardless, it's absolutely stunning.

The cabin must be on stilts, given its height, which is nearly equal to the treeline, but you can't tell with the dense thicket that surrounds the base. I first notice the enormous tinted glass windows that overlook where I'm standing. It must cost a fortune to keep them as clean and pristine as they are. The roof is the color of wet moss, its peaks reminding me of something out of gothic literature. The gravel leads me to a pathway of large, impeccably cut stones, each one spaced perfectly apart. My gaze follows the many stairs that lead up to the front door, the mossy hue matching that of the roof.

As I climb the vine-ridden stairs, I lift my hand from the iron railing and run it along the exterior of the house. By the texture alone, I'm guessing its cedarwood, although it's been stained to look more like cherry oak. When I reach the top landing, I'm nearly breathless, but I'm pleased to discover a keypad near the door. I pull my phone from my back pocket and scroll through the email correspondence I don't remember having with Xero.

Code: 0745#.

Again, I can't help but notice the synchronicity. Seven. And forty-five. Both numbers in the strange message I'd received. And the cabin address being the exact date of my birthday?

Curioser and curioser, the Alice in me murmurs.

I rest my hand on the doorframe, trying not to get too far ahead of myself, and take a deep breath. I punch the code into the keypad, the light just above it switching from red to green. I'm met with another set of stairs as I push the door open. My legs are gonna *burn* tomorrow, let me tell you.

With a sigh, I slide off my boots and place them by the welcome mat, then begin yet another daring ascent. On my way up, I realize that, *technically*, I'm breaking and entering. I bet Albeck would have a fucking field day if she ever caught wind of this, but I don't allow that thought to travel any further than it already has.

My mind flits to Xero and how he'd come to my rescue at the exact moment I'd needed him. Frankly, I hadn't *known* that I'd needed him, but I'd been more than willing to accept his help—even though I still don't understand why or how all of this is happening. The guilt around coming here uninvited begins to claw at me, but it isn't enough to get me to leave. I've allegedly been here once before, and so, from my perspective, I'm a welcome guest.

Logic: 10/10.

When I reach the landing at the top of the stairs, I can't help but clutch the railing as my other hand flies over my mouth to suppress a wildly inappropriate squeal.

Holy. Fucking. Shit.

The first thought that enters my mind is that this *must* be a movie set. It has to be. Everything is expertly curated—from the rustic furniture, to the ornate fireplace, to the luxury kitchen, to the hallowed cherry oak floors I currently have the insane privilege of walking across. Modern artwork with a flair of the paranormal dons the walls, and it feels like I'm walking through a gothic-style Addams family mansion, but with just the right number of homey touches to undermine any hint of, well . . . *creepiness*. As a matter of fact, it's quite cozy.

The living room is lined with black leather sofas and chairs, with a few sangria-colored pillows to boot, and to the right is the kitchen, the black marble countertops and rectangular glass cabinets shining like the glorious beacons they are. From over my shoulder, I notice that there's both a front patio *and* a back patio, each with their own giant sliding glass doors, and that there are even more stairs leading to who knows where.

As I'm making my way to yet another set of stairs that are located at the back of the cabin, I hear something that gives me pause.

Footsteps.

Climbing.

Shit.

I dart across the living room on the balls of my feet, hoping that I'll be able to see something out the windows, but the trees are so dense, it's like I'm floating among them. I freeze in place at the soft beeps as the code is punched into the door, the lock clicking as it releases.

It has to be Xero.

As much as I want to hide, there are two dead giveaways that the cabin isn't empty: 1) my car's in the driveway, and 2) my boots are sitting idly at the front door. I hear rustling just below me . . . then the removing of a coat. The voice in my head tells me to *do something*, to run to the landing and announce my presence—but another part of me says that he already knows. That he's somehow . . . *expecting* me to already be here.

I wait by the window, halfway petrified, as heavy boots hit the stairs. Eventually, a russet head of hair emerges from the stairwell and turns toward me. Our eyes meet for a brief moment before my gaze flicks to what he's carrying in his hands. Relief washes over me.

The corner of his mouth pulls into a smile as he draws closer. Without saying anything, he extends one of the cups to me. I follow his lead as he tilts the drink to his mouth. The moment the taste of chai hits my lips, I instantly feel myself relax. I let out a small sigh, savoring everything about this moment. Our eyes meet again, his expression even softer than before. I can't explain why it feels so comfortable, being around him—or how my senses scream that we've somehow done this before . . . but the look on his face tells me that I'm right.

Best chai in town.

At first, I'm positive I've just heard him say those exact words out loud—but they're floating through my head.

Unspoken.

I angle my head at him, confused.

You said so yourself. At the café, remember?

I nearly drop my beverage, searching his face for some sort of explanation. "I can . . . *hear* you," I whisper, my heart suddenly pounding.

Good. He angles his head, eyes glinting. *I just needed to be sure it really was you.*

13

IT'S A GOOD thing one of us has catlike reflexes, otherwise we'd be spending our time cleaning up spilled coffee instead of talking about . . . well, whatever *this* is.

Even though his hands are full—again—he tells me to sit and gestures toward one of the couches. I turn away from him, making sure to take my time settling in so that I can think. But if I'm thinking . . . *can he somehow read those thoughts, too?*

Suddenly, I don't know what to think. I don't know how to feel. All I know is that someone I've *just met* has communicated with me telepathically. Like, that's even a thing?!

Don't get me wrong, I've always believed in things unseen, but having it actually happen? So unexpectedly? My shock is entirely warranted.

I watch as Xero takes a seat in the armchair, setting his drink on the table between us. I study his face, waiting for more words to enter my mind, but none come.

I slouch back into the leather seat, defeated.

"Hey now," he says teasingly, "why the long face?"

"I think you know why."

There's a familiar glimmer in his eyes as he says, "Ever heard the old adage *walk before you run*?"

Somehow, I manage to stifle my disbelief. "Pretty sure you were just 'running' a second ago. In my *mind*," I shoot back.

His silence is unnerving.

"So it's all true," I start, knowing what I want to say, but stumbling over how to say it. "This cabin. Me being here. For four days. With you." The last part makes my throat go dry.

He takes a long swig of his drink. "I suppose it is."

"You suppose? Or it *is*?" I press.

"It is," he answers quietly. "True."

"At the café, at open mic night . . . that was you I met on the patio, wasn't it?" It certainly doesn't look like him now—not with the way he's currently dressed. He neither confirms nor denies the statement, but the look on his face brings me back to the day we'd first met in the lecture hall. He'd sought me out for an assistant position which means . . . he must have been looking for me. He must have *known* about me—and about Professor Haven.

Suddenly feeling a little cautious, I scoot away from the edge of the couch, turning my gaze to the window. I can't figure out what to say, so I don't say anything.

"Look," he finally says after an extended silence, "I know this is going to sound certifiably insane, but I've been . . . trying to find you."

I slowly turn back toward him, my eyes shooting daggers. "No shit."

He straightens, clearly taken aback by my candid response. "I'm not talking about in a weird 'serial killer' kind of way. Honestly, it baffles me to think you even have such a thing here." He shakes his head, seeming to catch himself. "That came out wrong—"

76

But I've already latched on to the oddity in his statement. "What do you mean . . . 'have such a thing *here*'?"

Crimson blooms across his cheeks. "Listen, this is just as confusing for me as it is for you, okay?"

I swing my legs around so that my entire body is facing him. "I highly doubt that, Xero. You just spoke to me . . . *without* speaking!" Even as I say the words, I realize that, indeed, I do sound exactly as he'd said—certifiably insane. "I wasn't imagining that, right? You're not here to strap me up and wheel me in?"

He guffaws, shaking his head. "Nothing like that, Elara. I promise."

The way he says my name sends an electric jolt through *all* the right places.

"So, what *are* you doing here? What are *we* doing here?"

"As for *my* being here, I wanted to make sure you were okay." The honesty in his voice is undeniable. "As for us? Well . . . that remains to be seen."

I'm about to tell him that he'd better start talking—and *fast*—but he seems to read the urgency in my expression. *Or maybe he's accessing my thoughts at this very moment.*

With his elbows resting on his knees, Xero clasps his hands together, his thumbs making circles over his olive skin. He drops his head before releasing a long, steady breath. "The truth is . . . I don't fully remember. One day, I woke up here, in this cabin, without any recollection of how I got here."

I lean in closer, not wanting to miss a single word.

"On the counter were car keys, a driver's license, a university badge, a class schedule, and this." He digs around in his jacket pocket before producing a small piece of paper with a portrait on it.

I take it from him, my eyes fixed on the black-and-white sketch. There's no questioning it. *It looks exactly like me . . .* but with a few minor differences. From what I can glean, there's no discoloration in my hair (otherwise there'd be shading), my eyes seem to be larger and wider-set, and my cheeks are raised, leaving me with an even more angular profile than the one I already have. I gently turn the portrait over, but there's nothing on the back.

I study it for a few more moments before returning my gaze to Xero. "*This* is how you found me? No name, no address, no information at all—just a sketch of a woman who slightly resembles me?"

He tilts his head, confused. "*Slightly?* I've never seen anything more accurate."

His words are flattering, but I'm having a hard time believing that he was able to scope me out using just this portrait. "Okay, yes, I'll admit she looks like me, but there are some major differences. I mean, just compare our facial structures. She looks more whimsical, more *ethereal*"—my voice catches on the word—"almost like she isn't even from here," I finish in a whisper.

I'm instantly brought back to an earlier moment in our conversation. Xero's voice plays in my head. *It baffles me to think you even have such a thing here.*

". . . but that's because *she* isn't from here, is she?" I say slowly, my heart fluttering in my chest. My grip loosens, the sketch falling to the ground at my feet. "And neither are you."

He moves so quickly that I hardly realize just how close he is to me now. He takes my hands in his—they're so warm, like a furnace. It makes me want to move in even closer but, somehow, I resist the urge.

Look at me.

He's doing it again. Speaking without speaking.

I lift my gaze, my eyes locking on his.

Is this okay?

My mind freezes for a moment. For reasons I can't explain, it *is*. It's okay that he's this close to me. It's okay that he's holding my hands. It's okay that he's, well . . . *in* my mind.

I nod, hoping he'll continue.

You're right, Elara. I'm not from here. The thing is, I don't know exactly where it is I'm from. All I know is that when I woke up here, with no recollection of anything, I felt this sort of inclination, this urge, to find you. The portrait and the CU badge on the counter were only confirmations of what I already knew to be true.

You'd think it'd take time for me to process what he's just said, but the words sink in with such ease—like butter on warm bread. I decide to try my hand at this whole telepathy thing. *Can you hear me?*

Brow raised, he sits back slightly. A smile tugs at the corner of his mouth. *You catch on fast.*

I return the smile. *I'm a quick learner. Always have been.*

You have questions, no doubt.

I nod, briefly forgetting that we aren't actually speaking. It's unreal how clearly I can *hear* his voice in my head, as if he actually *is* talking to me . . .

How long have you been here?

Only a week or so, but it feels a lot longer.

It took you that long to find me? I tease.

His face falls. *I spotted you the first day I got here.*

My heart skips a beat. I think back to the stranger outside the café, outside my apartment window, the feeling I had on the rooftop . . . but that first one has me circling. "There's light to be seen here, yet." I repeat what had been said to me at open mic night, studying his face for a flicker of recognition, but there isn't any.

Had my assumption been wrong?

I can't help but feel a little disappointed. But I want him to keep talking, to keep sharing, so I push my doubts aside.

"The last thing I wanted to do was frighten you"—his voice sounds even better in person than in my head—"and I wanted to be certain it truly *was* you. Didn't take long though. There's no denying what I felt when I saw you from across campus that first day."

"And what did you feel?" He's still holding my hands, and I can feel them growing warmer.

"I felt . . . *connected* to you. In more ways than one. When you consider all of the students on campus, all of the people that were brought into my awareness . . . that tether just wasn't there."

"*Tether* is an interesting choice of words. Almost as if you feel . . . bound to me?"

A hint of fire flashes across his eyes. "Not bound, no."

"Then what?" I press.

"I feel . . . protective. Fiercely loyal." He pauses before speaking the next word. "Devoted."

Devoted? I don't think I've *ever* had anyone use that word—not about me. Actually, I'm *certain* I haven't. It throws me for a loop. "Why did it take you this long to confront me? If you've known since day one . . ."

"Like I said, I didn't want to frighten you. I've also been trying to figure out, well, everything else." His expression turns downtrodden, as if he's failed somehow.

I gently squeeze his hands until he brings his gaze back to mine. The spark that once ignited his irises is gone. "Maybe you weren't meant to," I whisper. "Figure everything out alone, I mean."

I can tell my words hit him in a way most guys wouldn't show. But Xero isn't most guys. He closes his eyes and gently nods his head. "So you'll help me?"

"Seeing as you just taught me how to communicate telepathically?" I wink. "I mean, it's the least I can do."

With his hands still clutching mine, he brings them to his cheek before brushing his lips across the top. *I'm so happy I found you.*

My heart flutters. *Me too.*

And for that brief moment, the turmoil and confusion of the past week fades away entirely.

14

IF YOU HAD asked me a month ago if I thought I'd be spending the weekend up in the mountains, in a cabin, with a guy like Xero, I would have laughed at the notion. This is a far cry from the more recent life situation I've found myself in—single, jobless, struggling to stay afloat no matter how much effort I put in . . .

Being here pulls me away from all of that. Here, I don't have to think about Professor Haven and what did or didn't happen. I don't have to think about the Boulder County Police and what Albeck suspects or doesn't suspect. I don't even have to think about my future at the university because it all feels so infinitesimal compared to the fact that I—that *we*—have supernatural abilities. Is that even the correct term? I don't know, nor do I really care! It's the most exciting thing that's happened to me, well . . . *ever.*

Xero and I had stayed up the night prior, just talking and drinking tea by the fire. He'd even managed to pull out my favorite board game, Scrabble. A worthy opponent he'd turned out to be.

I could have stayed up into all hours of the morning with him, but there's only so much to talk about when the majority of your life is a blur. I could feel his longing—see the waves of sadness crashing in his eyes—whenever I'd bring up an old memory or something that reminded me of times past. Little does he know, there's plenty I'd like to forget.

My father, mostly.

My ex, too.

I wake to the sound of automatic blinds inching their way upward on the window across from me. I don't remember falling asleep, and I certainly don't remember coming into this room. I rub the sleep from my eyes, lifting the blanket just slightly to see that I'm still fully dressed, sans my boots, of course. I turn over in the bed and groan, pulling the sheets up higher so they'll cover my head, when I spot Xero standing at the door, breakfast tray in hand.

I sit up, a little more rapidly than I would have liked, and begin smoothing my hair. Believe me, I know what I look like in the mornings and this is *not* what I was hoping he'd see . . . and on our fourth encounter, no less.

But who's keeping track?

"I didn't mean to wake you," he says, his eyes shifting from my face to what I'm sure is the equivalent of a bird's nest atop my head. His mouth rigs to the side. "May I come in?"

I don't want to be rude and, if I'm being honest, I'm starving—and whatever he's got on that tray looks beyond appetizing. "Sure, come on in," I say, scooting over to make room.

He sets the tray down next to me before taking a seat at the edge of the bed. "I hope it's okay," he says quietly.

I look at the spread before me. There's a bowl of orange slices, honeydew melon, strawberries, and purple grapes, and next to that, a plate with a butter croissant and a couple of apple-filled pastries. *All of my favorite things.* I give him a toothy grin. "I was about to ask how you knew, but it seems that'd be a rhetorical question."

The sound of his laugh fills me up from the inside out. "Did you notice? I even tried my hand at making a chai tea latte." He points to the coffee mug at the far left of the tray. "I can't make any promises, seeing as Kensie is the town's pro barista, but I thought I'd give it a shot."

"Seems you've learned a lot in your short time here."

"I will admit, some things do come a bit easier than others . . ." He falls silent then, his expression growing troubled, but before I can ask what's wrong, he shakes it off and says, "What are your plans today?"

I hadn't really considered that. It dawns on me that I may have overstayed my welcome, seeing as I wasn't technically invited here to begin with, but something tells me he's asking for a different reason. "Well, now that I know Professor Colter gives her assistants every other Friday off . . . I'm not really sure."

"Well, you are more than welcome to stay. In fact," he says, popping one of the grapes into his mouth, "I'd much prefer it."

I try to hide my smile as I take a bite of one of the pastries. "I think I can swing that."

His eyes glimmer with delight. "I'll let you finish up here. Meet me downstairs in ten?"

I nod before taking a sip of the homemade chai tea latte. *Damn, that's good.*

He's halfway out the door when he turns around and asks, "Oh, do you have a heavier jacket, by chance?"

I look at the one I wore here, which is now folded neatly on the dresser—no doubt Xero's doing. I angle my head at it before saying, "Just the one. Why?"

"Because where we're headed, you're going to need it." He grins, taps the doorframe twice, then vanishes down the hall.

I fork a few more berries, hurriedly cleaning both the plate and the bowl, before bouncing over to the mirror to freshen up. *Not as bad as I'd expected.* I tighten some of the strands in my messy bun, throw on a swathe of lip balm, and dab some rose essential oil on my wrists and neck.

You know, just in case.

Trying not to seem too eager, I take my time going down the stairs. About halfway down, I can see Xero wrapping himself in a heavy wool coat. Even though my footsteps are nearly silent, he seems to sense my presence. He turns over his shoulder, fleece pullover in hand. "Thought you might want to wear this underneath your jacket."

"Thanks," I say, taking the red-and-black flannel from him. "My boots are one more flight down." I can't help but notice that he also isn't wearing boots yet, and that his socks match the flannel he's just given me. He looks part rugged-outdoorsmen, part little kid—and I love it. I tuck my chin in an effort to hide the warmth I feel rapidly spreading across my cheeks—and throughout my entire body.

Seems I'm too late. "Mine are as well." He smiles before dipping into a dramatic bow and gesturing toward the next flight of stairs. "After you."

Once our boots are on and we're outside, I can't even begin to express how thankful I am for this fleece pullover. With the wind chill, it feels at least twenty degrees colder than what the temperature reads—not to mention, we're currently climbing *up* the mountain, which is only making it colder . . . and windier.

"I'm surprised," I say, half-shouting from behind him, "I didn't think it got this windy in the morning."

He slows his pace so I can catch up before turning over his shoulder. "Never know what you're going to get up here—it's always a bit of a mystery. I promise though, the view is well worth it."

It takes us a solid thirty minutes of straight-slope hiking to get halfway to the top. I hadn't even noticed the bag draped over his shoulders until he swings it around and pulls out two water bottles.

"My, my, look who came prepared." I take a seat next to him on the boulder that overlooks the entire town. The view is breathtaking. "Wow, you were right. Definitely worth the hike."

"I bet you're glad you ate a hearty breakfast." His tone is playful and I'm afraid that if I look at him, I won't be able to resist kissing him.

I keep my eyes straight ahead. "Sure am, thanks to you."

"Well, don't get too comfortable. This is just one of two things I want to show you."

At that, I break my gaze from the view and look directly at him. "There's *more*?"

"I told you . . . well worth it."

I hold his gaze. At first, I'm searching his face for clues, but then find myself studying it for other reasons. There's so much familiarity, not only in the physical sense, but on an intangible level as well. Only briefly have we touched on the fact that he isn't "from here"—but what that ultimately means, I don't know.

Seems he doesn't either.

And just like that, my thoughts have ruined our potential connection. Xero's no longer looking at me—or sitting next to me, for that matter—but is zipping up his backpack with both our water bottles in tow.

"Come on," he says, urgency lining his voice. "I think you're going to like what I'm about to show you next even more."

"If that's even possible." I don't speak up enough for him to hear me, but I can tell by the look on his face that he *did* indeed hear me, loud and clear.

I follow close behind him up the steep slope, the climb getting more treacherous by the minute. I'm relieved when we finally reach a landing that *isn't* on an incline—that is, until I look up at the rocky wall I assume we're about to scale.

I take a quick glance at my feet. "While these *are* hiking boots and all, I don't quite think they're equipped to handle, well . . . all of *that*."

He raises a brow at my overly emphasized hand motions before chuckling and shaking his head. "We're not going up." He points along the side, to a nearly invisible edge that leads *around* the wall of solid rock.

Somehow worse.

I'm momentarily distracted by the sound of . . . "Is that running water?"

He perks up. "Good ear. There's a waterfall just on the other side. It runs all the way down the mountain—just wait until you see the way the sunlight refracts off of it."

"Say no more. Lead the way."

We inch our way along the barrier, taking our time so as to not plummet to our deaths. I notice that every few steps or so, Xero stops to make sure I'm doing okay. Little does he realize, I was born for this kind of stuff.

I mimic his hop-skip once I reach the edge, and it's a good thing he's there to catch me because the sight alone is enough to knock me off my feet. I've never seen a waterfall as gigantic (or as miraculous) as this one. Purples, blues, and greens bounce off the rippling waves, creating a sort of kaleidoscope as the water rushes by. I kneel by the stream and dip my hand in. Surprisingly, the water's *warm*—hot, even. At second glance, I notice the rising steam. "It's a hot spring?"

He nods. "A welcome respite from the biting cold."

I stand back up, mesmerized by the beautiful cavern and the many mysteries it promises to hold. "You're right," I say, taking a step closer to him. "I do like this even better."

"Worth the hike?" He closes the space between us.

I don't dare move. "Yes. More than worth it."

At this point, we're close enough that I can feel his breath on my face. His eyes search mine—hungry, *ravenous*—although I don't know what for. I mean, I have a few ideas . . . but he's hard to read. *Ha—the irony.* I attempt to tap into his thoughts, but I'm met with a brick wall. How does he do it so easily with me?

Just relax. His voice enters my head.

I've never been very good at that.

A smile. *That's why I brought you here. To unwind.*

I angle my head. *I see your game. Smooth.*

No game. Just something I remembered. His forehead creases, almost as if he's in pain. *It's familiar, is it not?*

As much as I don't want to, I break my gaze to look at my surroundings once more and . . . he's right. It *is* familiar. I've been here before. With him. I know it.

I can *feel* it.

He lifts his left hand and gently brings my focus back to him. His skin is just as warm as the waters in that spring. I nearly melt beneath his touch.

Elara.

My eyes close as his voice floats inside my head.

Elara.

I'm spinning in a memory I can't quite place. One that doesn't belong to me, but somehow feels like my own all the same. His presence, his voice, his touch . . . I'm wholly convinced that this is not the first time and yet, we've only just met. Stars explode across my vision, paving the way for more memories I can only hope will be made clear soon.

"Elara."

I hear it this time, his voice. Slowly, I open my eyes. It's only as he's pulling away that my attention is drawn to something there is no mistaking. There, on his left wrist, is silver ink. Silver *markings.*

And they're identical to my own.

15

I REACH FOR his wrist, mostly out of shock, grabbing it a bit more harshly than I'd intended. Xero doesn't flinch but, instead, studies me with apparent curiosity. I might go so far as to say perplexity, but given our newfound history—whatever *that* entails—I know that's a long shot.

My suspicions are confirmed as he says, "You have one just like it."

I release his wrist and pull the fleece lining up just far enough for him to see. "Identical." Almost instantly, I'm brought back to that night—the one where I'd received the strange message. I haven't told him about it.

Is it possible he already knows? Did he experience something similar? Finally, someone to talk to about this!

My thoughts are racing faster than I can keep up with, but they come to a grinding halt the moment his voice enters my head. *I woke up with it.*

My heart sinks. So no transmissions then.

What transmissions?

Shit. Didn't mean for him to hear that, but I guess once the gateway to my thoughts is open, there's no hiding anything. Good to know. I tuck that nugget of wisdom into the back of my brain for later.

I turn away from him then, suddenly feeling intrusive—*or like I've been intruded on?*—and break the connection. It seems to work because I hear him sigh behind me.

"Sorry. I guess you're still not used to that."

"That's putting it mildly." I rub the back of my neck before slowly turning back around. "No need to apologize, though. I don't know what girl in their right mind would ever complain about a guy being able to anticipate their every need—" I clamp my mouth shut before he gets the wrong idea. Or maybe it's the right one? *Ugh.* I try to get a grip on my thoughts, but the effort is futile.

"You seem flustered."

You don't say.

He smiles again.

Dammit.

"Okay, okay, no more," he says, raising his hands in jest. "It's just so easy."

"I prefer to hear your voice anyways." I wait for the blush to crawl across my cheeks, but it doesn't.

"And I yours."

Oh. There it is.

He turns away, but not fast enough for me to miss his smile. He removes his jacket, shirt, and pants, then suddenly dives into the water. He emerges from the surface, steam eddying from his hair, shoulders, and chest.

"Well?" he says, and it's then I realize I don't know how long I've been staring for. "After a hike like that, a refreshing swim is exactly what's called for."

He's right. In more ways than one—and while I'm not hesitant . . . I also kind of am.

He turns around so that his back's facing me, as if to point out what a perfect gentleman he is. He dives back under and swims a few feet, and it's only when he rises for a lungful of air that I admit he's convinced me.

I remove each layer, tossing them on the ground next to me, until my undergarments are the only things that remain. I walk over to the edge and dip a toe in, a satisfied shiver running over my cool skin. I'm immediately warmed from the inside out as I hop into the water, making sure to keep my shoulders beneath the surface to avoid the draft in the cavern.

"I take it I can turn around now?"

"I don't see why not," I reply as I swim over to him. I try not to focus too much on his incredibly toned physique, but it's been years since I've felt attracted to anyone—not so much that as *connected* to someone else.

The reflection off the water hits his eyes just right, drawing out an aquamarine hue I hadn't realized was there—as if his eyes somehow have the ability to shapeshift. "You're looking at me like you've never seen me before."

"Am I?" I splash him in jest. "If I'm being honest, you do look a bit different wet—" I clamp down on my tongue, instantly realizing the many implications of my statement. But Xero's laughing before I can even attempt to cover my faux pas.

"I suppose I could say the same about you."

Heat builds in my body, the natural hot spring only amplifying what's already there. I drift toward him, not realizing just how quickly the distance between us is closing.

With the waterfall pounding behind him, the water beading along his brow, his cheekbones, his jaw, and the way his hair slides back so smoothly as he runs his hands over his head, I'd swear he's doing it all on purpose.

There's a moment when our eyes meet, his gaze locking on mine, and I sense that he's about to reach toward me but he resists; pulls back for some reason or another. "Did you know that water is a conduit?" His attention is on the waterfall now.

"I can't say that I do. A conduit for what?"

"Follow me," he says somewhat cryptically, heading for the back of the cavern.

I swim after him, dipping underneath the side of the waterfall, trekking further and further into the monstrosity. It grows darker and darker, narrower and narrower, until we finally reach the center of what looks like another cavern. Light pours in from the naturally-formed skylight above us, the echo from the waterfall barely audible.

"This is . . ." I want to say *stunning. Breathtaking.* But I'm rendered speechless—as I should be.

"I found it the very first day I got here," he says, reaching his hand out and pulling me out of the water. "I can't really explain it, I just felt a sort of . . . magnetic pull."

"I can see why." I join him on the wool blanket I'm assuming he'd left behind from his last visit. "I mean, who wouldn't?"

"I've tried to make it out here every day since. Working at the university gets in the way some, but, luckily, it's even more beautiful at night." He points up at the sky. "You can see everything—and I mean *everything.*"

Without meaning to, my gaze tracks to his wrist. "You know what that is, right?"

"It's the Taurus constellation."

"Exactly." I take a deep breath. "Except, unlike you, I haven't always had mine. It only just showed up . . ." My words trail off as I notice Xero starting to lean back, his face paling to a ghostly white. "Hey," I say, suddenly feeling very concerned. "Are you okay?"

His eyelids begin to flutter, his mouth parting briefly before closing again. His throat bobs, as if he's trying to speak, but can't. I enter full panic mode when his eyes start to roll *all the way* back.

"Xero?"

Slight convulsions overtake his body, but they're not intense enough to be classified as a seizure. Whatever's happening though . . . isn't good.

"Xero?" I say again. I start to reach for him, thinking maybe I can shake him out of whatever's got its hold on him, but as I go to do just that, something *impossible* happens.

My hands don't make contact.

He's here, laying right in front of me, and I can physically *see* him . . . but I can't touch him. I move my hands around— back, forth, up, down . . . nothing. I can't feel the texture of his jacket, the warmth of his skin, the beating of his heart. *What the actual fuck?*

And then, as if I've entered into a realm where every law and rule of our reality has been rewritten, his body begins to *shimmer.* I sit back on my heels, taken aback by both the strangeness and beauty of what's unfolding right in front of me. His body appears less and less dense as it begins to take a similar form, just in thousands of tiny pieces instead of one cohesive unit—like small projections of each and every molecule. I look up at the skylight, almost expecting to see some extraterrestrial craft hovering above us, but I only see cyan blue. I bring my gaze back down to find that Xero's now . . . *gone?*

"Oh my god," I say, feeling like I've actually lost it this time. "Oh my god." That's the only phrase I can seem to mutter as I pick myself up off the blanket and whirl around, hoping that he's somehow going to appear behind me. "What *was* that? What just happened?" I run my hand along the side of my jaw before squeezing the bridge of my nose. "Think," I say, feeling both petrified yet also astounded by whatever I'd just witnessed.

My eyes fall to my wrist. *What have I read about this?*

Alien abduction? I look to the sky. *No.*

Currently in a dream? I pinch myself. *Nope.*

Figment of my imagination? I shrug. *Possibly . . .*

I look back down at the ground at the blanket, then remember our clothes, *and his bag,* are on the other side of the waterfall. I can't seem to move fast enough. I dive back into the water, propelling myself forward like a professional swimmer. I grunt as I half-push-up my way onto the stone surface, doing a quick scan of the area, past our clothes and . . . *there.* His bag. I crawl over to it, nearly scuffing my knees along the way, before pulling it onto my lap and rummaging through it. Two water bottles. Some snacks. And his cell phone. For reasons unknown, the cell phone gives me pause. The images play out in my mind once again.

Shimmering.

Projecting.

Disappearing.

Sounds a lot like teleportation, which I know doesn't exist here—at least, not that we know of—but there's something that *does* that falls along the same lines . . .

Astral projection.

Except Xero may not have been "projecting", per se—he may be full-on astral *traveling* as we speak.

Did you know that water is a conduit?

It can't just be a coincidence that we came here, that he asked that very question, that he disappeared just minutes after asking it . . .

Which brings me to another thought. Perhaps that's what had happened to me. Just before I'd tapped into that strange message, I'd taken a shower. Could it be that water is a conduit for accessing interdimensional feeds on the astral plane? And because it'd been during "normal" waking hours, I'd remained conscious throughout it? The evidence is overwhelming. Seeing as we can't seem to explain what *really* happens when we sleep, what dreams *truly* are, and where our consciousness goes . . .

who's to say we're not astral traveling *unconsciously* every single night when we fall "asleep"?

Whether it's right or wrong, it's the only lead I've got. I consider waiting in this exact spot for him to return, but something tells me he won't be coming back here. If anything, he'll land right back where he was when he first arrived.

I stuff his clothes into the bag before stripping off my undergarments and pulling on my dry clothes. If water *is* indeed a conduit, I certainly don't need both of us disappearing into thin air, now do I? I swing the bag over my shoulder, moving as fast as I can toward the cavern's entrance. I get a nice stride going, determined not to stop for anything or anyone along the way. *Back to the cabin it is.*

16

THE FIRST THING I do when I step foot inside is call out Xero's name. I drop the bag and blanket at the foot of the stairs before making my way up to the living room. I glance at the couches, the chairs. *Empty.* I sneak around to the kitchen. *Also empty.* A single glance out the window that overlooks the patio tells me he isn't out there either, so I backtrack and head up one of the other flights of stairs. He isn't in the room I slept in which means . . . maybe he's in *his* room? I quickly realize I haven't yet ventured over to that part of the cabin.

I hurry along the hallway, cracking open random doors to check and see if I've found what I'm looking for. *Washroom. Laundry room. Linen closet* . . . A door at the end of the hall, slightly ajar, catches my eye.

That has to be it.

I race over to it, careful not to make too much noise in case Xero *does* happen to be in there. No need to startle him any more than I'm sure he already feels, what with spontaneously disintegrating at a subatomic level and all.

I see no reason to announce my presence so I swing the door open, but my heart sinks in my chest at the sight of a perfectly made bed. I'm about to close the door and search the rest of the house when something pulls me back in. What was the word Xero had used? Oh, right.

Magnetic.

Without explanation or reason, I head straight for the nightstand. Seems he's left one of the drawers open, and sticking out of the small crevice are a bunch of yellow sticky notes— much like the ones in the CU observatory. Intrigued, I begin to reach for them, then stop, realizing that this is a total and complete invasion of privacy.

Really? We're going to go there? After he's been continuously reading your thoughts without permission?

Against my better judgment, I shimmy the drawer out a bit farther before grabbing the pile with both hands and tossing it onto the bed. It's mostly chicken scratch and there are a lot of scribbles—even more things are crossed out and rewritten again, quite poorly, I might add. I try to think back to the handwriting on the notes in the lab to compare, but these are different. Definitely not Professor Haven's, which gives me some relief.

I continue sorting through the notes, unable to read the majority of them, before finally coming to my senses. *This is wrong. Put them back.* Somewhat reluctantly, I listen to the voice in my head and return the pile to the drawer, making sure to leave it slightly ajar, just as I'd found it.

I try to suppress the panic rising within me, now that I know he isn't in the one place I was certain he would be. And seeing as I've checked almost everywhere else in the house . . . *Breathe.* I lean against the edge of the bed and close my eyes. I inhale deeply through my nose. *And exhale.* I sit like that for a few moments, not wanting to open my eyes and come back to reality.

Eventually, though, I have to.

I fall onto the bed, my legs hanging off knee-down at the edge, nearly gasping at the ceiling—or lack thereof. I mean, it *is* a ceiling, but it's made almost entirely of glass. The tops of the pine trees create an idyllic frame of the sky. I can only imagine what it looks like at night with all of the stars and constellations. It makes me wonder if he gets much sleep. *I sure wouldn't, not with a view like this.*

I don't carry that train of thought much further, though, due to the wave of exhaustion that's currently washing over me. I scoot myself to the top of the bed before fluffing one of the pillows and resting my head on it. Gaze still skyward, I notice some storm clouds encroaching on the spotless canvas. It only takes minutes (*why is it things seem to happen faster in higher altitudes?*) for the blue to disappear, revealing a churning, stormy gray. Raindrops begin to hit the glass, the pitter-patter a welcome reprieve from my overactive mind. My stare remains fixed on the glass above me until I feel my eyelids succumbing to the rhythmic pattern, and I drift off to sleep.

When I wake, I'm surrounded by darkness. I groggily turn over—momentarily forgetting where I am and what had happened earlier that day—but not for long. As I fling my arm over the side, it hits something.

On the bed.

Next to me.

A body.

Alarmed, I scramble to a sitting position, frantically reaching all around me for a light source—a lamp switch, my phone, his phone . . .

His phone.

"Xero?" I whisper, squinting in the darkness. I gently place my hand on what I think is his back, moving my arm up his shoulder to confirm. I trail up his neck until I reach his head. *There's no mistaking this hair.*

It's then that it dawns on me . . . I can *feel* him. My hand isn't floating through him, all ghostlike and shit, like it had earlier. Unless that had been a dream?

I'm certain that it wasn't . . .

Feeling overjoyed, I lightly shake him. "Xero, wake up. Wake up!" My eyes have mostly adjusted to the darkness now. He turns over, the glowing silver ink on his wrist catching my eye.

"Go back to bed, Elara," he mumbles, clearly half-asleep. And then . . . *"Elara."*

Instantly, his eyes shoot open as they settle on me. I've never seen anyone move so fast. Within mere seconds, he's sitting up and has me embraced in one of the tightest hugs I've ever felt.

You're okay!

You're okay! I think back. I'm not even upset that he's in my head. I'm just happy he's here, that he hadn't disappeared for good. The thought alone makes my stomach turn.

He pulls away from me, then puts his hands on my shoulders. Even in the darkness of the room, I can see the glimmer in his eyes, the tousled state of his hair, the concern etched all over his face. It surprises me when he speaks, *out loud.*

"You saw it, right?"

I search his face, confused. "Saw what?"

"What happened back at the cave?"

So that confirms it—not a dream. It's funny how he says it so nonchalantly, as if vanishing into thin air is commonplace. Yeah, maybe for magicians. *Or wizards.*

"Yes," I stammer, "I—I saw it all right." I shift my focus away from him, suddenly feeling the urge to search the room for bugs, cameras, hidden mics . . .

I don't think we should talk about it verbally, I communicate.

He furrows his brows, then nods in understanding.

You disintegrated right in front of my eyes.

He nods again. *It's happened every time I've gone there.*

There? Where did you go? I have my suspicions, but I keep quiet. I'm obviously asking for a reason.

Hard to say. I can only remember bits and pieces—but I think I went back to where I'm from . . . where we're *from.*

That last part throws me for a loop. *We? I don't understand. I didn't go with you . . . I was still here.*

Last week. Those four days you can't account for . . .

His response hits me right between the eyes. *Do you mean to say that you somehow . . . took me with you?*

I must have. How else can you explain that?

"I can't," I murmur, briefly breaking our connection; but something he's just said snags in the corner of my mind. *You said you only remember bits and pieces . . .*

He takes my hands in his and gives them a light squeeze, as if what he's about to say is *that* unbelievable.

We weren't here, Elara. On this planet—dare I say, even in this realm. The more it happens, the more I'm convinced it's . . . it's . . .

Astral travel. I don't mean to interrupt, but I can't help myself. *I've read about it in as many books as I can find, watched countless documentaries—and given what I experienced last week . . . well, it fits the bill in more ways than one.*

You experienced something similar last week?

I give a fervent nod of my head. *That's what I was about to tell you before you vanished. And I think you might be right. I think, somehow, you took me with you.*

Do you remember anything?

My shoulders drop. *Not a thing.*

A long (mental) silence stretches between us.

I nearly jump at the sound of his voice.

"I think we should go back to your apartment."

Back to my apartment . . . The way he says it makes it sound like we've known each other for years. My head begins to spin at the thought of how fast all of this is happening. Not to mention *all* the things I haven't yet told him—the details of the (now confirmed) otherworldly transmission, what I saw in Professor Haven's office, the shadow entities that night in the observatory . . .

Don't move.

I bring my attention back to Xero. A pit forms deep in my stomach at the expression he's wearing. It borders on the edge of fearful, but it's more "protective determination", if anything else. I'm not sure what has him so worked up until I see it. The reflection in the glass. Tinted with silver and green.

Shit. He needs to know. I'm about to tell him when he squeezes my hand tighter.

Do not let go of my hand.

His voice is so firm and demanding in my head that I could have sworn he'd spoken the words out loud. *Xero—*

Do not let go, Elara.

I want to scream, to shut my eyes, to run and hide, but I stay put. I do exactly as he says, squeezing his hand even tighter in reassurance.

I don't know how I know . . . but I already sense what's coming next. The door to the bedroom is hurled open. Silver light, tinged with a sickly green, floods the space around us. My eyes travel to my wrist, the one with the markings. I blink once, twice. Mine is glowing *orange.*

I glance at Xero's wrist. So is his.

My gaze meets his once more. I can feel pulsing all around us, my eardrums thrumming as the intensity heightens. Xero's face is washed in the strange hue, making him look even less human. The pulsing grows stronger, the reverb bouncing around the inside of my skull. The urge to cover my ears is unlike anything I've ever experienced—well, except for that one night where I encountered exactly *this*.

I keep still, my gaze pointed directly at his, our hands firmly intertwined. I can see the tension mounting on his face as whatever is here draws closer, but, other than a slight muscle tick in his jaw, he's as still as a statue.

Xero's voice enters my head. *Three . . . Two . . .*

I don't know what he's counting down to. All I know is that wherever we're about to go, we're going together. I brace myself as the world around me bursts in a flash of orange, brighter than the sun itself.

17

W H E N I C O M E back to, I'm not sure what to think. The first thing I notice is the denseness of my body—actually, of my *entire being.* There's a sense of heaviness not only within me, but all around me—as if all of existence is weighted down by ten tons of rock, and that weight is being added on, over and over and over again.

My mind feels different, too. Murky, almost.

I move my head slowly to the side, looking for . . . I'm having trouble remembering what. Where had I been just moments prior?

A sharp pain jolts against my skull, and it feels like an echo of all the trauma I've endured in my life thus far—my damaged relationship with my father being at the forefront, along with my miscarriage and ass of an ex-fiancé. A swell of broken promises rises and falls, like tidal waves storming a beachfront. It might feel like more of a threat if I weren't so . . . what's the word? *Apathetic.*

I've hit low points in my life, sure, but nothing like this. Nothing like the complete and utter indifference I feel toward everything and everyone at this very moment.

But how did I get here? And where is here?

I attempt to search for the answer, to try and *remember,* when I realize that I don't really care.

I don't recognize this person, this Elara.

I don't care to.

I don't care not to.

I'm trailing a string of incomprehensible thoughts when something shakes me out of my seemingly endless spiral. A light. Silver. Then green . . .

My mind momentarily snaps back to recognition, to giving a damn. *Xero.*

I look around me for the first time, noticing that he doesn't seem to be anywhere nearby—wherever *nearby* is. It's dark everywhere I look, except in the spot where I saw the strange light. I shift my focus back in that direction, watching as the colors undergo a sort of "shift-change". Each color is only visible for a few seconds before the next one takes its place . . . and repeat.

I lift my head, trying to make sense of what I'm seeing. There's no sky—in fact, it seems wherever I am is enclosed. Now that I'm aware of this observation, I suddenly find it very hard to breathe. *But I've been breathing just fine. There must be oxygen here.*

Unless I don't need oxygen.

Oh, these unrelenting thoughts.

I look down at my hands, not sure what exactly I expect to find, but it certainly isn't this. Much like Xero, it seems I've taken on some sort of spectral form. My fingertips buzz with electricity, the particles in my hands broken apart into millions of tiny pieces, just waiting to be stitched back together. I'm not sure if *this* was the shadow entities' intention, but I'm guessing not so much.

Xero must have had something to do with it.

Even though I now know my body is floating in particulates and can't possibly be "dense", I can still feel the layers of heaviness that make up my mind. I try not to think about it and instead focus on my surroundings—which is a whole lot of nothing. It's dark and empty and void of, well . . . everything.

There are no plants. No sky. No sun. No *life*.

Unless maybe there *is*, and I just can't see it.

I find that possibility even more unnerving.

I attempt to communicate with Xero in my mind, hoping that he'll somehow be able to pick up on the transmission. There's no doubt he's *way* more skilled in that arena, seeing as he somehow got me here, all in one piece—well, *pieces.*

Xero, I say silently. *Come in, Xero.*

Great walkie-talkie speak on my part. I shake off my nerves and try again.

Xero, it's Elara. Are you there?

Radio silence. Pun intended—seems I've got a slight sense of humor in astral form.

I wait a few more moments before starting to lose patience. Another thought occurs to me. *What if he isn't here? What if he's lost in some other dimension? What if we can't connect?*

The panic gremlins creep into my thoughts once more, doing whatever they can to keep me feeling worried, afraid—

To keep me feeling *heavy.*

I hack their plan almost immediately. I don't know how I know, I just *know.* I intentionally flood my mind with images of Xero the first time I laid eyes on him. The first time he spoke to me. The words he both said and didn't say. The connection we made . . .

Elara.

It's faint, but, somehow, I manage to pick up on it.

It's him. I know it.

Xero.

One more time.

Xero.

. . . Wrist.

The word is clear, but I don't know what he . . .

Oh. The markings.

I look down, trying to focus on the silver ink that's no longer stationary on my "arm", but is instead dancing like autumn leaves caught in a stormy gust. I recall the markings turning orange just before I'd been sent *here*, but that isn't the case at the moment. In fact, they're hardly even silver.

Trying, I communicate. *How?*

Focus. His voice is crystal clear now—which means he must be getting close. Or so I assume.

I keep my focus on my swirling wrist, trying not to get too freaked out at the fact that my body isn't actually "a body" at present—at least, not in the physical sense. I've never done drugs before but *damn*, if this isn't trippy as *fuck*.

I don't know if it's because I've been staring for too long or what, but a faint purple begins to emanate from the very spot I've been focusing on.

Purple. I find it fascinating that, somehow, we're effectively communicating with one another via one-word phrases—although, let's not forget, he *has* said we've done this before. If I didn't believe him then, I certainly do now.

Yes. Good. Wait.

Three words this time. Something tells me to keep my eyes on my wrist, so that's what I do until I receive further instruction. And then . . .

"Here."

It's a voice that isn't Xero's.

I'm not sure a chill *can* run down my spine in astral form, but—a *massive* fucking chill runs down my spine. I'm keenly aware that the voice came from behind me and, as tempted as I am to turn around, I don't want to risk losing my connection with Xero. If we lose each other, there's no telling what might happen—and, judging from the foreboding nature of that voice, it probably isn't good.

Bad, I communicate. *Hurry.*

Instantly, I feel the ominous presence of whatever's approaching—similar to the slow suffocation of all that is well in the world. Darkness encroaches, filling me with every gut-wrenching, heart-breaking, tormenting emotion the mind can grasp. Fear is a very powerful thing. But pain?

Even more so.

Fearing the pain only causes more pain from the illusion of fear itself. An endless loop. A vicious cycle. The pattern of all patterns.

Debilitating.

Incapacitating.

Devastating.

It claws at my mind, threatening to force its way through— but I won't let it. I can't.

Xero! The urgency is clear as fucking day.

The faint purple near my wrist grows stronger, brighter. Hope springs within me.

Ahead.

He doesn't have to say it twice. I look directly in front of me and—there he is . . . the most glorious thing I have ever seen. Like mine, his body is also in particulates, but as he moves, they seem to string together, forming beautiful rainbow-colored waves. I've honestly never seen anything like it. In all of my years of research and studying, I've always known that everything is energy, but this . . . this *defines* it. What I'm looking at right now is the absolute essence of *every single thing* in this vast, infinite, ever-expanding Universe.

I can *feel* the resonance between us, more clearly than I ever could before. And, while I can't explain it, I don't need to. The feeling is more than enough. It's *real*.

Something pulls at me from behind, but I remain focused on Xero—that is, until I hear another familiar voice.

"Elara."

I nearly freeze. After multiple semesters' worth of lectures, I'd know that voice anywhere. *Professor Haven.*

Fortunately (or perhaps not), I'm pulled away just in time.

18

THE BLARE OF a semi-truck's horn is the first thing I hear. My eyes shoot open, only to be covered immediately by the back of my hand. Per my current view of my Jeep's sunroof, the sky is exceptionally bright today. The interior of the car suddenly grows dark as the semi passes by, and it's then I'm fully aware that I'm in the backseat of my car—which means Xero must be at the wheel.

All at once, what we've just been through comes barreling in. I grab the back of the driver's seat headrest and pull myself all the way up. Just as I'd suspected, Xero's at the wheel, doing well over ninety down Highway 36. I don't blame him. Given everything that's happened, I'd be booking it, too.

He glances at me in the rearview mirror. "Good to see you're awake." The way he says it puts me slightly on edge—as if something traumatic had happened that I can't seem to remember.

Pretty darn close to it.

I'm about to ask where we're headed when we pass a familiar exit. *We're headed back to my apartment . . . just like he'd said.* I can't even begin to sort through my thoughts, so I don't try to.

"Do you feel all right?"

"All things considered?" I let out a long sigh. "I guess so." But my stomach turns as I remember something that hadn't come back to me until just now. "We were . . ."

Xero nods. *We were taken.*

Hearing his voice in my head again has a strange way of soothing whatever's wrong. *Who were they? And where were we?*

That remains to be seen. But I know I've visited a place like that—he pauses—*many, many times before.*

His response is unsettling. "*We're* not from there . . . are we?"

He seems a bit startled by my breaking the silence, but he answers all the same. "No. We're not."

A wave of relief washes over me. I decide this next part shouldn't be spoken aloud. *Whoever they are . . . I think they have Professor Haven.*

He slowly takes the exit that goes straight through town and to my apartment. *What makes you say that?*

You didn't hear him?

I didn't hear anything. I was focused on getting us—on getting you—away from there as quickly as possible.

Perhaps I'd misheard. Perhaps one of them had pretended to be Professor Haven. That whole place had given off a very *Loki, God of Mischief,* kind of vibe. But something tells me otherwise . . .

We round a corner and turn into the parking lot, sitting in silence as Xero parks in my designated space. At this point, I'm not even going to try to act surprised. It's obvious that he somehow seems to know things he can't possibly know—and yet, here we are.

I open the car door, feeling a little shaky on my feet once they hit the ground. Xero takes me by the arm to steady me. *Side effects of astral traveling.*

I smirk. *You don't say.*

I don't know how to feel about the fact that we both seem . . . *unfazed* by all of this. That our demeanor is, more or less, lighthearted. I'm certain that if I were to tell Kensie, it'd be a completely different story—which is exactly why I've kept as much of this as possible to myself.

I'm happy to see that Xero had managed to repack my things before we'd left the cabin—both of which I have no recollection of. I'm sure we'll have plenty of time for him to fill me in . . . *Ugh.* My gaze travels up the many flights of stairs I have to climb. It might as well be Mount Everest.

Like a true gentleman, Xero takes my bag and my coat, throwing both over his shoulder. He extends his arm to me. I link mine with his, using my other hand to grip the railing.

"There you go. Easy does it."

I roll my eyes at him, wishing I didn't feel so pathetic and helpless right now. But without him, there's no way I'd make it up these stairs. He's patient and slow and takes his time, unlike every other male on this planet.

When we reach the fourth floor, Xero fishes in his pockets for my car keys, which also conveniently holds my apartment key. He unlocks the door, then leads me inside toward the couch. I gently lower myself onto it, not wanting to disrupt my body—and whatever healing process it's going through—any more than I already have. Complete and utter disassociation (and disembodiment) will do that to a person.

I notice that Xero makes sure to lock the door, even going so far as to twist the knob twice, before bringing over two glasses of water. He sits on the couch next to me and pats his lap. I try to swing my legs up and over, but it's no use. My brain doesn't seem to be fully communicating with the rest of my body at the moment.

It's clear he senses my frustration because he smiles, then gently lifts my legs, one at a time, until they're resting on his lap. He studies my face for a few moments before scanning the rest of my body. I don't feel the slightest bit uncomfortable under his heated gaze.

"You should be feeling like yourself again soon."

"You sure about that?" I tilt my head toward my bedroom. "The last time something like this happened, I was out of commission for four days, according to you."

"True, but you *were* conscious this time. That'll help speed up the process."

"Why is it that you seem to be just fine?"

"More practice, I suppose."

"Right. Your daily cave visits."

His face falls then, and I can't help but wonder if it's because of something I've said.

Listen, Elara. I think we're in a lot more danger than I originally thought. This isn't the first time you've come into contact with . . . them?

Only one other time. At the university. Right after Professor Haven went missing.

They're looking for something. Although I don't know what, I can feel it. The urgency. The desperation . . .

I attempt to ask my question again, even though I didn't get an answer the first time around. *Where were we?*

A shadow falls over his eyes, which indicates he knows something he's not telling me.

It's okay, I reassure him. *You can trust me.*

He looks sad now. *It's not that I don't trust you. It's that I don't want to say it if it doesn't actually exist. I don't want to speak it into existence.*

Well, technically, you're not speaking . . .

He raises a brow. *Thoughts are still made manifest, whether they're spoken aloud or not.*

I wait for him to continue, but the only thoughts currently in my head are my own. *Please. Tell me.*

He runs a hand along his jaw, debating. Finally, he says, *If my instincts are correct, we were taken to Nibiru.*

At first, I'm sure I haven't heard him correctly. *Nibiru? As in Planet X? The . . . nonexistent planet?*

I know all about it, thanks largely to Professor Haven and his borderline obsessive research assignments—but they, more often than not, turned up empty. Null. But hearing Xero say this makes me think the voice I'd heard right before we were pulled out of there *did* indeed belong to Professor Haven.

"How could we go to a place that allegedly doesn't even exist?"

"It may not exist *here*," Xero says quietly, "but that doesn't mean it doesn't exist elsewhere."

I know what he's going to say next and, for once, I wish I didn't. I beat him to the punch. "We have to go back there, don't we?"

He places his hands just above my knees, then gives them a light squeeze. "Eventually, yes," he whispers. "But first, we need to find out *why*."

19

THAT NIGHT, I find myself in a lucid dream. Xero's there, looking as enticing as ever—but, honestly, when doesn't he? We're somewhere I can't quite put my finger on; somewhere beautiful and mysterious and idyllic, yet oddly familiar and all too inviting.

I take his hand and begin to walk—*although it feels more like floating*—across an exquisite landscape of towering neon-colored florae, shimmering orbs refracting the light, and iridescent waves carrying the sounds of infinite oceans. We float higher and higher, even though there's no physical way of telling which way is up and which way is down. It's all based on sensory perception. And let me tell you, I am not *at all* prepared for how highly attuned my senses are to his.

Our upward trajectory comes to a stop, but we're still "moving" in the sense that we're floating. His hand wraps tightly around mine as he pulls me in closer. And closer.

Endless lifetimes.

The phrase hangs between us, but it isn't heavy or tense. Instead, it carries with it meaning and purpose; knowledge and truth.

We're so close now, I can feel every fiber of his being buzzing with electric currents, as if they were my own. A tender embrace follows, filling me with the kind of happiness I've only ever gotten from simple luxuries—feeling the sand between my toes for the first time, or a popsicle from the ice cream truck on the fourth of July, or the smell of a library book after cracking it open and devouring its contents . . . Those moments you don't realize are really special until they become mere memories of what once was.

I can feel Xero's presence reach into my own—not taking or stirring or fixing, just *sharing*. In the joy. In the laughter. In the liberation. In *me*.

If these were physical sensations, they'd be akin to sex with someone you hold very dear—but this is different in that it's *not* physical. It's so much better than that. And that's because, in more ways than one, we've collided. Not just physically. Not just mentally. But on a *soul* level . . . in complete and utter unison.

I don't think it's possible to feel this way anywhere *but* here. Where there's separation and divisiveness, how could you? Absolute unity is an enigma—and always will be amidst density and polarity. Amidst a place like Earth.

This moment between us stretches and stretches, until I'm fairly certain time doesn't exist at all. When he said we've done this before . . . *this* is what he meant.

It has to be.

Like an island breeze, we drift further away from "reality". I don't mind one bit. Being that I'm in a lucid dream (or so my mind says), I know that, eventually, there will come a time where I'll have to wake up. To end this. To return to the doubt, the fear, the duality—all that it is to be human.

But what if we could stay? What if we didn't have to go back? I much prefer this over the reality of my rapidly crumbling life. Of my incarcerated father. Of Professor Haven missing. Of cops knocking at my door. Of potentially putting Xero, or Kensie, or *anyone* in harm's way. Now that I've experienced this, it feels far too risky.

Far too *selfish.*

Realizing that my thoughts have somehow overtaken me in a place where that probably shouldn't be possible, I redirect my attention to where Xero *should* be—but it seems our connection had been lost somewhere in between my mini tirade of life's qualms.

Instead, I find myself still floating in an ever-expanding cosmic chasm—the colors, sounds, and pulses deepening the further I travel. *But where oh where is Xero?*

I spot what I *think* is him at the far edge of a brightly lit portal—a wormhole if I've ever seen one. I didn't think anything could get any brighter or any more magnificent, but it seems I stand corrected. It reminds me so much of a kaleidoscope that I could almost swear I've somehow reverted to my childhood-self, a curious girl peering into the looking glass.

Static fills my head, followed by a momentary buzzing, and it's then I realize that whoever this is *isn't* Xero—but they certainly seem to know who he is.

He's found her, I take it?

The voice is foreign to me, almost . . . *non*-human.

Yes, but it hasn't come without its trials.

The professor, you mean?

They're talking about Professor Haven—they have to be. *Focus, Elara. Don't let your thoughts run away with you. Not now.*

The second voice is softer, but still androgynous. *I told you, didn't I? That this was a risk—*

A risk well worth taking.

There's a long pause. *That remains to be seen.*

That last phrase sits with me. The way it'd been said . . . Xero's used that phrase before—but I know that this *entity* most certainly is *not* Xero.

These voices must be of his kind, where he came from, I think to myself. *And somehow, I'm tapping into this feed, this transmission . . .*

I watch in utter amazement as the shining, glimmering portal vanishes right before my very eyes. Not surprisingly, the voices go along with it. In almost the same moment, my surroundings begin to fade, becoming dimmer, and dimmer . . . until the "lucidity" of my dream is no more.

Not if I can help it.

My eyes flutter open and, although I'm somewhat disappointed to be back *here*, I do find some comfort when I see the bright red numbers that read 3:33 A.M. on my alarm clock. I glance down at the floor, noticing that Xero's curled up in a tight ball, his head hanging off one of the very small pillows from the couch. Why he didn't sleep *on* the couch, or in the bed, is beyond me.

I gently place my feet on the ground and tiptoe around him toward the kitchen. Surprisingly, I don't feel all that groggy, but something's nagging at me, although I can't quite place what . . .

I open one of the cupboards and grab a glass before turning the faucet on. As I'm absentmindedly watching the water fill the glass, a light flashes by one of my windows, somehow hitting the glass just perfectly. *The colors.* I nearly drop the glass as I recall my "dream".

I rush over to Xero, half-full glass in hand, and drop to my knees. I shake his shoulder lightly, but man, is he *out*. "Xero," I whisper, finding my voice. "Xero!"

Still nothing. I scan his body, just to make sure he isn't in astral form (which he isn't), before dipping my fingers in the glass and flicking water at his face. If water is a conduit, can it *un*-conduit him as well?

Logical or not, it seems to do the trick.

"Elara?" There's alarm in his voice as he directs his attention from me to the door. "Is everything okay?"

"Yeah, yeah, everything is fine," I say hurriedly, shifting my legs underneath me so that I'm sitting more comfortably. "I just had the craziest dream—well, except, it *wasn't* a dream."

He sits up then, rubbing the back of his head. The blanket falls off of him, revealing that he's shirtless. I try not to look, but I can't help it—especially not after what I'd just experienced *with* him.

"I was lucid the entire time," I say, talking as fast as I can so I don't lose a single detail. "You were there with me and it was . . . well, it was beautiful. Indescribable, really." My eyes fall to his bare chest as if somehow *that's* a natural response.

His mouth rigs to the side.

"Sorry," I say, getting my thoughts back on track.

"You never need to apologize to me."

I don't think he means for it to sound so sultry, so *inviting*, but in his half-asleep state and the rasp in his voice, it couldn't be more so.

"You were saying?"

"Yes, right," I say, blundering like an idiot. "Well, we were there, together, until we weren't. And then you were gone and—"

He's searching my face, his expression suddenly very serious. "And what?"

"Well, I think I tapped into something . . . *again*. And they were talking about us. About *you*."

I have his full attention now. "What did they say?"

"They said . . ." *Come on, Elara. Think.* "They said something about you finding me. And they mentioned a professor, which *has* to be Professor Haven. And they said something about this being a risk—"

His stare is so intense, I can hardly breathe.

"What was a risk? Professor Haven?"

"No." I shake my head slowly. "No . . . I think they were referring to you—and me."

He looks stumped, and the expression he wears is a direct reflection of how I feel inside.

"They sounded just like you," I continue, my voice dropping to a whisper. "I think they . . . *know* you. And that you know— *knew*—them."

"Know," he says. "Time is merely a construct. All that happens, happens in the present."

I don't even mind the philosophy lesson—not when he's sitting in my bedroom, shirtless. *Get a fucking grip,* I scold myself. *This is important.*

"So . . . what does it all mean?" I ask.

He considers my question for a long while. "It means that they know about you. They know I'm here." A muscle ticks in his jaw. "And that, for some reason, they've gone to great lengths to keep us from knowing *why.*"

20

AFTER WHAT'S FELT like an incredibly long weekend, Xero and I find ourselves back at the university. It's strange having to behave like we've just met one another in front of Professor Colter, but I'd much rather be dealing with this than sitting at home, alone. At least this way, my mind is occupied— and the fact that Xero is here doesn't hurt either.

We're sitting in her exceptionally large office, red ink pens in hand. Call Colter old fashioned, but she prefers to have all assignments printed out and marked up. Her and Professor Haven have, er *had*, that in common.

As it currently stands, I'm sitting at the round table in the middle of the room; Xero's perched himself in one of the leather armchairs; and Professor Colter is typing away at her desk. I try not to look at Xero too often, but it's hard when I can feel his gaze burning a hole in my head. I briefly look up from the paper I'm grading and catch his eye. He smirks, adjusts his glasses, then quickly drops his head. *Damn, he looks good today.* Very Clark Kent-esque, if you ask me.

I snap out of my Superman daze as Professor Colter clears her throat. I try to give her my undivided attention, but it's proving to be difficult. *Go figure.*

"How many more?"

The question is directed at me. I gather the papers in my hands and hold them up for her to see. "About five or so left."

"Glad to see you're getting the hang of it, although I suppose it isn't much different from . . ." She clears her throat again, clearly not wanting to speak our long-lost professor's name aloud. She glances over at Xero. "How about you?"

Xero mimics the motions I've just made. "About the same as Ms. Friis."

My neck prickles at the formality. I've never heard him sound so . . . proper. *I fucking love it.*

"Well, it seems you two have your work cut out for you." With two more stacks in each hand, she winds around the side of her desk and drops the first stack in front of me; the second, in front of Xero. A glance at her watch indicates that she's leaving. "I'm off to lunch. Can I get you two anything?"

"That's very generous of you," I reply with a warm smile, "but I'm all set for today."

"Same," Xero says, giving her a small nod.

"I'll see you two in about an hour. Don't be late."

"Never am," Xero mutters so only I can hear.

"Have a nice lunch!" I clamp down on my tongue.

That sounded way too eager, Ms. Friis.

I look at Xero. *Not this again. While we're at the university, can we please use actual words?*

He sticks his bottom lip out in a pout. *Are you sure?*

I fling my pen at him. *Yes.*

"Fine. You win. No need to resort to violence."

"Oh, *I'm sorry*, did my pen hurt you?" I grab the stack of papers off the table and plop into the armchair next to him. "I just don't want to risk anyone walking by and noticing that we seem to be having a full-on conversation *in complete silence.* Might raise a little suspicion."

He waggles his eyebrows. "Maybe that's a good thing. Might liven things up a bit."

"Oh, we've had enough *liveliness* for a lifetime—*twenty lifetimes*, in fact."

"Oh, really? Tell me, just exactly how does that math add up?"

I give him a playful punch in the arm. "But really though," I say, letting out a long sigh, "doesn't this just seem so . . . *mundane?*"

He angles his head at me, curious. "Go on."

"Well, given our most recent . . . *experiences*, doesn't it seem like going to work and paying bills is a bit, well, *insignificant?*"

"You said it, not me," he says with a laugh, putting his hands up. "But in all seriousness, yes. This is fucking *stupid.*"

I can't help but grin. "To think just a couple of weeks ago, I was *so* worried about submitting a late application, losing my job, being *fired* from said job, paying my bills . . ."

"And then you met me."

The way he says it sends my chest fluttering as if it were brimming with dragonflies. "Yes," I say. I'm speaking in nearly a whisper now. "And then I met you."

He holds my gaze, a faint ray of light entering his olive-green eyes. "I never meant to disrupt anything."

Quite the opposite, in fact.

He grins. *I thought we weren't doing this.*

"Damn it," I mutter under my breath. "There's no getting by you, is there?"

"Afraid not."

I can't explain it but, right then, it feels like a dark storm cloud enters the room. While all of this is so new between us, it also feels tried and true. It's hard to imagine how things were *before* he showed up—unannounced, unexpected, but *more* than welcome. The rest of my life feels like a giant blur up until he'd waltzed on in. Before Xero, my life had been a cacophony of excessive stargazing, late night essay grading, oversleeping, and a general disdain for nearly everything and everyone. Don't get me wrong, I have ambition (well, sort of). I do my part. But I never really knew *why*.

Xero's starting to feel like a big part of my *why*, like we're a part of something larger. It feels important . . . like something that might *actually* make a difference— although I don't know how, exactly. All I know is that, before I met him, I was facing one direction, and one direction only. But now . . . well, it's as if we've built our own damn compass, our own map, our own . . . *future*.

I realize my thoughts have run away with me again when I notice that Xero's standing by the door, clearly waiting for me to join him. I glance at the untouched stack of papers sitting across from me.

As per usual, he knows what I'm about to say before I even say it. "We have to eat too, you know."

"Fair point," I say as I swipe my coat from the armchair. "So, what'll it be?"

"No afternoon chai today?"

Not until I tell Kensie what the hell is going on. I groan, wishing that I had more answers—and time. "Not today, no. But what I could really go for . . ."

"Happens to rhyme with chai?"

I laugh, shaking my head. "Thai it is."

Our lunch date started off great—that is, until my two favorite people just so happened to walk through the door. Chief Albeck and her number two. Okay, so I don't as much mind Detective Blatter as I do Albeck, but given the looks on both their faces, it would appear I should be *very* concerned.

There's no need for Xero to turn around. I've already communicated everything he needs to know, sans words.

"Fancy seeing you two here," Blatter says as he approaches our table. "I've been coming here for years, can't quite seem to get enough of the pad thai." He pats his protruding stomach for emphasis. "I see you have good taste."

I look down at my half-eaten bowl of noodles, then give him as warm a smile as I can muster. "There's no denying it, they *are* delicious."

"So, lunch break?" Xero directs his question straight at the chief.

She tips her hat forward. "Thought we might join you."

"Actually, we were just getting ready to go . . ." As if on cue, our server appears with to-go containers and the bill.

Albeck seems put off by my hastiness. I can tell by the way she narrows her eyes at me and purses her lips.

"Afraid we missed you the other day, Elara," Detective Blatter says as he takes a seat at the table next to us. "We were hoping to follow up on a few things."

"About Professor Haven? Any word?" I can feel my heart pounding in my chest, but my voice comes out smooth and steady.

"Nothing yet," he admits. "I'm guessing the same goes for you?"

"You're the first person I would have called."

We need to go. Xero's voice enters my mind in a very commanding fashion.

"Well, we have to get back to the university. Papers to grade and such." I hurriedly scoop my pad thai noodles into the to-go container. Thankfully, and somehow without my noticing, Xero's already taken care of the bill.

"New job?" Albeck questions.

I nearly freeze as I remember what I'd owned up to in our first interview. About being fired just moments before Professor Haven had disappeared. "Got lucky, I guess."

"Hmm," she murmurs, her eyes flicking to Xero before settling back on me. "Are you planning to be out of town over the coming weeks?"

"Seeing as I have to work, no. No plans to be out of town—at least not right now."

"Good," she says unnervingly. "Might want to keep it that way."

The entire time Xero is ushering me out the door, I'm wondering what she'd meant by that. He grabs my to-go bag from my hand and combines it with his. He seems frazzled, which is very unlike him.

"Hey," I say, gently pulling at his arm. "What's wrong?"

"Honestly," he says, not taking my hint to stop walking, "I'm not entirely sure. But the way Albeck watches you, talks to you . . ."

"I know. It's like she suspects me or something."

"It's more than that, Elara."

This time, I tug on his arm, *hard*. "What is *that* supposed to mean? What do you know that you're not telling me?"

"I saw the warrant in her pocket." He shakes his head. "It had your name on it."

His words come as a complete shock. "Tell me you're joking."

His eyes fall to the ground. "Afraid not."

I look around me, realizing that where we've stopped is just a few blocks away from my apartment. Seeing as we'd walked to the restaurant, I decide to book it to my apartment as fast as I possibly can. My mind is whirling with different scenarios, most of them bad, some of them unreasonably hopeful—but the only scenario I need see is the one I'm looking at the moment I arrive.

Damn police searched my apartment.

21

FROM THE MOMENT that we arrive, I can tell something's off—which isn't all that difficult when your apartment is the size of mine. I walk through the door with caution. At least *that* hadn't been busted down.

I figure the police must have gotten a key from my landlord. *How embarrassing.* Probably safe to expect an eviction notice to be tacked to my door any day now.

I settle on the kitchen first. Nothing seems out of place. I move to the living room area, which I had left a bit of a mess, but again, nothing appears to be out of order. But just behind that, near my bed, things seem to have been rifled through—particularly along the wall.

I storm over to one of the built-in shelves, feeling both angry and relieved at the same time. I pull out the thick three-ring binder that's already sticking out half an inch. I *know*, for a fact, that I haven't touched this binder in at least fifteen years . . . not since I changed my last name.

I flip through the legal documents—the petition, the applications, the court order—it all seems to be here. But that's not what concerns me. What *concerns* me is Chief Albeck knows. Or perhaps it was Detective Blatter who'd found the binder? *Wishful thinking.* I scold myself for not keeping this under lock and key.

"Everything all right?" Xero's voice interrupts my escalating internal tirade.

"Fine," I say, slamming the binder shut and tossing it back on the shelf. "Everything's just fine."

"Certainly doesn't sound that way." He walks up behind me and wraps his arms around me at the same moment I lean my forehead against the wall. "Nothing's been taken, I assume?"

"No. Thankfully, they didn't *seize* any of my *assets.*" I almost laugh out loud at how ridiculous I sound. *Who would have thought I, Elara goddamn Friis, would be saying those words?*

I exhale a deep sigh. "I suppose that's what I get, even after following all the rules my entire life, being an 'upstanding citizen' of society—even with all that, an invasion of privacy is still on the docket." I lift my head, sighing once more before muttering, "Unbelievable."

"I *would* offer my condolences, but it seems I'm at a loss. I can't possibly imagine what that feels like."

I turn around to face him, meeting him in his embrace. "It's fine. There are just some things I prefer to keep to myself, that's all."

"Like whatever's in that binder?"

I nod. "*Exactly* what's in that binder."

He pulls away from me slightly before taking my hand and leading me over to the couch. I fall into it, wishing I could just fall back asleep and lucid dream again. At least *there*, there's no pettiness. No crime. No fear or worry or invasion of privacy. Makes me wonder how Earth got so fucking turned around.

From the couch, we're both surveying my apartment in complete silence, when I just so happen to focus on the wall clock right behind Xero's head. Professor Colter pops into my mind.

"Shit, we're late," I say, starting to get up. "We're so, *so* late." The last thing I need right now is to get fired . . . *again.*

"Whoa, hang on," Xero says as he pulls out his phone and holds it up. "I already sent her an email. She responded about five minutes ago. She says she hopes you feel better."

"You told her I was sick?"

"I told her we had thai."

We look at each other with a smile and say, at the same time, "Food poisoning."

"Nice cover. And . . . thanks for that."

"Don't mention it. Besides, it seems we have more important things to deal with."

"Oh yeah? Like what?" I joke.

He adjusts one of the pillows behind him, clearly at a loss for words. "So, what now?"

"Well . . . we can't go back to the university."

"Right."

"Café's probably not a good idea either."

"Darn"—he sucks in a breath and narrows his eyes in jest—"I really could have gone for a latte."

"You and me both." My shoulders slump. Feeling like a prisoner in your own home was *not* on the menu today.

Xero echoes my thoughts. "Well, we could just stay here, seeing as we don't have much of a choice anyway."

For some reason, the way he says it gives me an idea—a *brilliant* idea. "Come on," I say tugging on his arm. "I have a feeling you're *really* going to like this."

Even though it seems I've caught him off guard, he doesn't resist. He's laughing, stumbling a little as we head for the door. "Changed your mind, have you?"

"You got to show me something," I say, keys jangling in hand. "Now it's my turn."

22

I PUSH OPEN the door to the rooftop, relishing the autumn breeze as it hits my face. "Here we are," I say as I hold the door open with my foot. Xero joins me shortly after. "I know it doesn't look like much right now, but just you wait until dusk. Watching the stars appear is, dare I say, *magical*."

"Can I take that as an invitation?" His eyes gleam.

"I suppose so." I walk to the center of the roof until I'm standing next to him. "I know it's not exactly *in* the mountains like your cabin"—I pause, realizing that I may have just brought up a tender subject—"but the view from up here is really something."

"Seems I'll have to take your word for it—until I can see it for myself."

"Oh?" I say, teasing him right back. "Is my word not *good enough*?"

He meets my gaze, eyes smoldering like hot coals on a winter's night. "Au contraire, it's *more* than enough."

He's already got me hooked *without* an accent or speaking another language. This just might be the thing to reel me all the way in. *Like I'm not already there.*

"I'm humbled that you invited me up here. Seems like a fairly secluded spot—like somewhere I'd go to think after a long day."

That makes two of us. As per usual, he's hit the nail on the head. Thankfully, the synchronicity is beginning to surprise me less and less. "Well, it's the least I can do after I showed up at your cabin, unannounced and uninvited."

Olive eyes simmering, he slides a sidelong glance my way before saying, "You're always welcome, Elara."

A chill runs down my spine. "I'll keep that in mind."

He breaks eye contact to look over his shoulder, surveying the space. "Well, since we're staying here until dusk, you know what would make this even better?"

"Pillows, a blanket, maybe some food?"

"And a bottle of red?"

Take me now. "I think I can scrounge something up."

"I can come with you, if you'd like."

While his offer is tempting, I feel the need to . . . *freshen up.* "I'll only be a minute. You stay here and reserve our spot."

He salutes me, his tone playful. "On it."

I don't think I've ever raced down the stairs this fast. I make it to my apartment in record time, hoping that I do, indeed, have that bottle of wine I'd promised. I pull a few wool and fleece blankets from one of the cabinets and throw them onto the couch, then gather some pillows. It dawns on me that perhaps I *should* have taken Xero up on his offer. I could definitely use another set of hands to get all this stuff up there.

I make for the kitchen and, in true gentleman-fashion, he's waiting just outside my apartment door. He pushes the edge of it with his foot before leaning against the doorframe. "Seems like an awful lot for one person to carry."

If I could freeze any moment in time, this would be it. Between the way he's studying me and the way he's standing, his clothes fitting in all the right places, I can hardly think straight. The angled head, the tilt of his glasses, the slightly raised brow . . . "I suppose I underestimated how much *stuff* there would be," I admit.

He ducks into my apartment and heads straight for the kitchen, searching the countertop for the wine rack that doesn't exist.

"Top cabinet on the left," I instruct as I dig in another cabinet for some snacks. "Although I can't make any promises . . ." When I look up, pretzels and crackers in hand, I'm delighted (and honestly a little surprised) to see him turning over a bottle of vintage red.

"Wow, I'd forgotten about that." I set the snacks down and walk over to where's he standing.

"It was tucked away in the very back." His fingers graze mine as he hands it to me. "Saving it for a special occasion, I presume?"

"Seems I was . . . until I forgot about it." My throat closes up as yet another failure in my life resurfaces: failed engagement aka a failed attempt at "normalcy"—whatever the fuck that is.

He senses my discomfort immediately. "We don't have to—"

He tries to take it back, but I pull away and shake my head. "No. I'm happy you found it. A wine this good deserves to be enjoyed. And there's no one I'd rather enjoy it with than you."

My words seem to have stirred something within him. He moves closer to me, which doesn't take much, seeing as we're already in the extremely small space that is my kitchen. I can feel myself holding my breath as the musky scent of amber and mahogany fills the air around me. *Damn him for smelling so good.*

This time, as he reaches for the bottle of wine, I let him take it. I hear it *clink* on the countertop behind me, his arms boxing me in on either side. He closes the gap between us so that my chin is nearly touching his chest.

I tell myself not to look up, but I can't resist. We've never been this close before—well, in my "dream", yes, but in real life? Physically? No.

My eyes travel up his flannel shirt, along the front of his neck, past the growing stubble on his chin, only to pause at his slightly parted lips. I feel my chest heave a sigh as my gaze travels the rest of the way to his eyes.

Olive green pierces the very depths of my soul.

For the first time in a long time, my thoughts are neither here nor there. I'm so enraptured by him, by this endlessly still moment, that anything other than complete and total presence feels . . . *forbidden*, somehow.

He lifts his right hand and slowly brings it to my neck, my cheek. His touch is so tender and yet I feel like I've just been jolted with a thousand megawatts of electricity. I shudder at the sensation, wondering if he's felt it, too. Based on the way his mouth rigs to the side, I'm assuming so.

I move my hands so that my thumbs hook in his front pockets, pulling him even closer. "I could stare at you all day."

"Likewise," he whispers.

His eyes flick to my mouth, and never have I wanted anything more than I do in this very moment. His head lowers just enough for me to meet him halfway, and I do.

We seem to skip right over the "introduction" because the minute I feel his mouth on mine, we're exploring each other in ways I didn't even know were possible. He hoists me onto the counter so that we're eye level and slips in between my legs. Even through my jeans, I can feel the length of him hardening against my inner thigh. I wrap my arms around his neck, drawing him in even tighter, wanting to feel every ripple, every breath, every *movement* of his body against mine.

His mouth slides down to my neck. I throw my head back so hard, I nearly hit the back of it against the cabinet. I let out a faint groan, which only seems to rev him up even more. With brute strength, he picks me up and carries me to the couch, not bothering to move the mountain of pillows and blankets I'd gathered earlier. We're half-standing, half-laying, our hands and mouths exploring every inch of each other.

Although I'm certain we'd both prefer to stay as we are, eventually, we have to come up for air. Not coincidentally, we pull away at the exact same time. He's panting, as am I, and I can feel his heart racing beneath his chest. "Well, that was nice."

"And expected," I say, flashing a grin back at him.

"Expected?" He pushes himself up off the mound of blankets before helping me stand all the way up. "Not what I thought you were going to say."

"I thought that that was a given—you knowing my thoughts and all."

"Only when there's a direct invitation."

I raise a brow. "Is this a new rule I'm unaware of?"

"It can be." He presses a light kiss to my forehead. "I'm just honoring your request, that's all."

"How chivalrous of you." Even though the words come out somewhat sarcastically, I *do* mean them.

"Seems I may have jumped the gun." He takes my hand and leads me back into the kitchen. "True chivalry would have involved waiting until we were on the rooftop, at dusk, to kiss you."

I tug on his arm and pull him in before planting a kiss on his cheek. "I much prefer it how it just happened."

"Yeah?"

I nod. "Yeah."

He seems both surprised and delighted by my response. "Good to know." He takes my hand and spins me around, grabbing the bottle of wine in the process. "What do you say we take this to the roof?"

I reach across him and swipe two wine glasses from the counter. "Lead the way."

23

I'M DOING MY best not to look so hot and bothered after what's just transpired in the kitchen, but to say I'm struggling is an understatement. I'd thought my dream was "next level", but *nope*—that steamy few minutes between us definitely takes the cake.

Xero sets down the bottle of wine and spreads out the wool blanket, topping it with one of the fleece blankets, then sets up the *second* fleece blanket for us to crawl underneath. With empty wine glasses in my right hand and two pillows tucked underneath my left arm, I join him on the blanket. I gently set down everything I'm carrying and pull the blanket over my legs. *It's freezing.*

I'm intently watching him as he opens the bottle with a corkscrew when a thought occurs to me. "So, I take it Professor Colter's not expecting you for the rest of the day?"

"That would be correct," he says with a grunt. The cork makes a loud *pop!* as he pulls it out. "As I figured she might, it seems she assumed I wouldn't be too far behind you in the food poisoning department."

"Yeah, who's stupid idea *was* thai food anyway?"

He lets out a belly-deep laugh. "No matter. Seems it's worked out in our favor."

"What makes you say that?"

He angles his head at me before giving me a knowing look. In this lighting, his eyes appear almost more jade-colored. Striking all the same. "Well, we're here, on your rooftop, about to drink some wine. Would you rather be marking up essays?"

"I suppose that would depend on the essay."

He brings his hand to his chest in mock offense. "I must admit, your quick wit is one of the things I love about you."

Heat rushes to my cheeks. "Good to know," I say, instantly regretting the *un*-wittiness of my response—but I refuse to let my nerves get the better of me. "So, are you gonna nurse that bottle all day or actually pour us a glass?"

And she's back, folks.

"Yes, ma'am," he says, putting on his best southern accent. "Don't have to tell me twice." He hands me a *very* full burgundy glass, then holds his out to cheers.

I clink mine with his. "To thai food."

He grins. "To thai food."

We've been up here for so long and have been so engrossed in conversation (amongst other things) that I've completely lost track of time. The sky is now darker than dark, and we'd finished the bottle of wine about an hour ago—*I think.*

I'm mid-laugh with my head resting in his lap, my cheeks hurting from all the smiling. "What a great day."

"Agreed," he says. "Absolutely stupendous."

"*Stupendous*," I say in a terrible English accent, finding the word exceptionally funny. *Well, that's a bottle of wine for ya.*

I lift my head when I hear his phone ping, realizing that mine's made the exact same sound. He shifts his weight forward, digging around in his back pocket until his phone is in hand.

"Were you sitting on that the entire time?"

He shrugs. "It would appear so . . ." His voice trails off as he reads whatever's on the screen. "Do me a favor and check your phone."

His tone has completely changed, or maybe it's just the wine talking. "On it." I reach over to the side of the blanket, swiping at the ground until my fingers finally grip the edge of my phone. I unlock the screen, feeling confused as multiple news alerts bombard my vision.

"Did you get these, too?" I ask.

He quickly glances at my phone, then nods. "Seems like the entire county did—"

"More than that," I interrupt as I press play on one of the news clips. "It's national news."

. . . *Strange disappearances at well-known universities across the nation have plagued students and faculty over the last week,* the newscaster reports. *The first missing persons report in a string of what is now twenty, and climbing, occurred in Boulder, Colorado at CU in the Astronomy Sciences Department, which is now becoming a major staple in recently filed reports. Many are now referring to the disappearances as abductions due to the likeness in academic department, which, it seems, is somehow being targeted . . .*

I try to ignore the knot forming in my stomach as I press the pause button on the video, not caring to hear the rest. My voice is hushed as I begin to speak, but Xero shakes his head at me.

Not out loud, he communicates.

I nod in understanding. *Do you think this has anything to do with what happened at your cabin?*

I think it has everything to do with it.

You said we were on Nibiru—

Yes.

—a nonexistent planet, I finish.

An audible sigh. *Yes.*

I told you, right before you pulled me out of there, that I heard Professor Haven.

I know.

A taut silence stretches between us.

The more I try to wrap my head around it all, the more jumbled my mind becomes. *Do you think that's where the others are?*

While I don't want to assume anything, it is likely.

"Xero," I say slowly, "we have to do something."

It's amazing how quickly the mood can shift from playful and fun to somber and near life-threatening.

"I know." Those are the only two words he speaks before he's in my head again. *But we can't risk trying to get back to Nibiru by going to the cabin. It's too dangerous.*

But we made it out . . .

The strain of what he's about to say pulls at his eyes. *Just barely, Elara. They found a way to separate us. If I hadn't found my way back to you . . .*

Well, this is news to me. While I'd known we'd lost each other momentarily, I hadn't realized we were on the brink of being separated to the point of no return. *Why didn't you tell me?*

Because I've only just found you.

There's so much sincerity in his expression, I can't possibly be upset. I know he's telling the truth, but it still hurts to think he hadn't been forthright with me. *And even with that knowledge, you're still willing to go back?*

I don't know if 'willing' is the right word. But I'm becoming increasingly aware that my purpose here is much more complex than I realized. A pause. *And yours is, too.*

Me? I search his face for answers. *How do you mean?*

The way in which we're connected . . . your ability to astral travel, to witness me astral traveling . . . that isn't by coincidence. It's by design.

The thought of my being here for a purpose larger than the average "human experience" is both exhilarating and downright terrifying—but somehow, it all makes sense. My interest in the cosmos, my fascination with the metaphysical, my extensive work with Professor Haven in Astronomy Sciences . . . *hell,* I'm even named after one of Jupiter's moons. In a way, this *not* happening would make even less sense.

"So, what do we do?"

Xero shakes his head, clearly at a loss for words. I can't help but follow his gaze as he looks up at the sky.

The idea of all ideas hits me. *Of course.*

I spring to my feet before tugging on Xero's arm.

"What's happening?" he asks, confused by my sudden shift in demeanor.

"We need to go," I say as I hastily gather the blankets and pillows in my arms.

He follows my lead, swiping the empty wine bottle and crimson-stained glasses from the ground. "Okay, but *where* are we going?"

I pull him toward the door. "To the one place where all of this is bound to make sense. The observatory."

24

WE DECIDE TO walk to campus and, after our dalliance with red wine, it feels like we make it in no time. A blustery wind sweeps across the trees, blowing even more leaves onto our path. Between the crunching beneath our boots and the howling of the wind, it's impossible to hear anything else. Fortunately, the campus is mostly empty, save for the few students filtering out of the twenty-four-hour library.

When we make it to the Astronomy Sciences building, I reach into my bag to pull out my badge, but Xero's already beaten me to it. The lock on the door clicks, and we're admitted into the building. The sensors detect us, the lights automatically flickering on as we venture down the hallway. We wait, in silence, for the elevator to make its timely arrival to take us up.

I notice that I still feel a little uneasy being here, even though Xero's with me. The observatory has always been a favorite of mine, but ever since that night . . .

Xero interrupts my thoughts as we gain access to the observatory. "After you." I can tell he's deep in thought because those are the first words he's spoken since we got here.

I survey the room. At first glance, it doesn't seem like much has changed. I don't know why that makes me feel slightly disheartened, but it does. *Maybe because when you're looking for clues, the more obvious the find, the easier it is to figure things out in the end*—or so all of the crime documentaries say.

"Any idea what we're looking for?"

I turn over my shoulder to look at Xero. He seems just as lost as I am. *Great.* I run my hand along one of the desks, doing another onceover of the room. "The last time I was here, I was looking up the coordinates for the Taurus constellation." I walk over to the telescope, searching for the one sticky note that had caught my eye last time. I peel it off the surface and walk over to Xero. "This is what I was looking at" . . . *before they arrived,* I finish communicating silently.

Coordinates to Aldebaran?

I nod. *Written in Professor Haven's handwriting.*

He keeps his eyes fixed on the note. *You're sure?*

Yes. Trust me, we've spent enough semesters working together that I'd recognize his handwriting anywhere.

He hands the note back to me before walking over to the computer and punching the coordinates in. The telescope whirs to life, all of the components clicking and clacking as Xero inputs the command. He seems to be even more well-versed in the software than I am, because he's able to bring up the image on the mainframe computer. That way, we can both look at it at the same time.

"Why Aldebaran?" he asks, his tone more curious than anything else.

"I'm not sure." I keep my eyes focused on the star, its glow even more mesmerizing as Xero zooms in. "All I know is that it's Haven's favorite."

"Odd choice." His words are clipped. "Not much to study seeing as not much is really known about it."

"Perhaps that's *why* he was studying it."

He seems to consider this. "Touché."

Ten minutes go by. Nothing worth noting happens.

"This is getting us nowhere, huh?" I pull one of the chairs out from underneath the desk and fall into it. I'm not sure if it's the aftereffects of the wine or all this thinking—or a combination of the two—but I feel a massive headache coming on.

As if he can sense it, Xero looks at me. "You look pale. Are you feeling all right?"

I wave a hand in the air to indicate that I'm fine when, in fact, I can feel myself steadily getting worse. "I think I'm just dehydrated. Or maybe it *was* the thai."

"Now wouldn't that be karma?" He starts digging around the observatory, probably looking for a mini fridge or a case of water. No luck. But then, he quickly raises a finger in the air like some cheesy character in a sitcom. "Hang on just a second. I think I remember seeing a mini fridge . . ." His voice trails off as he leaves the room.

I look back at the mainframe, the dull ache in the back of my head morphing into a slow, painful pulse. I place my palm on the back of my neck, realizing just how cold my skin feels to the touch. I know better than to look at a reflective surface—that would be like looking into a mirror when you're already sobbing, only to have the sheer image make you cry even harder.

In an effort to distract myself until Xero returns with what I hope is some cold water, I zoom the telescope out so that the entire Taurus constellation comes into view. I hear Xero's footsteps approaching, but before he makes it into the room, I see something rather *unusual* on the screen. A flash of light appears out of nowhere, and multiple flashes follow.

For reasons I can't explain, my stomach turns in on itself, the pulsing in my head grows deeper and denser, and I briefly get the sense that I'm about to pass out—for real this time. Xero appears next to me, water bottle in hand, but he isn't looking at me. He's looking at the screen.

"What the . . .?"

So you see it, too.

He whirls toward me, no doubt hearing the immense effort it took just to get that simple sentence across to him. "Drink this," he says firmly as he unscrews the cap to the water bottle.

I take it from him, my fingers feeling weak as they grasp the flimsy plastic. I take a long, slow drink, trying to focus on how good the water tastes instead of the heavy metal tune that seems to have taken center stage in my head. "This can't just be from the wine. And it can't be from the thai either."

"Agreed. We shared everything and I feel fine."

"What do you think it is?" *On the screen,* I clarify.

"They certainly aren't shooting stars," he murmurs, getting a closer look. "And to see so many lights, clustered around a single constellation like that—"

"It's unheard of," I finish.

"It's unseen," he adds with a nod.

"So," I say, taking another gulp of water, "what could it be then?"

"From an astronomer's point of view, I'd think an asteroid collision is a safe bet."

"But that many?"

"Good catch. From *my* point of view, it almost looks *intentional.*"

His words give me pause. "You mean like an attack?"

"*Exactly* like an attack." He glances at the half-empty water bottle in my hand. "You were feeling fine all night, weren't you?"

"Yeah. Great, actually. Why? Am I still pale?"

"Improving, but not by much."

I roll my neck from side to side, hoping that maybe it'll get the blood flowing to my cheeks. "What's odd is that whatever *this* is didn't hit me until we got here."

"On campus?"

I finish the water bottle, then shake my head. "No, *here*—in the observatory."

Xero looks like he's about to say something when my phone rings. I reach for it, feeling confused when I look at the screen. I swipe my thumb to answer it, hoping it isn't the Boulder County Police Department, namely Chief Albeck—but it's so much worse.

Hello. This is a collect call from an inmate at Boulder County Jail. This service is provided by—

I don't wait to hear more. I immediately hang up the phone and fling it across the table. "Fuck," I mutter, knowing *exactly* who would have been on the other end of that call. *But how? After all these years, how could my father possibly have gotten my phone number?* My thoughts revert to my apartment and how it'd been searched—and that damn binder.

Police: 1; Elara: 0.

The alarmed expression on Xero's face tells me I have some explaining to do, but this is the one thing I haven't told him. For some reason, it's something I don't *want* to tell him. The only other person on the planet who knows (well, besides the police now) is Kensie.

I don't want to lie to Xero. Not to mention, I know I won't get away with it. The guy can read me like a book. But today has just been . . . *too much.* The fact that I'm not feeling well isn't helping either. At this juncture, all I want to do is go back to my apartment, curl up in bed, *alone*, and be whisked away to some dreamland—anywhere that isn't here. Then, with a clear head (hopefully), I can meet up with Kensie and talk more about what's just happened—and *eventually* fill Xero in.

When I return from my thought spiral, I realize I still haven't said anything and Xero's still standing there . . . waiting.

His patience is unlike anything I've ever witnessed before. I bow my head and lower my eyes, hoping that my silence speaks volumes. Luckily, it seems to.

"Let's get you home."

I look up at him, hoping he can sense how sorry I am for suddenly shutting off. "I'd like that," I say, somehow managing to keep my emotions at bay.

He shuts down the computer, grabs his badge, and interlaces his fingers with mine, holding me close as we walk, stride for stride, out the door.

25

AN UNEVENTFUL SLEEP is just what the doctor ordered. I wake feeling fully refreshed, calm, and at ease . . . until yesterday comes hurtling in like the meteor strike it was. I look to my left, at the empty space beside me, feeling like such an ass after what could not have been a better day with Xero.

He hadn't asked any questions when we'd walked back to my apartment last night *and,* without my even saying anything, he'd just known that I'd wanted to be alone. A kiss on the forehead and a wave goodbye later, I'd found myself in that exact situation—back home, in my bed, entirely alone.

I glance at the clock, realizing that I still have a few hours before I need to be at the university. Hopefully the "food poisoning" story won't raise too many questions with Professor Colter. Just in case, I decide to make myself look slightly more haggard than usual. Not exactly a stretch, either, because I *do* feel that way.

I send Kensie a quick text before taking my time getting ready. Once he's confirmed he's working at the café and has a break coming up in fifteen minutes, I decide to hit the road. I can tell another storm is on the horizon, meaning clear skies won't be on the radar any time soon—at least, not for the next couple of days.

No stargazing for us.

I pull into one of many open parking spaces directly in front of the café, feeling grateful that it's so empty. The last thing I need is someone eavesdropping on this conversation I'm about to have with Kensie. He greets me at the door with a charming smile. "Snagged the far table in the back, next to your usual spot," he says as he brings his apron overhead. "And don't take this the wrong way, but you look like hell."

"Thanks," I say flippantly. "That's exactly the look I was going for."

"May I ask *why?*" The disdain on his face is more than apparent. "By the way, I haven't seen you around. Started to worry me. Not to mention, it seems your spot's in the process of being taken over by a group of loud, obnoxious freshmen."

I snort, unwrapping my scarf from around my neck before throwing it onto the table. Almost immediately, I fixate on the delicious beverage that's just waiting to be consumed. "Let them have it. With Chief Albeck on my ass, I'm not sure how often I'll be stopping by anyway."

Eyes wide, he slides into the seat across from me. "Is it really that bad with the police?"

I sigh. "You don't even know the half of it."

"Well, fill me in! Clearly, I've got all the time in the world," he says, motioning to all of the empty tables.

"Well, *somehow*, they got a search warrant. So that's something."

His jaw drops. He sets his drink down, readying himself with unbridled hand gestures. "Hold up. They searched your *apartment*? Shit. Were you there when it happened?"

I honestly hadn't even thought about that—until now. "Thankfully, no."

"Well, that's good, at least. Saves you a little awkwardness, but damn, that blows." He shakes his head. "Do you know if they took anything?"

"I don't think so, but I definitely noticed that some of my stuff had been moved around. I know they went through a few things." I take a deep breath, trying to figure out how exactly I want to approach what I want to ask him next. "Kensie," I say, lowering my voice, even though there's no one around, "when you spoke with the police, *before* I arrived, did you happen to mention anything about . . . my father? Or my last name?"

He reaches across the table, dreadlocks swinging adamantly in his defense. "Of course not. I would never."

I force a smile. "I knew you wouldn't. I'm sorry I asked. It's just that things have been so . . . *weird* lately."

"You're tellin' me. I'm sure you're also well aware of the new disappearances that are happening all over the nation. It's unreal." He takes a sip of his drink. "But since you asked, now *I* have to ask . . . what's going on with your father? Do the police know something?"

I trace my finger along the rim of my cup. It's such a simple question to which there is no easy answer. "Last night, I got a call from Boulder County Jail."

"Stop." His eyes grow so wide, I can see the white around them.

"It was a collect call. From an inmate. Not too hard to put two and two together." I pause, briefly wondering how things would have played out had I actually answered it. *Probably not good.* I push that thought away and continue, "And then, in my apartment, after they'd clearly searched the place, I noticed that the binder where I keep all of my legal documents had been rifled through."

"Your last name," he says, slowly drifting back in his chair. "Hence the question."

I nod. "It can't really be a coincidence that the same day the police may or may not have discovered my last name is the same day I get a collect call from an inmate."

"No shit." He sucks in a breath. "I hope you haven't been going through all of this *alone.*"

At that, I can't help but smile. I try to hide it, but what's the point? "Not exactly."

"I knew it!" He waggles his eyebrows. "You've been with that guy . . . Xero, right?"

I shrug. "It's possible."

He throws a napkin at me from across the table. "I *knew* there was something going on there! Spill. Now."

The thought of sharing what Xero and I have with someone else, even *if* that someone is my dearest and closest friend, immediately makes me freeze up. "It's really recent. Still really new. But yeah. I guess you can say we've been hanging out."

"Oh, I bet it's been more than that, E."

Now it's my turn to throw the napkin at him. "You're such an ass. But you're also right."

"I know," he says proudly, flinging his dreadlocks over his shoulders in signature Kensie fashion. "I'm just happy to finally be in the loop. Took you long enough."

Even though he's good at covering it, I can sense the hurt in his voice. There's so much more I want to tell him, but I don't think *anyone*—not even someone as open-minded as Kensie— would understand. And *that's* saying something.

"I'll be sure to circle back and keep you updated on any new developments," I say, mocking the many business patrons we often make fun of. Oh, the bits and pieces of conversation you happen to catch when your perma café status directly correlates to that of "fly on the wall" . . .

I wrap my scarf back around my neck, checking the time as I get ready to leave. Like an idiot, I'd nearly forgotten about my markings. I quickly pull the sleeve of my sweater back down before giving Kensie a hug.

"Don't be a stranger, m'kay?"

"I won't."

I'm halfway out the door when he rushes up beside me. "Made you one for the road. On the house, of course."

I plant a kiss on the side of his cheek. "You're the best, you know that?"

"I *do* know that—but I'll never turn down the chance to hear it." He grins. "Tell Xero I say hi!"

I roll my eyes at him and laugh. With my spirits fully lifted, I head out the door.

26

AFTER A SHORT drive from the café to the university, I'm standing in front of the department building. I don't know exactly *why* I'm hesitating . . . or maybe I do. After the way I'd left things last night, and my "needing space", I wouldn't be surprised if Xero decided he needed space from *me*.

I push open the door, my thoughts and emotions stirring with reckless unease. I feel more than guilty not telling him everything I'd just openly shared with Kensie, especially after the night we'd had. Well, *nights*, actually. Xero's more than gained my trust. He more than deserves to know what's going on . . . even if that means roping him into a past I wish didn't exist.

Since it's during regular class hours, there's no need to swipe my badge to access the lecture hall. I pull on one of the doors, immediately noticing that some students have already trickled in and taken their seats all over the hall. I make my way down the stairs, keeping my gaze pointed down, so as to not draw any attention. The last thing I need is to answer an academic-related question when my mind is anywhere but.

I make it to the front of the hall, unbothered and seemingly unnoticed. When I look up, I'm surprised, and a little distressed, to see only Professor Colter behind the desk. I glance at my watch. Five minutes before class starts—*Xero's always on time*. More than that, he's always *early*.

Worry curls in my stomach. I force a smile as Professor Colter waves me over. It seems our "day off" has left her feeling frazzled—an unusual sight—because there are papers and pens strewn all over her desk, and she seems to be looking for something.

"Glad to see at least *one* of you is feeling better." She doesn't make eye contact as she continues rifling through the mess on her desk.

"Xero isn't here?" I try to keep my tone calm, indifferent, but even I can hear the apparent concern.

This time, she does look up. "*Mr. Sivalla*," she corrects me, "has not reached out to confirm otherwise."

"But that's so unlike him."

She raises a brow. "Is it now?"

"I just mean . . . well, he's quite punctual, isn't he?"

"That's quite the observation for someone who's been here for less than a week." She clicks her tongue against the roof of her mouth, as if she somehow *expected* a romantic relationship of sorts to manifest between her two assistants.

Ask and you shall receive.

I open my mouth to respond but decide against it.

"I've emailed, called, and texted him," Professor Colter goes on wearily. "No response. Perhaps you can try? I doubt he'd, oh, what do all the kids say? *Ghost* you."

As off-putting as it is to hear a fifty-something-year-old professor use slang, I give her full points for the effort. I manage to maintain my composure as I say, "Certainly. I'll reach out to him right now and I'll let you know the minute I get a response."

She angles her head toward the side door, as if to say, *I'm about to start class and I don't have time for this.*

I force yet another smile before marching over to said side door, phone in hand. I push it open just enough for me to squeeze through, making sure it closes as quietly as possible. I can hear the blare of the sound system as the professor turns it on, and the subsequent static as she attaches her mic to her lapel.

My fingers are flying across my phone as I send Xero a text, then an email, then another text. I wait a total of what feels like thirty minutes, when it's only been thirty seconds, before picking up the phone and actually calling him. It automatically goes to voicemail. I try once more, thinking that *maybe* he was trying to call me at the exact same time—technology can be funny in that way—but again, it goes straight to voicemail.

I start to pace back and forth, feeling the familiar rise of panic as it flutters within my chest. I've made it all the way up and down the hall at least ten times without a response. I can hear Professor Colter talking on the other side of the wall. *Five minutes into the lecture.*

It crosses my mind to leave, to drive back to my apartment or maybe even up to the cabin, but I can't leave Professor Colter. We're both already skating on thin ice as it is—but the idea of "holding down a job" right now is so fucking *trivial* when compared to the fact that Xero could very well be in danger. And knowing what I know, that is a very likely possibility.

I do everything I can to try and calm my nerves. Perhaps he overslept. Perhaps he's astral traveling. Perhaps he just needs a little space. I reprimand myself for last night. I shouldn't have let him leave. I shouldn't have shooed him away like the annoyance he most certainly is *not*. Funny how, in the end, a guarded heart does very little guarding and a whole lot of hurting.

It's then my mind reverts to the news alerts we'd both received last night. No mention of students disappearing, only professors—but seeing as Xero fits right in between the two, maybe something had gotten to him? We've both already been taken once . . . *what if it'd happened again?*

The worst part is . . . I have no way of knowing. The last thing I want to do is head to the police station and report another disappearance, especially when there's likely no record of him. That's sure to be a one-way ticket to a life behind bars, just like my father.

Whoa, Elara. You're getting ahead of yourself.

I take a deep inhale, my chest shuddering at the motion, then breathe out as I slump against the wall. The rational thing to do is . . . get through this day. To assist Professor Colter in her lectures. To wait and see if Xero shows up because, mostly likely, he will. Because there are a million other reasons he's running late besides the worst-case scenarios I've drummed up in my head.

I start to collect myself, one bit at a time. I pull my sweater down and straighten the bottom of it before smoothing my hair. I tuck my phone into my back pocket and push open the door. *Yes, this is the rational thing to do.* The problem is, I've never been one to *choose* rational.

I suppose there's a first for everything.

27

I MANAGE TO make it through three of Professor Colter's classes without any word from Xero. I'm worried, to say the least, but grading papers serves as a welcome distraction. I'm so engrossed in one of them that I'd almost forgotten my predicament—until one of the lecture hall doors had opened. My heart had skipped a beat, thinking maybe it was him, but it was a just a severely tardy student.

I'm now sitting in Professor Colter's office, grading the last of the essays, when she walks through the door with a loud sigh. I watch in complete silence as she falls into her desk chair and removes her glasses, squeezing the bridge of her nose. "I appreciate you staying a bit later than usual, Elara. I know it's less than enjoyable to make up the slack. That's exactly why I requested two assistants versus just one." She puts her thin, wire-framed glasses back on before looking directly at me. "How much longer do you think you'll need?"

I hold up the paper I'm currently grading. "Actually, this is the last one."

"Hmph," she murmurs. "Maybe I don't need two of you after all."

"Xero graded the majority of them, before the whole thai food incident." I swallow, hoping she won't see right through my lie. "Seems we make a good team after all."

From the faraway look on her face, I can tell she's completely disinterested in everything I'm saying. I don't blame her. I'm sure the last thing she needs is for her *assistants* to be acting like lovestruck freshmen. Playing "hooky" is *not* what I'd had in mind, but Xero had made it sound so enticing—*and enticing it had been.*

"Still no word from him, I take it?"

I shake my head, checking my phone for emphasis.

"Well, whenever you do hear from him, please tell him to contact me right away."

"Is he in trouble?" I regret the question the minute it leaves my mouth.

"I'm not entirely sure yet. I suppose it depends."

Even though her tone is harsh, I can't help myself. "I just know that this job means a lot to Xer"—I catch myself—"*Mr. Sivalla.*"

"Elara," she says with a sigh, raising her brows from behind her glasses. The way she looks right now reminds me of a librarian I hated in the fourth grade. "You do not need to fight his battles for him. He's an adult. As are you."

At first, I open my mouth to counter but . . . she's right. I'm probably only making things worse. I give her a curt nod before returning to the task at hand.

After the most uncomfortable fifteen minutes of my life, I'm surprised when Professor Colter tells me to take tomorrow off. After having felt smothered and suffocated for the entire day, I suck in a breath of fresh air the moment I step through the building's exit, allowing the crisp, edge-of-winter weather to pour into me.

I feel my phone vibrate in my back pocket, nearly jumping as I reach for it. Of course, I'm expecting to see Xero's name lighting up the screen, but it's Kensie.

Got another latte brewing for you, the text reads.

I know I was just there a few hours earlier, but until I hear from Xero . . . what else am I supposed to do?

Be there in five, I text back.

Normally, I would have walked to the café, seeing how close it is to campus, but something—namely Xero's lack of communication—told me to drive . . . just in case.

When I arrive, I spot Kensie with his earbuds in, swaying behind the countertop. I quickly scan the small space for that unmistakable dark head of hair but come up empty. Disappointed, I make my way to the counter, not even bothering to fake a smile for my friend.

"Yikes. What's got you so down?" Kensie asks as he slides a fresh latte to me.

"Xero didn't happen to stop in here, did he?"

"Not that I can recall." Kensie furrows his brows. "Why? Did something happen?"

"He didn't show up today. At all."

Kensie motions to one of the other baristas to cover him before leading me to a table in the very back. "I'm guessing you texted him?"

"Texted. Called. Emailed. The only thing I haven't tried is telepathy." It's only when Kensie laughs at my "joke" that I realize I'd said it out loud—and had been completely serious.

"I'm sure he just took the day off or wasn't feeling well or something. Did you try the cabin I so rudely wasn't invited to?"

I roll my eyes. "Still harping on that, are we?"

He raises his hands, palms facing me. "Just sayin'."

"To answer your question, no. I haven't tried the cabin. But that's . . . that's a good idea." *Or a really bad one, seeing as Xero was adamant to get the hell out of there after our last visit.*

"Hey," Kensie says, reaching across the table for my hand. "Are you okay? You seem . . . I don't even know the right word. *Shaken,* almost? It isn't like you." He looks me up and down. "You're starting to worry me."

"I'm okay, really," I lie. "It's just been a weird couple of days." *And it's about to get weirder . . .*

My phone rings and with a single glance, I know exactly who's calling. "*Fuck,* go away," I mutter, feeling an intense urge to throw my phone.

"Elara," Kensie says firmly. "Tell me what's going on."

"Remember how I told you earlier about getting that collect call?" My phone continues to buzz, taunting me.

"From the jail?" Kensie whispers.

I nod, my eyes flitting toward the phone. "It's him."

"Maybe you should answer it."

"I have nothing to say to him."

"Elara—"

"*Nothing,*" I reiterate through clenched teeth.

"What if it's Xero?"

I hadn't thought of that. But . . . "What would Xero be doing in jail?"

"Beats me. But I'll tell you one thing. That Albeck woman didn't seem to care for him. Not one bit."

"There's no way," I say, shaking my head. "I mean, on what grounds?"

"They searched your place, Elara."

Hearing him say it makes my blood run cold. "Well, it's too late now." I hold up my phone to show him the missed call from *Unknown.*

"You could always go down there."

"And implicate myself?" I scoff. "Not a chance."

Kensie shrugs. "It was just an idea."

I can tell by the way he says it that he's slightly offended. "Look, I'm sorry. I know you're just trying to help. I'm just all over the map today." I look at my untouched coffee. "Can I take this to go?"

"Anything for you." And just like that, things go back to the way they were.

Now, if only I could get that same result with Xero.

I know better than to drive an hour out of town—in rush hour—without checking my apartment *and* the rooftop first, so I do. No sign of him.

Allenspark it is.

I'm minutes from pulling onto Highway 36 when I veer off at a gas station. I drive over to the farthest corner and put my Jeep in park. Thankfully, it's getting dark, and even the bright overhead lights aren't illuminating the inside of my car. For some reason, I want it to be as dark as possible before attempting what I'm about to do. I make sure my doors are locked before closing my eyes. Deep inhale . . . and exhale.

Xero?

I wait patiently, trying to get "in the zone", as it were.

Xero, are you there?

I can't explain it but, somehow, the connection feels like it's lacking—possibly even severed.

I open my eyes and shake out my shoulders, rolling my neck a few times. I take another deep breath, in and out, then close my eyes once more. I try a slightly different approach.

Xero, please. Tell me where you are.

I wait. And wait. And wait.

Radio silence.

Ugh. There was a part of me that was really hoping that this would work, but it seems it's just cause for more concern. Tightness grips my chest as I consider all the ways I may have colossally fucked up. *I should have just told him. I should have just asked him to stay.*

But that's what I do. The minute I feel vulnerable, I shut down. I suppose I have my ex-fiancé (and my father) to thank for that—not that I want to be thinking about either of them at a time like this. Xero didn't deserve to be pushed away. Not after everything he's shown me. Not after everything he's done for me. Guilt coils in my stomach like a venomous serpent, patiently waiting to strike upwards and pierce my heart.

I'm not thinking straight as I cruise along the highway at a much faster speed than is posted. All I can think about is getting to that damn cabin—and what I might find once I'm there. In true Elara-fashion, my thoughts are taking me down a winding rabbit hole of worst-case scenarios.

Is he lost? Hurt? Struggling? Fighting for his life?

. . . Dead?

I stop the spiral in its tracks. No, if something so catastrophic had happened to him, I would have felt it. I just *know* it. *Unless our connection has been severed.*

"Stop it," I say out loud, even though I'm the only one in the car. Inner dialogue is a real bitch; and yet, I have a full-on conversation with myself the entire way to Allenspark. The back and forth in my brain only ceases when I turn up the steep driveway to cabin number 511.

A serious case of déjà vu washes over me.

I notice a car, parked off to the side of the structure, and, upon closer inspection, I recognize it to be Xero's.

Well, that's a good sign.

I walk up the incline, noticing that the exterior lights aren't on. *Not such a good sign.* I climb the stairs that lead up to the front door, not needing to pull out my phone to check the code, seeing as I'd memorized it the last time. The door clicks open, and I step inside.

The first thing I notice is how quiet it is—and not just because we're in a secluded area in the woods . . . but because the silence errs on the side of *eerie*. A chill runs down my spine as I climb the next set of stairs, using my phone as a light. It's completely dark in the cabin and, if I hadn't seen the car, I would have assumed no one had been here in days, which doesn't do much to calm my nerves.

I consider turning on the lights, but if there *is* someone here—someone who isn't Xero—I'd prefer to have the upper hand. Then again, I guess it depends on who (more like *what*) we're dealing with here. My hands shake with each step I take until I finally reach the landing. I blow out a long, steady breath as I point my phone's flashlight around the living room.

It's empty.

I walk over to the kitchen and turn on one of the lowlights. It makes me feel a little bit better, albeit not much. I slide open the screen door that leads to the front patio and poke my head out. I do the same for the back.

More stairs it is.

As I walk along the hall, I briefly flash the light into the bedroom I'd slept in. It looks exactly how I'd left it. I'm heading toward the end of the hall, nearing Xero's room, when I break off into a room I hadn't really noticed before. It appears to be a study. There's a safe in the corner of the room, but that isn't what catches my attention. Strewn all over the obsidian marble desk is something I haven't seen in *years*: physical *printed* newspapers. I flick the desk lamp on and take a seat, carefully folding and unfolding each of the papers. The dates vary, all the way from the 1960s to the 1990s to more recent times—but not too recent, seeing as everything's gone mostly digital now.

From the looks of it, it seems Xero's been busy . . . and quite interested in Boulder's "unexplained" disappearances. One paper in particular catches my eye, and I thumb through the pages to get to the article. It's from the early part of the millennium, right before 2010, and talks about sudden disappearances, much like the ones currently being reported on by the news.

I can tell by the barcode on the front of each newspaper that he'd borrowed them from the university library, so I carefully fold each one back up and put them in the order I'd found them in.

If I know Xero—and I'd like to think I do—it seems he may have unearthed something . . . a pattern of some sort, that perhaps other entities out there would rather keep hidden. *Or, best case, his discovery has allowed him to reconnect with wherever he came from.* The thought makes me smile. It also makes me wish I'd think along *those* lines more often.

I switch the desk lamp off, once again using my phone's light to guide me back into the hallway. The door to his bedroom is cracked open, just slightly. I push against it with my foot, pointing the light down at first, so as to not disturb him in case he *is* indeed sleeping. *Here's hoping.* Although it's empty, the comforter is halfway down the bed, and the sheets appear to have been slept in.

Before I can question my actions, I kick my boots off and slide underneath the blankets. The minute my head hits the pillow, I catch the overwhelming scent of amber and mahogany— *his* scent. The small clue gives me a tiny ounce of hope that he's been here recently, and that he could return at any moment.

I check my phone one last time for a message from him, even going so far as to lay there with my eyes closed and reach out to him telepathically. *Crickets.* With a sigh, I set my phone on the automatic charger on his bedside table and pull the covers up even higher.

I have no intention of leaving. His car is here, his bed smells like him, and there's a pile of research I need to ask him about in his study. It's too dark to go wandering off, so I tell myself at first light tomorrow, I'll hike up to the waterfall where I first witnessed him in astral form.

Which reminds me . . .

I turn my head to the still-cracked bedroom door. I throw the covers off of me, march over to it, and swing it shut as memories of silver and green light swim across my mind. *Nope,* we certainly don't need a repeat of last time, that's for sure.

28

MY EYES SHOOT open at the first sliver of sunlight that shines through the glass panes overhead. I turn to my left, already sensing that I'm still alone in the bed, but I check, just to be sure. It's still unmade from the night prior—*before I'd arrived*—although my tossing and turning has definitely added to the mess of blankets and sheets.

I stretch my arms overhead, wishing that I had one of Kensie's infamous lattes awaiting me—or better yet, the one Xero had handcrafted for me. *Mmm.* I pull on the sweater I'd worn yesterday and lace up my boots. I rummage around in my bag for my beanie before fashioning my hair into two bubble braids, the navy blue sticking out at the ends, and pulling the thick fabric down over my forehead.

I do a quick sweep of the house, checking each room and hallway that I cross, but everything appears to be in order. No sign of Xero in the middle of the night. No strangers either. *Thank the powers that be for that.*

I'm pleased to find orange juice in the fridge and a leftover half of a bagel. I snag both and, on second thought, grab some water bottles, two apples, and a blueberry yogurt. Who knows what condition he'll be in when I find him . . .

If I find him.

I stuff everything into my bag, down the orange juice, and take the bagel to go. I'm bounding down the stairs when I peek over the railing. His car's still here, covered by fallen leaves and pine needles. *Same spot as yesterday. Hasn't been moved.*

Another good sign, if my hunch is correct.

I look off into the distance, hoping my memory will serve me well in retracing the pathway Xero had used to get us to the cavern. All I know is that if I'm heading up, (and feel completely out of breath), I'm on the right track. I reach the first marker in record time—twenty-two minutes, to be exact—and immediately recognize the giant boulder we'd sat on during the first half of the hike. I grab one of the apples and tear my teeth into it, already feeling like I've worked off that bagel and then some—not to mention, I know what's about to come next.

Another steep slope.

And an even more treacherous climb.

I take a swig from my water bottle, salute the view below me, and continue onward. The sun is still rising, barely peeking through the trees, which gives me just enough light to see when I've made it to the enormous rock wall—the one I originally thought he was going to make me climb. Oh, how I would take *that* over shimmying along this narrow ledge . . .

Crossing my fingers that I'm *awake enough* for what I'm about to attempt—and that I'm not about to plunge to my death—I take my time moving along what is, for all intents and purposes, a very dangerous cliffside. The sound of rushing water beckons me, which means I'm getting close. I try *not* to think about the fact that I'm severely undercaffeinated, like, completely *de*caffeinated, as I take the last few side-to-side steps with my chest pressed against the solid structure, hands gripping what is, for the most part, completely smooth rock.

I blow out a long breath when I finally reach the safety checkpoint and hop onto stable, much wider, ground. I begin to scan the area, looking for Xero, which doesn't take long at all—mere seconds, actually. I spot him at the far end of the cavern with his back to me. He's sitting down with his legs crossed, arms resting lightly on top and appears to be . . . *meditating?*

Seriously?

I half-expect him to turn around, to sense my presence, but he remains as still as a statue. I don't want to startle him, but I also kind of do after what he's put me through the past twenty-four hours. I decide not to call out his name, realizing that, even if I did, there's no way he'd be able to hear me over the waterfall. I trudge over to where he's sitting, not entirely sure *what* to expect . . . but when I arrive, it certainly isn't this.

Xero's eyes are open. Vacant. Blank.

And he's just . . . *staring.*

Not at a view. Not at the waterfall.

But straight ahead.

"Hey," I say slowly, cautiously. Unease blooms in my stomach. "I thought I'd find you here."

He doesn't say anything. Doesn't move. Doesn't even blink. If not for the slow rise and fall of his chest, I'd be convinced that something much worse had happened.

"Xero?" I gently wave a hand in front of his face. Back. And forth. "Xero, can you hear me?"

Expressionless, and without response, he stares on.

Not knowing what to do—and trying to deflate my rising feelings of panic—I decide to sit next to him. I figure that *maybe* I can see whatever he's looking at, whatever has him so enraptured . . .

Except he's *not* enraptured. He's the exact opposite of that—lifeless. Unresponsive. Floating aimlessly within a seemingly invisible void, one that I desperately need to find the tether to.

I sit next to him and gaze out at . . . well, *nothing*. I try to calm my racing thoughts, to "empty my mind", as all the yogis say, but my mind seems to be pretty damn attached to the mounting panic and worry within me. I glance over and reach out for him, double checking to make sure that he *is* indeed here in physical form and not floating around, particle-style, in astral form.

All here. All in one piece.

What, then?

I'm seconds away from attempting to shake him back to reality when I hear a murmur. It's almost indiscernible, but I *know* it's him.

"One," he says quietly, before repeating it. "One." He moves his hands so that his middle and index fingers are extended in the number two position.

"Two?" I say trying to clarify as I mimic his hand signals.

He shakes his head—*painfully* slow. "One. One." The way he says it makes it sound like he's almost in a trance. The faraway look in his eyes only confirms it. He lowers his middle finger, but keeps his index finger pointed out, then points his *other* index finger out so that they make a sort of goalpost shape.

I copy this motion as well, except I bring my fingers closer together. *One. One . . . also kind of looks like eleven?*

"Eleven?" I don't expect to get an answer, so I'm surprised when he nods his head.

He's coherent. He must be . . . channeling something.

I wait, on edge, for the next clue.

"Why."

For a brief moment, I consider the fact that maybe he's just hopped into my head and is now asking questions. But he still seems to be in a trance, so that's unlikely.

"Why?" I repeat, feeling confused.

"A."

"A?" *Is he spelling something?* "Y . . . A . . ."

A small nod. "M."

"Y-A-M. Yam?" I confirm. "Eleven yams?" What the hell kind of message *is* this?

He shakes his head but doesn't say anything further.

"Eleven . . . Amy?" I try word-scrambling. "Eleven . . . May?" I stop, realizing that that last one definitely rings a bell. "May eleventh. The eleventh of May. My birthday?"

I'm even more confused now. *Of course* I know my own birthday. *Grrreat message.* But then I have another thought . . .

It can't be.

As if I've just unlocked the answer to the world's most impossible riddle, I watch as Xero closes his eyes and lifts his palms to chest height. Something begins to emanate from them. When they first appear, they're just tiny wisps of light, but, eventually, they transmute into full-on particles—*orbs*, even—of pure, unfiltered light.

Mouth agape, I watch as these particles and orbs dance in complete unison, only breaking their rhythm, their synchronicity, to take the form of . . . something else. I lean back, eyes darting as the particles begin to take shape.

Although his eyes are closed, the expression on Xero's face is one of complete and utter calm, as if he's pulling this image from the very depths of his soul. His breath is steady as the particles work their magic, arranging, then rearranging to create . . .

A portrait.

I nearly faint at the sight. It's clear as day. There's absolutely no mistaking who it is.

May. Eleventh.

The only other person I know of with my same birth date is the very woman glinting before me in magnificent beams of light.

BEYOND THE STARS AND SHADOWS

My mother.

29

I'M BOTH ASTOUNDED and shaken at the sight of her. How could I not be? While I'm aware that this is likely just a projection of Xero's consciousness, one that I'm somehow miraculously able to see, I can't help but wish that she were actually here, even if only in astral form.

To speak with her again. To hear her voice. To ask her *what had happened* all those years ago. To finally have some answers . . .

My awe turns to longing as the particles before me begin to dissipate and, slowly but surely, I can feel a *different* emotion rising within me—one I haven't fully allowed myself to feel in quite some time. *Anger.*

I'm about to shake Xero when, of his own accord, he comes back to. "Elara?" he whispers incredulously the moment his eyes settle on me. "You're . . . *here.* How are you here?" He looks around before running his hands along his legs, his arms, then patting his chest. "Oh," he says with a quick sigh, "We're *here.*"

I have no idea what that means but, if I had to guess, he's probably just traveled a *really* long way. "Do you know what you just did? What you just showed me?"

He regards me with a befuddled expression, clearly trying to gather his thoughts now that he's back in our "realm". "I . . . yes, I think I remember." He furrows his brows. "Wait—I *absolutely* remember."

"How?" I ask, on the edge of angry tears. "How were you able to find her?"

His face pales at my tone, my expression. Clearly this is not the reaction he'd expected, if he'd expected any at all. I'm guessing it's the latter since I'm not technically even supposed to be here.

He hesitates before saying, "I didn't find her. She . . . well, she found me."

I don't know what that means or how that's even possible. My head is spinning at the thought of him communicating with her as if it were happenstance. "I *really* need you to start talking, Xero. To explain this somehow . . . because my mind is whirling in a million different directions and I feel like I'm about to lose it."

He reaches for my hand, but I pull away. He breathes a heavy sigh at my reaction. "Elara, please. I've just traveled the farthest I've *ever* traveled. I've never felt so disoriented. I need a minute. Or two. Maybe longer." He seems to realize how harsh he sounds because he immediately adds, "I *know* this is a big deal. Huge. Life-altering. But I can't possibly offer you an explanation if I don't take the time to figure it out myself."

"I suppose that's fair," I murmur. "Doesn't mean I'm happy about it, though." I tug at one of my braids, not sure where we go from here.

"Come on," he says, pulling me to my feet. "Let's head back to the cabin."

I haven't so much as taken my eyes off of Xero from the moment we'd gotten back. I'm trying not to rush him, or to seem impatient, but the suspense is killing me. I mean, he just had contact with my mother—my *missing* mother.

We're sitting in the living room, me on the couch, and him in the armchair, just like before. I can tell by the way he slowly rises and begins to walk to the kitchen—and at a glacial pace, no less—that it's best if I get him what he needs. What *I* need is for him to sit down and sort through his thoughts, his experience, the *conversation*, if there was one. Right now, I feel completely in the dark.

I fucking hate it.

"Here, allow me," I say as gently as I can, even though I really feel like screaming. "What can I get you?"

He stops in his tracks and turns back toward the chair. It takes everything in me not to tap my foot incessantly as he sits back down. Regardless, he seems to sense my impatience. "Another water, please." He waits until I'm halfway in the kitchen when he says, "I know this isn't easy for you. And I know the time it's taking me to figure this out isn't helping to relieve that. Getting grounded again is a bit more challenging than usual."

I lower my head into the refrigerator, hoping to mask my expression. I can't possibly be frustrated with him. He *found* my mother—or *she* found *him*, whatever that means. Ever since she'd disappeared, I'd given up hope that I'd ever see her again. Blamed my father. Pushed any semblance of "family" far from my mind. Rejected it even.

But here's Xero, with *news* of her. Real, tangible news. Completely unexpected, yet somehow timely, if that makes any sense. As much as I'm trying to get a grip on my emotions, it's proving to be difficult . . .

First and foremost, we'd had an incredible night. Beyond incredible. We'd connected in a way we hadn't before—and then, I'd shut him out. Not intentionally, not on purpose . . . but sometimes what we *intend* isn't always perceived in the way we'd originally hoped for.

Second, I'd spent half of yesterday thinking he was upset or angry with me, seeing as he didn't show up to work and wasn't taking any of my calls or replying to any of my messages. The other half I'd spent panicking that something terrible had happened to him and that I might not ever see him again.

Third—after numerous unanswered phone calls from the prison, which I'm inclined to assume are from my father, I discover that Xero is okay and that he's somehow made contact out in the ethers with my long-lost mother.

So *excuse me* for being a bit frazzled and hopping from emotion to emotion. I am certainly *not* tall enough to ride *this* particular rollercoaster.

My thoughts having consumed me entirely, I realize that I'm still holding the refrigerator door open and I have no idea how long I've been standing here—but I'm assuming it's been a while.

"You okay over there?" Xero calls out.

I grab the water bottle, mutter a profanity or two to myself, then close the metal door. "You know me. Getting lost in my thoughts again." I consider tossing the bottle to him, but seeing as his motor skills may not be quite up to par, I walk it over to him instead. Definitely don't need to accidentally knock him out and cause him to forget everything that's happened.

Talk about me losing my shit.

"Thanks." Xero twists the cap open and downs half its contents within seconds. He exhales loudly before melting back into the armchair.

I'm twiddling my thumbs against the leg of my pants when I notice his breathing falls even deeper. He did *not* just fall asleep.

"Don't worry, I'm not asleep," he murmurs somewhat absentmindedly.

His comment makes me smile. "Good to know you're still in my head."

"Trying not to be, but your aura is pulsing." He opens one eye, then closes it again. "Red."

"And what does that mean?"

"Either you're passionate . . . or angry." His mouth rigs to the side. "Guessing it's the latter."

Even though he can't see me, I roll my eyes. "Happy you're amused."

This time, I actually get a full laugh. "You're much more than just *amusing* to me," he says, clearly still reading my thoughts, my insecurities. "Or have you forgotten the other night?"

My cheeks burn at the remark—and the memory.

"Of course I haven't forgotten." My sarcasm seems to have fled faster than a freight train. "But I'd really started to think you were avoiding me or something."

At this, he opens his eyes and leans forward, his gaze burning a hole right through the very core of my being. "Never. But you made it clear you wanted space. And I wanted to honor that request, even if I secretly hoped you'd change your mind and invite me to stay."

"Oh." The word whooshes out of me, unrestrained. Well, I can't be mad at him for *that*, now can I? Words escape me, but I don't seem to need them.

His brows furrow and his forehead wrinkles, as if he's remembering something.

Finally. I don't prompt him. I don't poke or prod. I just wait. It's very un-Taurean of me, but it's what's called for in a moment like this.

Thank you, discernment.

"Our encounter was . . . brief." Each word he speaks sounds more forced than the last. "At first, I didn't know who she was. But she was persistent, dare I say stubborn." He gives me a knowing look. "She never gave me her name, but she didn't have to. I could *see* her in numbers, almost in numerical form. Five. And eleven. I put two and two together almost immediately."

I'm sitting on the edge of the couch now, hanging on his every word.

"Once we connected, I felt the synergy. I *knew* she was related to you. It was a feeling more than anything else. But she said . . ."

His body is so tense now, his shoulders raised, jaw clenched, as if the memory is trying to escape him and he's desperately trying to hold on, to cling to every last remnant.

"She said . . ." I repeat softly. Waiting.

He looks up suddenly and points to the table. Right at my phone. "They need to be answered."

Surely he can't mean . . .

"The next time he calls," Xero says with a sharp inhale, "you need to answer, Elara. You need to speak with your father."

30

THE WORDS HIT me like a bullet to the chest. *That? That's* the message? Really? No *Hi Elara, it's your mother. This is what happened to me, this is who to blame, and I'm so proud of the woman you've become. I miss you, love you, and am always watching over you.*

Instead, I get: *Speak to your father.*

Fucking brutal. And most certainly *not* what I wanted to hear.

"All the other stuff was implied." Xero's voice is faint, just above a whisper. "But you're right. Perhaps I should have led with that. That was insensitive of me."

I gape at him. "You think?"

"You don't understand—"

"*Of course* I don't," I scowl. "How could I possibly understand when I wasn't even there? When she chose to contact you *over* me?"

"Let me finish."

His stark tone takes us both by surprise. I can tell by the way he blanches. His eyes hover away from me for a few seconds before returning.

"Go on then," I say, folding my arms over my chest.

"The way that she expressed for you to speak with your father . . . it was with such *urgency*. It's the thing she wanted me to remember most. I can still feel her resolve, her *determination*, to ensure the message got to you." He pauses. "But I do apologize for the delivery. Sincerely. That was crass of me."

I stare down at my phone, willing it *not* to ring. I trust Xero, absolutely. I trust my mother, too, even though my memory of her fades with each passing day. But knowing what kind of forces are out there, what was lurking in this cabin just one week ago . . . I can't help but question *why* she would have me talk to the very person responsible for her disappearance—for what I now know to be her *death*.

I shudder at the thought.

I suppose there *was* a part of me—a *sliver*—that believed she was still alive. That maybe she'd fled a shitty situation and started a new life for herself. That maybe she'd come back one day—like now, when I'm all grown up—to rekindle what we once had and make up for lost time. But that hope has been completely snuffed out.

That's two bullets in one day.

I squeeze the bridge of my nose, then let my hand fall to my chin. Xero's watching me in that way that he does, and I can tell he's trying not to barge in on my thoughts. I appreciate that more than he could possibly understand, especially right now.

The silence that stretches between us feels unending until he finally speaks. "I think what we both need is some rest."

I look to the stairs, remembering what happened the last time we decided to stay the night here. "Is it safe?"

If there's any doubt in his mind, he doesn't show it. "Safer than either of us would be on the road at this point."

I can tell his energy is drained and mine is, too, although in a different way. Rest sounds nice. Curling up next to him and falling asleep sounds nice. *Other stuff* sounds nice too, but let's be real, we're both way too lethargic for that.

"So," he says, starting to climb the stairs, "are you going to tell me what I missed? I bet Professor Colter is going to have my head for missing two days in a row."

I manage a laugh, sliding my hand along the wooden banister as I follow closely behind him. "I think she's caught on to the fact that we're . . ." My words trail off as I try to find a word that describes *what* we are, exactly.

"*Involved?*"

I give him a playful nudge in the shoulder. "I was kind of hoping for *more* than just 'involved'."

He stops walking then, and turns around. We've reached the top of the stairs and, even though he's only one step above me, I could almost swear that he's floating. With a sort of angelic nature, he picks me up at the hips and sets me down at the start of the banister. He's in between my legs again, just like he was in the kitchen at my apartment. I find myself wanting to recreate that moment—and perhaps make it even *more* memorable than the last time.

He's looking at me with such intensity, I can hardly breathe. His mouth unexpectedly pulls to the side as his gaze travels to my hair, which still happens to be in braids. I'd left my beanie downstairs, along with my phone. *Good. We don't need any unwelcome distractions.*

He brings his hands to my left braid and gently begins undoing it. I can feel each strand as it loosens, no longer pulling taut at my head. He moves to the right braid and does the same thing. I'm tempted to wrap my legs around him and pull him in close, but I'm curious to see what he's about to do. He delicately fluffs out my hair, running his fingers through it ever so slowly. When he reaches the end he asks, "Why blue?"

I look down at his hands, confused for a moment, then remember the navy hue ombré I'd managed to put in my hair. "It reminds me of the night sky. I figured this way, even when it's daylight out, I'm still holding a piece of the night and all its mysteries with me."

He runs his hands through my hair again, his fingers grazing, then stopping, at my neck. "It's never a simple answer with you, is it?"

To most, that would be a blow to the ego. Like being called high-maintenance or complex or "too much work". But I know the way he means it is the highest form of praise possible. That I have depth far beyond what any regular old soul could see— something very few get to experience in this lifetime.

He lifts his hands to the sides of my face, his thumbs gently caressing my cheeks. His eyes leave mine as they slowly trail down every inch of my face. He drops his mouth to just below my jawline, his lips soft and gentle against my skin. I angle my neck to give him better access before wrapping my legs around him and pulling him in. He curls into me, his face covered by my hair, his breath heated and yearning against my skin.

Without meaning to, I moan, but it only makes him kiss me more, harder. His mouth is on mine now, ravaging me for every ounce of desire I have to give. My hand falls between us, brushing against the length of him as he echoes my moan right back. I rake my other hand through his hair, tugging on it just enough for him to pause and look me in the eyes. I've never seen so much passion, so much *fire*, blazing behind anyone's eyes before—but there's also something else. Something I find even *more* enticing, *if that's even humanly possible.*

And that is . . . belief.

There's a sort of conviction about him, especially when we're together, that makes me forget all of my questions. All of my doubts. Like he's never been more certain of anything, ever, in his whole entire life.

And that certainty . . . is driven by *me*.

It's everything I never knew I wanted until he came into my life. Until he gave me the gift of that experience. To have that level of conviction and assuredness about anyone requires an insane amount of trust and . . .

Faith.

Acceptance.

Love.

We're both breathing heavily now, our need for rest having transmuted into something else entirely. He kisses me tenderly on the mouth, once, twice, before lightly dragging his lips over my jawline on the *other* side, moving from my neck to my ear. Hearing him pant nearly does me in.

I rope his hand around the front of my sweater, wanting to feel his touch on more than just my clothes. He seems to get the hint as I dip underneath his shirt and slide my hand across his stomach. He clenches, then shudders, as I run a fingernail up and down his skin. He mimics the motion, slipping underneath the hem and running his hand along my stomach, my sides, and up my back. I bring my hand just low enough to feel him again, wanting to tear every single article of clothing from our bodies.

He leans into me, growing hungrier, as he unclasps my bra and pulls it to the side. I hurriedly pull it forward and slide the straps along my arms before slipping it out from underneath, letting it fall beside me. His hand moves up until he's cupping my breast, tracing lazy circles over my nipple. His other hand is at the base of my spine, supporting me, and, at this point, holding me upright. I press my mouth harder against his and gently tug at his lip with my teeth. Between his hand circling, my hand stroking, and the moans we're exchanging, it's clear neither of us wants this moment to end—that we want to expand it into something *more*.

"Elara," he whispers when he finally pulls away.

I try to bring him back to me, but he resists.

"Look at me."

My eyes travel to his, stormy gray meeting deep jade.

"I want to take you into the bedroom." There's a glimmer in his eyes that's simultaneously darkened by shadows. "You have no idea how badly I want this."

His words wrap like a ribbon around my heart. Chest heaving, I say, "But . . .?"

"But I've already let my guard down long enough, just in this short time we've been . . ." He smiles. "Well, you know."

Everything he'd just ignited within me dissipates as dread curls in my stomach. "We're not safe." It's more of a confirmation than a question.

"We are," he assures me. "For tonight. As long as I'm not . . ." He blows out an exasperated sigh. "Distracted."

I *could* be mad about this. Most girls would be. But I'm not. It's refreshing to be with someone who cares about your actual well-being versus the superfluous stuff.

Even though the superfluous stuff *is* quite nice.

I give him a peck on the cheek, then pat the inside of his thigh to let him know I want to hop down. He grins, shaking his head at the way my hand lingers just a few seconds too long. He guides my hips as I hop down from the banister. "To be continued?"

"To be continued," he confirms. Then, he picks me right back up, wraps his arms around my waist, and walks us straight into the bedroom.

31

A S M U C H A S we don't want to, Xero and I wake up super early the next morning, seeing as we have to drive an hour, in traffic, to get to campus. We're both surprisingly energized after what had happened last night . . . okay, maybe that's not *so* surprising.

"Hey, you think you can arrange something with *wherever* you came from so that we don't have to go to work anymore?" I quip. "Because I'm not gonna lie, it's starting to get *really* old."

He shoots a sidelong glance my way from the passenger's seat. We'd agreed to take my car and ride together, which may or may not have been my idea, given the fact that I'd prefer not to "lose" him again. I'm hoping that the next time he ventures off on an astral journey, he'll take me with him—and I'm pretty sure it's hard to forget someone when they're glued to your side. Luckily for me, he doesn't seem to mind the company. In fact, I think he might like it more than he's letting on.

"I'll put in a good word," he teases back. He reaches across the middle console and delicately brushes my hair behind my shoulder.

The lightness of his touch gives me chills. I glance at him. "What are you doing?"

"I like being able to see your face. Your expression."

My cheeks heat as I recall him having said the same exact thing last night—except *last night,* I definitely hadn't been driving.

"Is that okay?"

I nod. "More than."

He doesn't say anything else, but I can feel him staring at me. It dawns on me that I still haven't addressed the fact that, at some point, I'll have to talk to my incarcerated father. As much as Xero probably wants me to open up about that—about my past—that future phone call is the *last* thing on my mind, as it should be. I decide that it's not today's problem.

At least I hope it's not.

We make it to campus in record time, thanks to an abnormally light rush hour. We both hop out of the car, our bags slung over our shoulders, when we simultaneously freeze mid-movement. Something feels . . . off.

What is it? I silently communicate.

Xero surveys the campus, watching the students like a hawk as they hurry to and fro. *More news.*

I'm not sure what he means by that exactly, but I don't have time to ask for clarification. He rushes past the Astronomy Sciences building, walking faster than I've ever seen him move before. A few buildings down, I burst through the door behind him, breathless, watching as he eyes the clock, then heads for the elevator.

"But the lecture—"

He shakes his head to quiet me as the elevator doors open, then pulls me inside. He's tapping his foot, completely focused on each number as it illuminates on the silver panel. We're out of the elevator in mere seconds, moving swiftly toward Professor Colter's office. I get an uneasy feeling as we approach, immediately noticing that the lights are off. Xero jiggles the door handle. Locked.

One look at my watch tells me that we still have at least fifteen minutes before the next lecture starts. "Colter's always in her office right before class, finalizing her notes and syllabus."

"Like clockwork." The lines etched in his forehead tell me that whatever he's thinking can't be good. "Come on," he says, leading me to the emergency stairwell. We bound down the stairs before entering the lecture hall. The hushed whispers fall as hundreds of concerned eyes turn to look at us. They tell us everything we need to know.

Professor Colter has *also* gone missing.

32

"SEEMS YOU GOT what you asked for."

We're standing outside the lecture hall, with a hundred or so other students, as the police swarm the building. Xero's statement catches me off guard, and I can't figure out to *what* he's referring. "And what's that?"

"Not having to go to work anymore."

I know it's supposed to be a joke—a really bad joke with exceptionally bad timing—but there's an edge to his voice as he says it . . . almost like he'd been *expecting* this somehow.

I'm about to say something that's borderline accusatory, but then think better of it. My attention is pulled to even more students piling out of the building. I back away slightly, retreating to the courtyard. Xero follows. I spot a bench not too far from where we're standing and walk over to it. There's complete silence between us as he sits down next to me.

I blow out a long, exasperated sigh before rubbing my hand over the back of my neck, but still don't say anything. Honestly, I don't know what to think right now.

"So," he says, his eyes searching mine, "where do we go from here?"

My eyes flick past him. "You tell me."

He follows my gaze just as the police are starting to tape off the doors and windows. "Looks like we might have some time off."

My chest begins to tighten as an unexpected bout of anger surges through me—not at him, but at *this*. At *all* of this. "These professors going missing can't just be a coincidence."

He regards me with a solemn expression, making it very clear that we shouldn't keep talking out loud.

Do you think they were taken like we were?

I think there's more to it than that, but yes.

I catch the shadows darkening his eyes, realizing something for the very first time. *You know something.*

I wait for his response, but it doesn't come.

You know something and you're not telling me, I try again.

Knowing he can't very well hide *anything* from me, he takes me by the hand and leads me across campus. Away from the chaos of the lecture hall. Away from the courtyard. Away from listening ears of any kind. And then, we're suddenly tucked back *behind* the library, in a truly stunning arboretum that I didn't even know existed. Boxwood trees line the winding mosaic pathway, as well as hydrangeas, peonies, and tulips, spiraling into the center of the garden. Small birds nestle into glazed terra cotta fountains, splashing about as they dip their beaks into the flowing water. The further we walk into the garden, the more I feel as though I've been transported to a faraway place—a place where people *don't* suddenly go missing.

Xero leads me to a canopy-covered swinging bench and pats the seat next to him. I gladly take it, knowing that the view from here—the inside looking out—is probably even more breathtaking than the one walking in.

"How is it that you've only been here a fraction of the time and have managed to find places like this?"

He shrugs. "I look."

Oh, how one answer can be so simple, yet so profound. When you're so used to your surroundings, rushing through your days, it's easy to forget to wander. To explore. To get lost. To forever remain open and curious. If Xero's taught me anything, it's that there's *always* something new to be discovered around every corner.

This is a prime example.

I've worked on this campus for longer than I care to admit and I *never* knew it had an arboretum—and that's probably because I hadn't been looking. The possibility of such a thing hadn't even crossed my mind. If it had, I would have spent many a day grading papers and eating lunch in total peace and solitude.

I'm so distracted by the newness, the *beauty* of it all, that I nearly forget why we walked so far away from the hustle and bustle of campus . . . why we tucked ourselves into this enchanted little corner in the first place.

I speak openly, knowing that no one could possibly hear us between the sheer distance and the bubbling of the many fountains. "So, what is it exactly that you know and aren't telling me?"

Xero shifts back and forth in his seat before looking down at his hands. I've never seen him . . . *uncomfortable* before. This is definitely new territory. Not just for him, but for the both of us.

"Hey," I whisper as I angle my body to face him. "You can tell me."

A muscle ticks in his jaw, but he starts to nod, repeating the motion a few times before finally saying, "Last night, after you fell asleep, I . . . I remembered something." He pauses, as if trying to gather the right string of words. "It was brief. Just a flash. But . . ."

I can tell the words are on the tip of his tongue, but it's like everything within him is trying to hold them back.

"But what?" I gently press.

"I think I know what happened right before I got here." His voice is so quiet now that I have to lean in to hear him—but he doesn't say the last part out loud.

I was intercepted by Nibiru.

I stare at him, trying to process what he's just said, but I can't. I shake my head, studying every inch of his face. "What does that *mean*, Xero?"

"It means that everything that's happened up until this point . . . might be my fault."

There's a brokenness to him now that I hadn't seen before. There's guilt. And shame. I can see it trying to claw its way out, but I refuse to let it get that far. What's happened to these professors, these missing people . . . it is *not* his fault. It can't be.

"Xero," I say calmly, "there is no way you have anything to do with any of this. You've been with me the entire time. Surely I would have noticed. You've been trying to figure things out just as much as I have—"

He shakes his head with such intensity that I shut my mouth immediately. "I was sent here for a reason, Elara. I've felt that. I've *known* it. But for *what* reason exactly, I haven't been able to figure out. Now that I know Nibiru intercepted me on my way here, it's starting to make sense. They wanted me to forget. They wanted us *all* to forget—"

Okay, now he's really lost me. "Forget *what?*"

"That's the part I *still* don't know. And it's like there's this ticking clock, counting down to *something* in the back of my head." He rakes a hand through his russet hair, his expression shifting from one of frustration to despair. "It's like I'm not figuring it out fast enough and because of that, things keep happening. Things that aren't supposed to be happening."

I have to admit, while it's strange to see him so vulnerable, on the edge of unraveling completely, I'm more drawn to him in this moment than in all of our prior moments combined. He's not trying to run. He's not trying to escape. By sharing this with me, he's refusing to hide behind the unknown. To bravely face the things that terrify the living shit out of him, with me at his side.

We've done this before. I pull some of the first words he'd ever spoken to me from my mind. I hadn't understood at first, but now? Now they ring truer than anything I've ever said. If only he knew how much reassurance, how much *confidence* he's given me . . . it's the least I can do to try and return the favor.

We've done this before, I repeat, *and we'll do it again.*

33

THE UNIVERSITY ISSUED a campus-wide dismissal of classes for the next week. Not surprising, given that a large portion of their staff has suddenly disappeared without so much as a trace. As we were being led off campus by security, I couldn't help but notice all of the yellow tape wrapped around many of the buildings. It's sad and confusing, yes, and if I didn't have everything *else* going on, I'd be feeling all of those feelings.

But honestly? Right now? I feel slightly relieved—like a major distraction has magically been cast aside. And I say "magically" because the university has given all remaining staff, *including* teachers' assistants, paid leave for the week.

As it should be . . .

Which means I don't have to worry about falling behind on my bills or stressing about money for an entire week—which I know doesn't sound like a long time, but for someone like me? It is. It may as well be a *lifetime.*

And I refuse to take a single second for granted.

We're back at my apartment now, even though I tried mentioning to Xero that we should head back to his cabin, but every time I do, he manages to change the subject. I know it may not be the "safest" spot for us, but it's the only place where he seems to be able to travel astrally—and if we're hoping to get answers, that's kind of an important part of the equation. The *only* part, really.

We're on the couch, his head resting on my lap, when my thoughts drag my attention behind me, to my bedroom. The strange message I'd received is plucked from my memory bank and placed front and center. Maybe it *doesn't* matter where we are. Where *he* is. Perhaps interdimensional travel is possible from anywhere.

I tap him on the shoulder, once, twice. His eyes flutter open. He gives me a lazy smile. "Did I doze off?"

I hadn't noticed, but I say, "It would appear so."

He grunts as he sits up, smoothing out his hair and his crinkled button-down shirt. He reaches for his glasses and slides them on, the thick frames doing even more to magnify those olive-green eyes.

I catch myself staring for a bit too long before I quickly say, "I have an idea. Come on."

Before he can protest, I hop up from the couch and walk us over to my bed. *Here comes a joke in three, two . . .*

"If you wanted a repeat of last night, you could have just said so."

There it is. I try not to read too much into the playful, somewhat *arousing*, edge to his tone as I make my way around the bed. "If we're going to stay here, especially with our newfound time off, we need to at least try to make the most of it." Even I'm surprised at how forthright I sound. "It's clear we need to go back to Nibiru, even if it's a risk—"

"*We?*"

I stop mid-sentence. "That's what we talked about before, is it not?"

He crosses his arms over his chest. "*Talked* about, yes. But agreed to?" He scratches his head mockingly. "That I don't recall."

"Well, if you think I'm letting you go alone, you're completely delusional. Which, by the way, I'm pretty sure *I* was the one on Nibiru in the first place. You had to come find me, remember?"

He falls silent.

"So, it seems Nibiru intercepted *me* and not *you*." As soon as I speak the words, I know they're trouble, and I immediately wish I could take them back. "Holy shit, Xero. Why would they intercept *me*?"

He regards me with a pained expression. "That's yet another question I don't have the answer to. But it's also why you need to take your mother's advice."

Back to this again.

"Has he called you since—?"

"No."

"Are you su—?"

"I'm sure."

His eyes don't leave mine. "When he calls again, will you answer?"

That question stirs up years and *years'* worth of conflict, something he can't possibly understand because he hasn't been here, on this *planet*, long enough. "I'm considering it."

He runs a hand along his jaw, clearly not pleased with my response. "What if he can tell you more about your mother?"

"And what if everything he tells me is laced with lies for his benefit?"

Well that's oddly specific.

It was meant to be, I shoot back silently.

"You have to give him a chance, Elara."

195

There it is again, that rising anger. "I don't *have* to do anything." I can feel my defenses firing on all cylinders, but they're brought to a sudden halt when I catch the unsettling look on his face.

Is that . . . fear?

Is he . . . afraid?

"I don't think your mother would seek me out if it weren't important—*dire,* even. Can we at least agree on that?"

I move slightly around the side of the bed. "We can."

"He can't hurt you, Elara."

I don't know how he picked up on that, but he did. Something I've buried so, so deep. Something I've tucked away into the furthest depths of my subconscious mind. Something I'd do *anything* to rid myself of. And here it is.

Revealed.

Uncovered.

Splayed out for all to see.

A ticket to a show only a masochist would buy.

"He's where he belongs. For more reasons than one."

Xero shifts his stance, and I can tell he's backing off. Retreating. Although to where, I don't know. I don't think he does either.

"I don't doubt that," he says, each word more strained than the last. "But the message I received was crystal clear. Your role in all of this is just as important as mine."

Tears sting my eyes as I try to decipher yet another fucking riddle. Why can't he just *say* exactly what he means?

"Because *I don't know*," he says quietly, answering my unspoken question. "But it's a feeling. A strong one. I can't ignore it—and neither should you."

"Well, I have a feeling, too," I say, still fighting back tears. "And perhaps, as someone who's been following them her whole life—and turned out damn near all right—I shouldn't be so quick to dismiss them."

Xero casts his eyes toward the ground. A small nod follows, his voice shaky as he says, "You're right. I'm just trying to do the best I can with the information I've been given. And, to me, this feels like it's coming from a pretty important source."

His words hit me square in the chest. Here we are, badgering each other and working against each other, when what we really need to be doing is walking through this together—as partners. As one cohesive unit.

"Okay, here's the deal," I say, compromising for once in my life. "If you lay here and do *whatever* it is you do to astral travel, I'll answer the next 'unknown call' I receive."

Xero raises a brow. "And the one after that?"

I narrow my eyes, knowing exactly where this is headed.

"I just want to make sure that you'll continue to answer the phone until you actually speak with your father. Things go amiss all the time with technology, especially when you're dealing with prison systems."

I give him a dubious look. "How could you possibly know that?"

"I can tap into more frequencies than you're even aware of."

Now *that* I believe.

"Fine. Deal."

"Okay then." Xero looks at the bed, assessing which side he wants to lay on. He chooses the right. I wait for him to extend his entire body out, his ankles nearly hanging off the edge. I stand, somewhat awkwardly, off to the side, not sure what my role is in all of this.

As if answering my question, he angles his head at the open space next to him. I slip my watch off my wrist and take out my earrings before joining him. Now we're both on my bed, lying on our backs, staring up at the ceiling. I feel his hand close around mine and, for the first time that day, I feel calm. At ease. Like everything might just turn out okay.

"So, what do we do now?"

He raises our intertwined hands ever so slightly, our inked-up wrists the first thing on display. "This is how you were able to come with me last time." An audible gulp. "Even though we ended up somewhere neither of us wanted to be."

The sheer memory gives me chills—and not the good kind. "The first time around, I was alone. This time, it'll be different. Because I won't be."

"That depends on if I can get this right."

"Get what right?"

"Using our connection to take astral form at the same time, in the same place . . . *and* end up in the same place, at the same time."

"What do I need to do?"

"Just focus on this, right here. The way our hands feel pressed together. Our connection. The ease with which we communicate. How it feels when we merge into one."

My cheeks heat at his last comment, but I cover it well. "Shouldn't be a problem, seeing as it's all really fresh in my mind."

Now it's his turn to blush. I turn my head slightly, just barely catching it.

"Are you ready?"

The question is heavy. Dense. But there's only one acceptable answer.

"Ready as I'll ever be."

34

ONE MINUTE I'M staring up at the ceiling, and the next, I'm rapidly blinking as I'm traveling through a sort of cosmic gateway. Greens, blues, pinks, and yellows swirl around me, twinkling like Christmas lights on the best-decorated house in the neighborhood. While I can still feel Xero's hand clasped tightly around mine, when I turn to look at him, he isn't there. *Don't panic,* I tell myself. *Focus on the feeling.*

Xero had made it very clear to stay focused on our connection—on things *unseen.* Astral traveling isn't so much about what you can *see* as it is about what you can *feel.* "Feeling" is the essence of everything. And that's probably how we got disconnected last time. That, and the other seemingly intelligent entities that had been involved.

As much as I want to keep my eyes open to witness the spectacular lightshow, I refuse to be distracted. I keep Xero at the forefront of my mind, focusing on his hand gripping mine, the warmth of his touch, the way his hands had slid down my neck and bare back . . . Okay, so maybe *that* isn't exactly what he'd meant, but I'm enjoying myself, nonetheless.

The heat emanating from my wrist momentarily grabs at my attention, but I don't open my eyes. Does it feel like it's on fire? Yes. Does my entire arm feel like scorched earth? Yes. But I keep my eyes closed, keep my *focus* on Xero.

When we finally arrive *wherever* we've arrived, it feels like both years and mere seconds have passed. I'm not sure how that's even possible, but Xero's there, in my mind, to help clarify my thoughts. *Time is but an illusion.*

Right. It doesn't exist here.

Can I open my eyes?

Almost, he says.

I hear a strange rustling and, while I'm desperate to see what's going on, I keep my eyes closed. I trust him. I don't want to do anything to accidentally screw this up. We're both here, still connected, still together. If I have to wait a few more seconds with my eyes sealed shut, then so be it.

"It worked," he says, nearly breathless. "It actually worked." I don't know how it's possible, but he sounds both far away and crystal clear at the same time.

"What worked? What's going on?" I say, trying to remain patient.

"Not everyone—every *human*—is fully equipped to see themselves in their true form. And when I say fully equipped, I mean many can't handle it. It's too surreal. Too *out of body*—"

"Why? Because they don't have a body?" I joke.

"Precisely."

Oh. I can't say I wasn't expecting that, but the thought of me as . . . *not* a body? Like how I'd been in my dream, as pure energy, but now in real life? Trippy, to say the least.

"Not to worry, though. In a sense, you still have your body and I still have mine. We were able to fully project ourselves astrally, although there are a few minor differences—"

Not wanting to wait any longer, I take that as full permission to open my eyes. When I do, I immediately feel as though I might pass out. "Oh . . . my . . ."

I've seen Xero in astral form before, sure—but that was on Earth. Here . . . well, my senses are heightened. Colors more vibrant. Sounds crisp and crystal clear.

Feelings *way* intensified.

When I first look at him, I can't help but notice the golden glow that outlines every floating particle that makes up, well, *Xero*. The form he's taken is glistening, shimmering—brighter than the sun itself . . . except I can look at him without going blind.

Not only that, but I can *feel* him on a level I didn't even think was possible. The longer I look at him, the more I see *myself* reflected in his astral form. I've never taken drugs before, but I swear, this is probably what taking DMT feels like.

"You are magnificent," I breathe. My voice sounds like silken honey as it wraps around the both of us, and a feeling of pure, unconditional love follows. It's so foreign, so *unfamiliar*, that I can't help but expend, by far, the strangest sound I've ever made. It lands somewhere between a gasp of total and complete shock and the happiest laughter you've ever heard—the kind that makes you laugh uncontrollably the moment you hear it. The thing is though . . . I'm not embarrassed by it. I'm not embarrassed by anything, actually. I can feel myself grinning from ear to ear (*like an idiot*, a human would say) and I just feel . . . happy.

Unencumbered.

Infinite.

He reaches out to me, and I gladly take his "hand", still smiling so much that my "mouth" *should* hurt, but it doesn't (which I'm sure is just another grandiose effect of this place) as he spins me around so that I can finally see what he's looking at. And . . .

Oh. My. Fucking. Shit.

I let out another strange sound, this one between a high-pitched squeal and a low, guttural, *"You gotta be kidding me"*. The seemingly endless expanse before us is unlike anything I ever could have dreamt up.

First and foremost, everything is sparkling, as if just touched by rainy, morning dew and kissed ever so lightly by the sun. Streams and rivulets of glorious platinum liquid run off into every corner, every crevice, as far as the eye can see. Floating pods in the shape of boulders, in all different colors, float above these deepening pools of liquid metal, moving of their own accord, dipping down only to open and release what appears to be rising steam.

Colorful waterfalls pour straight out of the sky itself, trickling down and through some of these boulders as they shift and change with the tide, hiding caverns and alcoves of their own behind steady curtains. And the sky . . . *oh, the sky*. It gleams with orbs and streaks, as if painting its canvas in purples and pinks, casting a miraculous highlight on the twinkling stars themselves.

It's then, as I'm taking it all in, that I realize I can't *hear* anything. That the soundtrack to this glorious place is one I seem to have made up entirely in my head. I lean forward, listening, but it's completely silent.

You're almost there, I hear Xero say.

It's so quiet . . .

You've seen it. Witnessed it. Observed it. Now close your eyes and feel into it.

I do exactly as he says and close my eyes. The image of this picture-perfect place is burned into the backs of my eyelids. Instantly, I feel beauty. Harmony. Tranquility.

I feel *free*.

There's a sudden burst of recognition as a wave of light travels through me, all the way from the top of my head, into my heart, deep down into the very core of my soul. It embeds itself, pulsing, beating, perfectly in tune with the heartbeat of this place.

And then I hear it.

The most miraculous symphony I've ever heard.

The rushing of the streams, although it doesn't sound like water, but more like the *glug glug* of wine as its poured from a bottle, then delicately swirled around a glass. The boulder-like pods sound like a violin quartet as they move and sway and dip and shift places. And the orbs, streaking across the sky, sound like the turning of pages of an old library book, an ever so soft *swish.*

Far off in the distance, I can see more ethereal structures, floating and moving as if, somehow, they each have a consciousness of their own and aren't willing to take up permanent residence anywhere. It's only when I look down that I realize I'm hovering just above one of the platinum lakes. I glance at Xero, instantly seeing a reflection of myself before seeing him again.

"This is . . ." There isn't even a word to describe it. For the first time in my life, I am truly, irrevocably speechless. Stunned. Shocked. Amazed. On the verge of passing out from the sheer *is-ness* of it all.

"Where . . . *are* we?" I hear myself say the words, but deep down, I know. I've been here before. *We've* been here before—like we keep saying.

Xero doesn't answer. Just waits for it to come to me.

So certain. So assured.

He has every right to be because within seconds . . . it does. I glance down at my wrist, recalling the message I'd received from the unknown voices.

Forty-five. Star system. Seven.

"Star system Messier 45. Seven as in The Seven Sisters star cluster in the Taurus constellation," I whisper. "The Pleiades. We're *in* the Pleiades."

Xero doesn't say anything to confirm, but he doesn't need to. I can *feel* it. This is right. This is exactly where we are.

"They also mentioned Haven . . . Haven must be here, somewhere. Must be connected to this somehow. And—"

The *other* piece of the message. The other name.

Axel Volaris.

I feel myself shudder as the knowledge begins to pour through me. Suddenly, it all makes sense. Suddenly, I know more than I ever thought I could. Recognition takes hold. I visualize the letters before me, unscrambling them and, sure enough . . .

X-e-r-o S-i-v-a-l-l-a.

A-x-e-l V-o-l-a-r-i-s.

I turn to face him, the Xero I've come to know so well. "It's *you*. It's always *been* you." The words are a mere brush of air as they leave my lips in pure disbelief.

"*You're* Axel Volaris."

35

THE REALIZATION SEEMS to hit him at the same time it hits me. This is the first time I've seen him speechless. The first time I've seen him in complete and utter astonishment. The first time I've seen him recognize what must be the undeniable truth.

"Elara." He reaches out to me, his voice pained.

I meet his raw, aching stare. Suddenly, the tranquility and peace I'd felt just moments ago begins to roil within me, like hot lava bubbling to the surface. Flames ignite—in my legs, my chest, my back, my *mind*—dancing to a rhythm I don't yet recognize or understand. I gaze at my astrally-formed hands, watching as the particles speed up, pulsing faster, dancing *wilder*. I feel a revolution stirring. Rising conflict. Incontestable anger.

Rage.

"Elara, don't!" His voice is far away as the ground beneath me shatters, collapsing in on itself. I hadn't realized that I'm no longer floating, no longer impervious to the effects of the environment around me, as I fall into the darkening abyss, into what looks like a massive black hole.

"Elara!" I've never heard him scream like that before. It'd rip my chest straight open if I weren't so fucking angry with him. Even though I'm falling, even though I can no longer see him, can no longer see which way is up, which way is down, or left, or right . . . I can clearly see the memory of Professor Haven, standing in front of me, *blaming* me for something I did not do.

Something that Xer—*Axel* did.

It cost me my job. My livelihood as I'd come to know it. And whether things may have played out differently than they had doesn't actually matter. Because he could *never* possibly understand the feeling of having the floor ripped out from underneath you, over and over and over again. As it had been my whole entire life.

My mother. My father. My ex-fiancé. My miscarriage.

My job might seem small in comparison—but that's exactly it. It was *all* I had left. And if he hadn't shown up—if his email hadn't suddenly appeared in my inbox—my story would look entirely different.

No job. No money. Evicted. Homeless.

No fallback. No support. No *life*.

Not one I'd want, anyway.

Does he *know* how close I'd been? Can he even begin to fathom it? The complete and utter despair I'd been on the precipice of?

When I finally manage to pull myself out of my rage-spiral, I'm in a place that looks very different from the one before. This is most certainly *not* The Pleiades. Before I can get my bearings, a familiar voice speaks.

"Hello, Elara."

A chill lodges in my chest. *Xero?*

"Yes and no," he responds, clearly able to read my thoughts. "Just a more . . . *refined* piece of this puzzle."

Slowly, I turn around. From what I can tell, I'm still in astral form, but it's . . . different. Denser. It feels a lot like how I felt in Nibiru.

My eyes land on what looks like Xero . . . but it *isn't* Xero. I can just tell. By the demeanor. The expression. The strangely ominous presence. All *feelings*, but they don't discount what I *know*.

"You're Axel," I say, taking in the sight of him. "Axel Volaris."

"Who are we *really,* if not each other?"

I don't respond to that. The last thing I need is a *different* version of Xero speaking in even more complex riddles. Might as well be a foreign tongue.

I narrow my eyes at him, unable to pull myself away from the sight. Where his body *should* be is a tapestry of interwoven black spirals and swirls, floating like a strange mist that desperately wants to leave, but is being forced to stay. He doesn't have limbs, as far I can tell, but his chest and neck seem to grow out of a vine-ridden blackness, the one that makes up his very shape. His skin, if you can even call it that, is gray, dashed with flecks of silver, and platinum lines run along the outer edges, outlining his upper half in a demonic sort of way.

But his face . . .

His face is my only indication that he *might* be Xero, just in another form. The eyes are not olive-green, but a deep, deep gray—almost black. His hair, which is usually tousled and shaggy is smoothed back like an oil slick. And it's *long.* It meshes and melds with the mist as it trails down the back of his neck, subtly converging with the ever-present darkness. He does not wear glasses, but there are small scaly-like patches embedded in his skin—around his hairline, covering his ears, and lining his jaw. They appear on the sides of his nose, too, almost reminiscent of the skin of an old, dried-out reptile.

Even with all of these *new* features (don't know if I'd say they're necessarily "improved"), I can still feel Xero's presence—although it *is* different, in a way that words can't quite explain.

"You're here because you shifted."

His voice startles me, like a baby rabbit in a shaken cage. "Because I *shifted?*" I echo back.

"Oh, right, right, right," he says as he looks up, conversing with what I assume must be another entity. "Too much, too soon. Or too much always? It seems I've finagled the two once more."

I haven't a clue what he's talking about—or *who* he's talking to—but something tells me I ended up here because of how I'd been feeling earlier. Regardless, I much prefer *Xero* to *Axel*.

"Well now, *that* hurts my feelings," he says, drawing out each word. "Dear, dear Elara—you haven't even given me a chance."

It's absolutely pointless to think my thoughts if he's just going to read them anyway, so I decide to speak them out loud. "Why are you intervening?"

He raises a hand to his chest in mock surprise. "Why, whatever do you mean?"

Okay, I'm calling it. I *hate* him. The way he talks. His tone. His mannerisms. The "cheeky" remarks. *All* of it.

"Hate is a strong word, Elara. Especially for someone you've only just met."

Condescending. We can add that one to the list, too.

"Seeing as I can only be summoned, I most certainly did not intervene." He lets out a childish laugh, one that sounds like nails on a chalkboard. I cringe. "Seems you need to do some reassessing." He makes a *tick-tock* noise with his mouth. "Take some accountability, perhaps? Nobody likes a victim—especially not men like *Xero.*"

My temper flares. "Okay, first of all, *fuck* you. Second of all, there is no 'reassessing' that needs to be done. I don't know *what* I'm doing here, or *how* I got here, or why you've seemed to assume the identity of someone you're *clearly* not, but I demand that you leave. Now."

"Feisty today, aren't we?" He leers at me, which is all the more infuriating. "Well, Elara, seeing as *you* were the one who summoned *me*, that makes said demand null and void."

I can feel my anger mounting, yet again, so I turn away from him to regain my composure. There *has* to be a way to work through this. There has to be a way to reconnect with Xero. *How did I get here? How could I have fallen so far, so damn deep, into . . . this?*

"It happens to the best of us. Believe me."

"Can you *not* be in my head for, like, one second?"

"No can do, I'm afraid. I'm here to stay."

Xero? I grab at my wrist, trying to feel the tether that usually binds us—and, while I do feel *something*, it's not the *usual* something. *Xero Sivalla. Come in, Xero.*

"*Prrr*-esent!" Axel touts.

"For the last fucking time, get *out* of my head," I growl through clenched teeth.

"You know, Elara, the more you try to resist me, the longer this is all going to take." He looks up into the void again, making faces and furrowing his brows as if there's someone there.

There's not.

"This has to be a dream, a *nightmare*," I clarify, trying all the cliché things to wake myself up.

"Far from it, dear. This is as real as it gets." Another look into the abyss overhead. "I'm *trying*, but the girl can't seem to take a hint!"

"Okay, so . . . this isn't real. It can't be. It also isn't a dream. Or a nightmare," I try to reason. "Which leaves only a couple of options. Either I've completely lost my mind and am now under the influence of some heavy dose of medicine at a psych ward, *or* I'm in the middle of astral traveling and got caught in some sort of limbo." I glance at the vexatious presence before me. "And based on this entire interaction, I'm going to assume it's the latter."

"Orrr," he purrs, "perhaps there's another option. One that makes complete sense, but seeing as it's one you won't necessarily like, your stubborn denial is keeping it at bay?" He lifts a brow. "How very Taurean of you, I might add."

"*Right*, and what would that be exactly?" I retort.

Axel tosses his hands up in mock defeat. "I'm just here to ask the right questions." Another glance at the sky. "Yes, that's what I just said. We're so close. Don't you *dare* rush me—"

"You sound insane, you know that? *Who* the fuck are you talking to?" I throw my arms at the nothingness above us.

"Why, my dear, dear, child," he says, his smile turning lupine. "I'm talking to *you*."

36

WHEN I FIRST come back to, I have no recollection of what's happened. I wake up in my bed, like I do every morning. I brush my teeth, turn the rickety heater on, and slip my feet into some faux fur-lined slippers. I watch the coffee maker as it *drip, drip, drips* into the pot, and it's only when I go to rinse out a mug and see the water swirling down the drain that I suddenly remember.

I rush to my bedroom, nearly tackling my nightstand as I search for my phone. I hear a *ding* in the distance, over near the bathroom, and immediately look up to find it—but the minute I do, I wish I hadn't.

At first, I'm hit with a wave of both happiness and relief at the sight of him, but that wave quickly crashes into full-fledged fury as recent events begin to flood in.

"What the fuck are you doing here?" I demand as I march over to him.

Axel shrugs before carelessly tossing my phone. I manage to make a miraculous catch as I continue to approach him. He doesn't seem to be rattled by my behavior in the slightest. "Well, *at some point,* we had to make our way back here." He frowns, clearly disgusted. "Although I can't imagine *why.*"

I scowl at him. "Where is Xero," I say through gritted teeth.

"Does it really matter? Especially when the upgrade," he gestures to himself, "is as good as this?"

"Gross," I say. "I'll ask once more. Where is he?"

"He'd want it this way. You certainly did."

"Stop. Talking." I hold my hand up, directly in front of his face. "Now."

Axel makes a zipping motion across his lips and that's when I notice it. I grab at his arm, turning his wrist so that it's facing me. "No," I breathe. "No, no, no, no . . ."

"You look like you've just seen a ghost."

I try to find my words, shaking my head in disbelief.

"Are you going to ask me again, or are we finally done with this relentless back and forth nonsense?"

I can't stop staring at his marks. The exact same ones as mine. The exact same marks as Xero's. "How—?"

"I think this will go a lot smoother for you if you just accept what is."

I want to scream. Run. Rewind. There is *no way* that the person standing in front of me is *Xero*—not the Xero I've come to know . . . and love. *Fuck.* It all hits me at once. How much I miss him. How I would do anything just to hear his voice again. To feel the heated tension between us right before we kiss. To wrap myself in our connection. To feel alive, understood, and whole. I take a deep breath, willing my racing thoughts to calm. He may not be right in front of me, but he's still here. No one is ever really gone.

Right?

My thoughts run haywire.

I'm expecting a smartass remark from Axel, but it doesn't come. A flicker of hope ignites deep in my chest. What was it he'd said? *Accept what is?* I carefully think through what I want to say before speaking it aloud.

"Axel, if it isn't too much to ask, I need a minute to myself. Alone."

He doesn't budge. "You know where I'll be."

I resist the urge to roll my eyes and say, *Fine then, prick. I'll leave.* Instead, I give him as gracious a nod as I can muster, then walk into the kitchen, falling out of sight behind the cabinets. I grip the edge of the countertops, fingers drumming against the faux granite.

If he's reading my thoughts, then so be it. I glance down at my wrist, placing my palm over the markings. I breathe in and close my eyes, hoping that this will somehow protect me from Axel's intrusive nature, even though he bears the exact same marks—

Even though he claims to be Xero.

That they're one in the same.

The last thing I remember before Axel . . . is being with Xero. Astral traveling. In The Pleiades. Feeling euphoric, blissed out. Platinum streams and colorful waterfalls and floating boulders. A sky streaked with majestic pinks and purples. Ease. Tranquility. Calm. And then . . .

An unwanted discovery. Something that couldn't possibly be true. The scrambling and unscrambling of letters. Xero, Axel. Sivalla, Volaris. So much pain. And hurt. And anger. So much distrust . . .

And that's when I'd plunged.

Straight into the unknown.

Straight into the nether realm.

Straight into the *truth* of Axel Volaris.

I can't help but flash back to the shadow entities I'd seen that night at the observatory—those silvery green pools of light and how they'd flooded the halls. I also can't help but notice that Axel's presence is eerily similar. He isn't kind and warm and welcoming. He's cynical, snide, and overall, wildly unpleasant to be around. The opposite of Xero. Literally.

The exact opposite.

Disheartened, I peek around the cabinets of the kitchen to find that Axel is no longer standing in my bedroom. I lean a little bit farther to find him staring out the window that overlooks a whole lotta nothing. With the way he's just floating there, so silently, and with his back to me, he almost looks like a wraith. A silhouette of complete darkness, save for the light that allows him to even be seen in the first place. Almost like a . . .

Of course.

My heart nearly stops at the realization.

Axel wasn't lying. He *is* Xero . . .

You must have multiple parts to make up a whole.

What I'm looking at, what Axel *is* . . .

Is Xero's *shadow.*

37

"TOOK YOU LONG enough."

I regard him with lethal calm. "It seems you *were* telling the truth. Very Xero-like of you."

"I aim to please."

The familiar phrase stabs at my heart. I don't know how to respond, so instead, I decide it might be best to set up some boundaries—especially with the whole telepathy thing.

"Listen, I know that 'being in my head' is how you communicate, but I'd appreciate it if you'd ask first."

He looks me up and down, studying me, examining me. I'd feel the urge to cringe if I didn't just find out that he *is* Xero. *We all have shadows.*

"Well, seeing as you asked so nicely, I suppose that's fair."

"Really?" I'm more than surprised by how easy that was.

"I aim—"

"—to please, I know," I finish for him. "So . . . what now?" It's my turn to look him up and down. "Do you come with me places like Xero did? Like *that?*" I don't mean for it to come out as harsh as it does, but Axel doesn't seem to take offense.

"Xero chose to take human form. Axel does not."

"Are we speaking in third person now?"

"It helps to differentiate between us."

No sarcasm this time. It's a bit strange coming from him. Even though his snide behavior's been driving me up a wall, I much prefer it over this ominous, somber version.

"So, when we go out," I clarify, "people can't see you."

"Or hear me. *Although,* they may sense me." A malevolent grin spreads across his face, reminding me of every villain in every animated movie that's ever been made.

"So, they can't see you or hear you, but might sense you— I'm guessing you mean your energy." *Good to know. Talking to myself may raise questions amongst the commonfolk.*

"Precisely."

"Okay, and uh . . . how long do you plan to be with me?" Again, coming out way harsher than I'd intended.

"As long as it takes."

I'm about to ask him what that means when my phone rings. I briefly glance at the screen. *Unknown* flashes across it— and it's then I remember what Xero kept harping on.

Speak to your father. Answer the phone.

It's what he wants. It's what he said my mother wants. And if answering this call means it might bring Xero back somehow, I'm all in. I take a deep breath before saying, "I need to take this", then swipe my finger across the screen and book it outside, although I don't know why because I'm sure he'll still hear everything that goes on. But if the illusion of privacy is what I need right now, then that's exactly what I'll give myself.

The woman on the automated prison recording is halfway through her spiel. *Press one to accept . . .*

I pull the phone away from my ear and stare at the electronic keypad. *Don't overthink this. Just suck it up and do it.* I nearly close my eyes as my index finger punches the number one.

Connecting . . . please wait.

I take another deep breath, trying to picture Xero's face and *not* the unhinged shadow version of him that's terrorizing my apartment right now—anything to keep me calm. The line clicks and I hear a voice I haven't heard in over a decade.

"Elara?"

"Seth." *Calling him 'Dad' seems wildly inappropriate.*

"It's so good to hear your voice. How are you?"

"Why are you calling?" My tone is clipped, unforgiving.

"I . . . well, I petitioned for an appeal in the hopes that maybe they'll overturn my sentence or let me out on parole."

As fucked up as it is, my heart sinks at the news.

". . . I just thought I ought to let you know. It took a lot of digging to get your information, especially since I was unaware you'd changed your name—"

"Needed a fresh start," I say, not that I owe him an explanation. "So, is that all you called to say?" I grit my teeth, trying not to implode over the line. "That you royally fucked up and even though that's *still* the case and nothing's changed, they might just let you off the hook and make *your* life a little easier?"

Too late. Implosion to full-on rage in 3 . . . 2 . . .

"They're letting me have visitors now—"

I blink. *He. Did. Not.*

"—and, well . . . I thought maybe, if you're feeling up to it, that is, that we could talk. In person."

"This interaction has been more than enough, Seth."

"Elara . . ."

I don't wait to hear what he's going to say next. Eyes brimming with tears, I end the call and shove the phone into my back pocket. I furiously wipe at my eyes, smearing the tears before they have a chance to fall. "Mother fucker," I mutter as I shake my head and push open the door to my apartment.

Axel's sitting on the couch, with one knee crossed over the other, staring out the window. He doesn't bother to look at me as I walk in. "Well. That was rough."

I raise a hand, glaring at him. "Don't even start."

"Do you think that's what Xero had in mind?"

"Enough, Axel. That's enough for one day."

I'm about to fill a glass of water at the sink when the overwhelm of what's just happened begins to pile on.

Fuck this day.

I leave the glass on the edge of the counter before throwing on my coat and grabbing my keys. I don't bother telling Axel where I'm going or what I'm doing as I lock the door. In either case, I'm sure he'll tag along just the same.

38

I'M ON MY way to campus by myself—at least it feels that way. I glance at the passenger's seat, then at the rearview mirror into the backseat and out the window. No sign of Axel. I suppose that's a good thing?

But just because I can't see him doesn't mean he isn't there. *That* I've learned the hard way.

I grip the steering wheel tighter, wishing that Xero were sitting next to me. As relentless as his optimism could be at times, I could really use a heavy dose of it right now. *Will I ever see him again? Or am I stuck with Axel? Which begs the question . . . why the switch? Did I do something wrong?*

I sigh, trying to push the thoughts from my mind. At this point, I have a seemingly endless list of questions—*big surprise*—and stewing over them when I *know* I can't get any answers is a waste of time and energy.

As I pull onto campus, the first thing I notice is the empty parking lot, which is quickly explained by the never-ending strands of yellow caution tape strung up all over campus—like a house that's been TP'd for a lame Halloween prank. It looks like "class dismissal" has up-leveled its status to be campus-wide.

I grab my phone and text Kensie. *I know campus is closed, but hopefully you're still open?*

He responds almost immediately. *It's been slower than death, but still open. You should come by.*

He doesn't have to tell me twice. *On my way.*

I toss my phone, reverse out of the parking lot, and head down Main Street, arriving within minutes. When I get out of my Jeep, I circle the vehicle, looking all around for any sign of Axel. I don't see him. I don't feel him . . .

Either he's not here or he's very good at hiding.

No matter. I'm beyond thankful for the break—because honestly, who knows how long it's going to last?

I push the café door open to an underwhelming setting of empty chairs and an overflowing supply of fresh coffee beans. I frown at Kensie. "That bad, huh?"

He's wiping down one of the counters, although I don't know why because it's already spotless. "Closed campus means no exams, which means no students, which means no late-night cramming or need for my caffeination services. I thought I'd at least get a pre-Halloween rush." He sighs, tossing the dish towel over his shoulder. "I'm honestly surprised I'm still employed."

"At least there's that. Right?"

"I suppose. I'm just happy I get paid by the hour and not by customer." He gestures to the empty café. "Because if that were the case, I'd be beyond broke . . ." His voice trails off as he realizes that this entire conversation might be bordering on insensitive. "I mean, should I even ask about your job? I heard about Professor Colter."

"Yeah," I mutter. "I scared off two professors in one month. I've got a real hot streak goin'."

Kensie's about to start making our drinks, but I shake my head. I don't want one. Now they just remind me of Xero. I sigh. "Got anything stronger?"

"Double shot of espresso?"

"Load 'em up."

I can feel him studying me as he preps the espresso machine. "I'm tempted to ask where your boytoy is, but given the look on your face, maybe I shouldn't?"

"Boytoy?" I roll my eyes. "I wouldn't exactly call him that."

"Fine. Your man, your boo, your other half."

That last one stings a little, but I don't let it show.

"He's staying at the cabin for a bit," I lie, not knowing what else to say. It's not like I can fill Kensie in on the fact that Xero isn't *actually* Xero and now there's this weird shadow version of him named Axel hanging around.

Even I don't fully understand what's going on . . .

So how can I expect Kensie to?

"Are you two, you know . . . *good?*"

"Yeah," I say, my voice on the edge of cracking. "All good." I force a smile.

I know Kensie sees right through it, but I've also been around him long enough to know that he won't press further, especially when it's obvious I don't feel like talking about it. He's a good friend in that way.

"One double shot espresso for the lady." He scoots the demitasse cup across the countertop. "And for me, well . . . I'm sticking to chai. I don't need to be all wired and shit, especially when I have no customers. It'd only make time go by slower."

I've already downed my espresso by the time he finishes talking when I realize he *does* have a point. Maybe this was a bad idea. It's not like I need time to feel like it's moving any slower. If anything, I want it to magically speed up—to the part where Xero is back in my life instead of Axel.

"You look concerned. Worried almost. Talk to me."

221

It's hard to look him in the eye knowing all that I'm choosing to keep to myself. Even though I can't tell him about the whole Xero/Axel thing, I *can* tell him about what happened earlier. "I spoke with Seth today."

Kensie nearly drops his chai. "Your *father* Seth?"

"That's the one." I lean over the counter, propping myself up on my elbows. "He mentioned he might get parole after submitting an appeal or something like that."

"Shit. That's crazy." He angles his head toward one of the tables. "Wanna sit?"

"I'm actually doing better processing this while standing up."

He eyes me dubiously. "You're not exactly standing, Elara. You're . . . slouching. Maybe even wallowing?"

"I am not," I say defiantly.

"It looks like your spine is about to cave in on itself. It's distracting." He winces. "And painful to watch."

"Fine," I say as I straighten and pull out the nearest chair. "Happy?"

"Much better," Kensie says as he joins me. "So, back to Seth. He might be getting out early? That's . . . well, I don't know *what* that is. How'd he get your number anyway?"

"That remains to be seen, although I have a feeling the police chief had something to do with it."

Kensie wags his finger in the air. "I don't like that Albeck. Not one bit."

"We have that in common." I sigh. "Anyway, he basically invited me to come visit him."

"Shut up." Kensie nearly spits out his coffee on the perfectly polished table. "Bastard."

"My thoughts exactly."

"What'd you say?"

I shrug. "I hung up."

"'Atta girl."

"This last month has me all up in arms. I feel so on edge—"

"That might just be the espresso," he says with a wink.

I smirk before drumming my fingers against the table. "I don't know what to do. Campus is completely closed. I don't want to go back to my apartment, especially knowing that Albeck could show up at any minute." I glance out the window, hoping I didn't just stupidly manifest that. "I just . . . *don't know.*"

"Well, from the sounds of it, you've got two choices, maybe three. One, drive up to Xero's cabin. Two, go visit Seth." He makes a face. "Or three, stay here with me."

I give him a warm smile—one that's actually genuine. But it quickly fades when I catch a shadowy figure floating just outside the café windows.

Damn it, Axel.

"You know I'd love to stay here with you and commiserate over the lack of customers and the overall dumpster fire that seems to be everyday life, but you're probably right. I should head up to the cabin." I try to keep my expression neutral. I *hate* that I'm lying to him . . . again.

"Well, don't let me keep you. At least I did my part in getting you caffeinated before the drive."

"And I thank you immensely for that." I scoot my chair out and stand up, making sure I have everything before heading toward the door. "You *will* call me if anything happens, though?"

"Absolutely. Although things seem to be pretty uneventful around here." He raises a brow. "I expect you'll do the same?"

I nod. "Talk to you later."

"Drive safe!" he shouts as I walk out the door.

My attention immediately goes to Axel, who's standing just outside, peering nosily into the café window. "He seems nice."

"In the car," I mutter, trying not to move my lips. I don't need Kensie to look out and see me talking to . . . no one.

I unlock the Jeep's doors and hop in, putting the keys in the ignition, but Axel doesn't follow. He's staring at the vehicle with a strange look on his face. It's only a flicker but, for a moment, it almost looks as if he's afraid. He nearly gives me a heart attack as he suddenly appears in the passenger's seat, like a fine mist.

"I take it you just . . . float *through* things?"

"It'd look pretty weird to see a car door opening by itself, don't you think?"

"Point taken," I say as the engine revs to life. "We're going to Xero's"—I pause, realizing my faux pas—"I mean, *your* cabin. In Allenspark." I should know my way by now, but I still punch the address into the GPS.

"Whatever you say," he says clearly disinterested.

Let the longest hour of my life commence.

We're on the highway, in complete and total silence, when I realize the GPS has me taking an unfamiliar exit. "What the hell?" I murmur, studying the screen as I pull off. "Must be an accident up ahead. A detour maybe?"

I wait for the GPS to signal that it's re-routing, but it keeps me on the road, as if we've been intentionally heading this way all along. I'm about to pull over and check the coordinates when I see a sign up ahead that explains everything. *Boulder County Jail.*

I slam on the brakes at the stop sign and look to Axel. "Are you fucking serious right now? You messed with the coordinates?"

"Keep driving like that and *you'll* be the one in jail. Or worse." A visible shudder quakes his non-body.

Oh, how I want to smack him. Punch him. Throw him out of my car. "You've already intervened in my life enough." I begin re-typing the address into the GPS when the screen goes black.

Yep, I'm gonna lose it.

"In case you haven't noticed, *Elara*, that's kind of what I'm here for."

I hate how he says my name, like I'm a schoolchild.

"Just turn right, head to the prison, talk to Seth." His eyes glimmer with a strange sort of knowing. "He's expecting you." He brushes a piece of lint from his imaginary coat—his imaginary *body*. Ugh. "You can thank me later."

"You are insufferable, you know that?"

He points to the right without looking at me. "Just drive."

"And if I don't?"

Now he looks at me. "Are you sure *I'm* the insufferable one here? Or would you like to amend that statement? You Tauruses are so damn stubborn."

I grip the steering wheel tighter, my knuckles nearly turning white. "Stop speaking in riddles, Axel. And stop circumventing every single one of my questions."

He sighs, suddenly shedding all levity from before.

I straighten, realizing that he's actually listening to me for once. "I'm all ears."

"I'm keeping you from going the roundabout way—from making two trips when you only need to make one."

"Prove it."

"She's a tough one, isn't she?" he says while looking up at the roof of my car.

"*Axel*," I say, snapping my fingers. "Focus. Please."

"Your father has something to give you. Something important. And you'll need it once you arrive at the cabin."

I narrow my eyes at him.

"Like I said, I've already seen this play out, and, *again*, you'll thank me once we get there."

I really *don't* want to believe him, but I have to remember that Xero is still in there, *somewhere*. He wouldn't lead me astray. And, I suppose if I go in there and Axel turns out to be wrong, I can always ream his ass. *But if he turns out to be right . . .*

I put the car back in drive and turn right at the stop sign, as he's directed.

"I'm pleased to see you've made the right choice, although I already knew you would—"

I turn on the music to block him out for the remainder of the short drive.

39

I PULL INTO the lot that's designated for visitors, my heart hammering in my chest like a jackhammer. I pull into an open space, away from all of the other cars. I pull the jail's website up on my phone.

"Stalling?"

I ignore him, scrolling through the pages. *Aha, visitor hours.* My *aha* quickly turns into an *oh no* as I realize that I have no idea what cell block number he's in . . .

"Cell Block C-2," Axel says. "And visiting hours for that block are," he looks at the clock on my dash, "right now. Although I'd hurry if I were you because you only have two hours left."

I'm not even going to bother asking how he knows all of that because I'm sure it'll just be another cryptic answer that I don't have the energy to decipher. "Two hours is more than enough time."

He raises a brow at me. "Have you been to a jail before?"

"Well, no—"

"Whether you're an inmate or a visitor doesn't matter. The processing time is no different. Always takes longer, and they're sticklers for their rules." He cocks his head. "After all, it is the *law*."

I scowl at him before starting to gather my things.

"You can leave all that here. Just take your key and your driver's license." He pulls it out of the ignition and hands it to me. He answers my next question almost immediately. "Pointless to bring your phone. They're just going to take it from you once you get in there. But"—he digs around in my glovebox before producing a pen and small notepad—"take these with you." He pats at his jacket pocket. "Now go. You're wasting precious time."

I roll my eyes. "I'm going, I'm going. Just . . . stay here, okay? And please, for the love of wherever you came from, don't start anything."

"How can I when I'm invisible to everyone but you?"

Lucky me.

I exit the car, following the signs to "visitor check-in", like it's a luxury hotel or something. Oh, the irony. When I arrive, the first thing I'm asked is, "No purse?"

I hold up my car key and driver's license. "Just these."

The guard runs a metal detector down the length of my body. "Anything in your pockets?"

I show him the notepad and pen. "And these," I say sheepishly.

"Any more *ands*?" the guard asks sternly.

"No," I say before quickly adding, "sir."

"Who are you here to see?" he asks.

I watch as he scans a photocopy of my driver's license, unable to stop thinking about how much further along we, as a civilization, should be at this point. *I just traveled through a fucking wormhole, bending space and time—reality as we know it—and this fool is making a photocopy of my 'identity'.*

"Miss? The name of the inmate you're here to see?"

"Seth Wells." I cringe at my old last name.

His last name.

"Relation?"

Another cringeworthy question. "Father."

The man makes a note on the paper. "Admitted. Please wait on the bench until your group is called." He's about to assign me "a group" when he looks over my shoulder at the empty waiting room. "Disregard that. When you hear the door click, you can go ahead and enter."

"Got it," I say, maneuvering behind him. "Thanks."

I take a seat on the metal bench, wondering how they keep it both freezing *and* damp in here at the same time. I tuck my car key and driver's license into my pocket before pulling out the small notepad and pen.

Let's see if Axel actually knows what he's talking about.

After waiting for what feels like a century, the door finally clicks. I'm still the only one in the waiting room. I look to the guard who angles his head toward the door, giving me the green light. I take a deep breath and smooth out my coat before walking through the high-security door. Seriously, it looks like all those bank vault doors you see in the movies. It makes me wonder if *all* of the cell blocks are as secure as this one, or if these types of doors are reserved for the damned of the damned—a.k.a. my father's type. *Must have cost a fortune.*

I'm halfway into the decent-sized rectangular room, surrounded by glass partitions and metal stools, when I see him from behind the glass. My heart drops into my stomach, immediately regretting my decision to come here. *I'm not ready for this. I'm not ready for this. I'm not ready to see him—to face him.*

I approach the booth, trying not to notice how eerie it is being the only two in here, until I see the guard stationed almost directly behind him. I don't know why, but it makes me feel a little better, which is honestly pretty fucked up. It's not like Seth can reach me, seeing as there are inches of thick polycarbonate glass separating us.

He gives me a sad smile the moment he lays those amber-colored eyes on me. Eyes like molten copper. The last time he saw me, I was eleven, but there's no denying that he recognizes me. How can he not? I'm his fucking daughter.

He reaches for the telephone on his side and takes it off the receiver. I hesitate, but eventually do the same on my side. His voice is shaky, but still sounds exactly the same. My heart breaks a little as he says, "Elara, it's so good to see you."

I can feel myself soften, then harden again around the edges. "I wish I could say the same, Seth."

His demeanor doesn't falter in the slightest at my using his proper name. As much as I hate to admit it, he seems genuinely happy to see me.

"Last we spoke, I honestly wasn't sure you'd come at all."

"I wasn't either." I pause. "Sure, that is."

He looks down at the metal table, then at the glass that's currently separating us. "I'd love to hear what I've missed. What you've been up to. I'm sure it's a lot."

You can say that again. Over two decades' worth.

"I doubt we have time for all that."

So far, Axel's little "prophecy" is leaning more towards phony. I glance at my watch, wondering how much more of this small talk I have to sit through—and in that absentminded state, I briefly forget about my markings.

Seth's eye goes to them immediately. I tug at my sleeve, feeling like a complete idiot. I'm hesitant to meet his gaze, but when I do, I'm more than surprised to see that he *isn't* alarmed. Or shocked. Or thrown off.

His eyes flick to his arm and it's then I notice he's laid it on the metal table, faceup, with the sleeve pulled back just enough to see . . . numbers.

A code?

They seem to be written in pink highlighter, and how he managed to get ahold of one of those, I haven't a clue, but *this* must be what Axel was referring to.

"Like I said, I'd love to hear what I've missed," Seth repeats slowly, trying to get me to play along. It makes sense that they would record all phone calls, especially in a prison setting. I mean, does privacy even exist anymore? If I had to guess, he probably wants me to keep talking so as to not raise any suspicion with the guard.

"Right, okay," I say, switching the phone from my right hand to my left. The cord is hardly long enough to reach, so I have to angle my body slightly. "Well, I've been a professor's assistant at the University of Colorado Boulder for . . ." I dig around in my pockets, just now realizing how bad I am at multitasking. I keep talking, even though I'm hardly making any sense, as I click the pen and begin scribbling the numbers. 8 – 2 – 5 – 1. ". . . And so that's what I've been up to lately," I finish, having little to no recollection of what I've just said. "How are things going for you . . . in there?"

The guard shifts behind him as I slide the notebook off the metal surface and secure it back into my pocket, along with the pen. Seth mimics a similar movement with his arm before switching the phone over to that hand. I nearly hold my breath as the guard watches him for a moment, then repositions himself against the door.

"It's been tough being in here for so long, but I'm making do. Just wish I could have been there for some of your milestones."

It's nice to hear him say that, but it hurts, too. I'm having a hard time fully focusing on our conversation because I have no idea what these numbers mean or what they're for. And because I'm not in the mood to decipher another one of Axel's riddles, I'd much rather if Seth just told me—or at least gave me some sort of hint.

"You know, for your twelfth birthday, we'd planned a huge birthday party, all galactic and space-themed, of course. We had the invitations all ready to go, printed out on cardstock in the shape of Elara, Jupiter's eighth largest moon. No coincidence there. Even as a kid, you loved exploring in the woods with only the stars and the moon to guide you. Scared your mom and me half to death at times." He clears his throat and, for the first time, I think he might actually be telling the truth—that this isn't a part of our "play along". "Yep, you loved that cabin up in Allenspark. Even when you'd go wandering off, your mother and I never worried too much. We knew . . . we knew that you'd always be *safe*."

He's speaking to me *in* code *about* the code. "I think I remember that," I say, hoping I'm not about to sound too obvious. "It was in the spring—"

Okay, Elara. He knows about the cabin in Allenspark. How he knows, I don't know. Because that's Xero's cabin . . . isn't it? Deep down, I've known it couldn't have just been coincidence that the cabin numbers are 5-1-1. *Same as my birthday. Same as my mother's birthday . . .*

I stop mid-sentence, unable to talk *and* think at this caliber at the same time. Seth picks up where I'd left off, but I don't hear a word he says.

He said they knew I'd always be 'safe'. I glance down at the pocket I'd tucked the notepad into. *It's a code for a safe.* In my mind's eye, I scan the layout of the cabin. *The study.* There'd been a safe in the corner. I'd hardly noticed it because I'd been so distracted by the newspapers on the desk. I can feel myself starting to smile, my eyes growing wide with recognition.

Thankfully, Seth seems to pick up on it. "I'm so glad we were able to do this." He glances behind him and nods at the guard. "I have everything I need and, from the looks of it, so do you." The guard approaches to collect him. "Visit again soon, will you?" His eyes twinkle with something I never thought I'd see again. Hope.

I nod, suddenly feeling sad and nostalgic and angry all at the same time. "I will."

"Take care of yourself." He gives me a parting smile as he hangs up the phone, then waits for the guard to lead him away from the glass partition and back through the cell door.

I just sit there, staring at the now empty space where my father had been. Where we'd connected for the first time in over two decades. A swell of emotions rises within me, each one more confusing than the last.

What if I have it all wrong?

What if I have *him* all wrong?

That is *not* the same man who used to shout and yell and throw household items clear across the living room.

That is *not* the same man who punched the sliding glass door and shattered the glass.

That is *not* the man I remember as my father . . .

My deadbeat, broke-ass, good-for-nothing, borderline abusive, criminal *father.*

"Ma'am?"

I turn around to see a new guard, not the one who'd checked me in, standing at the high-security door.

"Your visit has concluded."

"Right, yes," I say, trying not to sound too flustered. I stand up and walk toward the door, much preferring the *other* guard—the one who'd called me "Miss".

"Would you like an escort to the parking lot?"

"No, I'm fine. Thank you."

"You sure? It's getting dark out there. Sun's about to go down."

"Very kind of you, but I'm good." I give him a polite nod before walking out the door.

I can't help but stifle a laugh. If only he knew what awaits me in my car, he'd understand why a darkening sky is the very *least* of my worries.

40

FROM THE MOMENT I spot my car in the parking lot, I can't help but roll my eyes. Axel is "sitting" (okay more like floating) on the hood of my Jeep, very John Bender-esque circa 1985's classic feature film, *The Breakfast Club*.

I whistle at him before making an obscene gesture to get back in the car. Now it's *his* turn to roll his eyes, but he doesn't say anything as he dissipates through the windshield and into the passenger's seat. At first, I start to freak out, momentarily forgetting that no one can see him. *Thank the cosmos for that.*

I climb into the car, not looking forward to the conversation we're about to have where I have to admit that he was right and that I should have listened to him all along.

"Got what you came for?"

"I didn't even know I was coming here to begin with," I counter as I click my seatbelt into place.

"There's no use trying to hide it."

I punch the coordinates into the GPS, giving him a menacing *don't you dare touch this* glare, before starting the car. "I'm not hiding anything, Axel."

"You're acting like you didn't just have the most interesting, unexpected interaction with your *father*, a man you haven't spoken to in over twenty years." He shakes his head. "But I can feel it. Feel *you*—"

"Well, please stop," I say, trying not to get flustered all over again. "I'm still processing what just happened. But to answer your question, yes. He very discreetly gave me a code. To a safe. At Xer—er, *your* cabin." I pause, putting the pieces together. "Actually, *my* cabin."

"I told you you'd thank me later."

I wait for the car in front of me to finish turning before getting back on the highway. "Yeah, thanks for that. I'm happy you misdirected me."

He seems to catch my slightly playful tone. "More like *redirected*," he says, matching it.

"Agree to disagree."

"That certainly seems to be our M.O., doesn't it?"

Wow, a serious question for once. "Axel, don't think I don't want to trust you. I do."

"I feel a big *but* coming on." He smirks at his lame joke.

"*But*, after this . . . I suppose you haven't given me any reason not to. Trust you, I mean."

He looks at me in complete and utter surprise. It's a truly rare moment that I can only capture with a mental snapshot.

"All right then," he says, quickly regaining his composure, "so what was the code?"

I'm able to recall it from memory. "Eight, two, five, one."

"Looks like you didn't need a pen and paper after all." He shoots me a sidelong glance. "Any familiarity there?"

"Sometimes I have to wonder why you ask questions you already know the answers to."

"I like to keep things interesting."

I peek at him out of the corner of my eye. "And that you do."

When we finally arrive at the cabin, it's nightfall. Fortunately, the last time I'd been up here with Xero, we'd left the exterior lights on, otherwise it'd be pitch black. I pull on the parking brake before getting out of the car and follow Axel's wraith-like wisps up the stairs.

"Have I asked why you decided *not* to be in human form?"

He stops halfway up the stairs and turns. "This is fitting, is it not?"

"Ever the master evader, aren't you?"

He still doesn't answer as he continues gliding up the stairs and floats right through the door. I wait just outside, letting a few seconds pass, before trying the door. Locked.

"Axel, are you really going to make me enter the code?"

I wait a few more seconds. Still no response.

"Ugh," I mutter as I input the sequence, only to enter the cabin and find even more darkness. I feel like shouting, but it comes out as more of a growl. "Seriously? You couldn't turn on a fucking light?"

I switch the lights on, not bothering to take off my boots, seeing as this is *my* cabin, as I've just learned—well, my family's anyways. So technically, I suppose I'm part owner. That's how that works, right?

When I reach the landing at the top of the first staircase, I can't help but feel a little sad. Seeing everything here, just as we'd left it, makes me miss Xero even more than I'd realized. My gaze travels to the couch, remembering the many deep conversations we'd had.

He has to know how I feel about him, right? Even back then, at that moment in time?

Guilt coils in my stomach. I've never been great at expressing myself. Never trusted anyone enough to do so. Every past attempt has just ended in disappointment. But with Xero it had been so easy. Simple. Like two pieces of perfectly cut cloth that had finally been sewn back together—until Axel had come in and ripped out all the damn stitching.

My thoughts scatter as I hear noises coming from upstairs. I quickly turn on one of the tableside lamps and bolt up the steps. As I'm walking along the hall, I spot the bedroom, but turn into the study instead. I push open the half-cracked door. Axel's hovering in the far corner near the safe, his arms crossed.

"Took you long enough. How was your stroll down memory lane?"

"Better than being here with you."

He raises his hand to his chest in mock offense. "Ouch. You're pretty brutal, you know that?"

"Tell me something I don't already know." I pull the notepad from my pocket as I walk over to him before kneeling in front of the safe. I hadn't noticed it before, but there are *two* dials, not just one—which means there must be two codes.

"Hey, genius. Looks like you missed something."

He floats down to my level and looks from me to the safe then back to me again. "What are you talking about? I didn't miss a damn thing."

"Seth only gave me one set of numbers."

"Really? You still can't call him your *father*?"

I wave a hand in the air. "That'll come with time, okay? Once again, stop evading the question. And, when you *do* answer, please, for the love of all that is holy, do not answer in one of your signature riddles."

Both his tone and expression are so serious, they almost have me backing out of the room and running for my life.

"Your father gave you the one you needed. You already have the other one."

I stare at the first dial. "Are you kidding me, Axel? There are so many number combinations. This could be anything!" I grunt in frustration, not only at the task at hand, but also at the fact that this safe is super old and isn't electronic. The last time I used a lock like this was in middle school in the girl's locker room.

I start trying different combinations—my birthday, my birth year, my mom's birth year, what I can remember of my dad's birthday—but they all yield nothing. "Can you at least give me a hint? Otherwise, we're going to be here all night."

He looks up at the ceiling to check with whatever invisible presence seems to have him by the balls. "No can do."

"Really? *This* is where you choose *not* to intervene?"

He shrugs. "There's always tomorrow."

I try a few more combinations before throwing my hands in the air. "Fine," I mutter. "Have it your way."

"I think there's some wine downstairs."

I look at him in disbelief. "You think I want to relax and have a glass of wine . . . with you?"

"What could it hurt? You never know, you might just learn something."

"Thanks, but I've learned enough from you for one lifetime. Not to mention, wouldn't it go right through you?" I gesture to his non-body. "The wine, I mean?"

"Not if I take human form."

I narrow my eyes. "You can . . . do that?"

"There isn't much I can't do."

"If you say so. After you, then."

He tilts his head. "Ladies, first."

"Beast before beauty," I counter.

A hearty laugh escapes him, completely throwing me off guard. It doesn't fit with his personality or his appearance, and yet he'd laughed like jolly old St. Nick himself.

"You win this time," he says, floating by me. "But only because you've accepted me in my true form."

I don't know when I'd agreed to that, but sure.

I follow him down the stairs, careful not to get too close to the black mist that makes up said "true form". A part of me wants to reach out and touch it—and another part of me tells me that today is not the day to die.

Nor is it the day to turn into . . . *whatever* he is.

I lose sight of him as he whirs down the rest of the stairs, past the living room, and into the kitchen. I hop off the final step, my hand sliding down the rest of the wooden banister, trying not to think about what Xero and I had experienced together just days prior. A knot twists in my stomach, heart aching.

"Red or white?" Axel calls from the kitchen.

"Shouldn't you know the answer to that?" I shout back.

"Red it is," he says.

"He chose right," I murmur to myself before taking a seat in the armchair. But when Axel turns the corner from the kitchen, I nearly fall back out of it. He's *walking*, on two *legs*, with two very full glasses of wine in hand, clad in black. The grayish hue and scaly patches have disappeared from his face, leaving an alabaster, yet more human-like, skin tone. His jet-black hair is still slicked back behind his ears, but it now curls out at the ends—very Loki-esque. And his eyes, that deep stormy gray, threaten to pierce me with each bolt of lightning that passes through them.

I try to silence the dull roar that's rising within me as he draws nearer. The last thing I need is for him to think I'm . . . *attracted* to him. Which I am. And I can't figure out why. Because he's Xero—Xero's *shadow*—and there's something about the darkness I've always been drawn to. I glance at the navy blue in my hair as a testament to that.

"It's a Cabernet," Axel says as he hands me the glass, "from before you were born."

"Thank you," I say, not sure what to do with that information.

He sits across from me, looking awkward as all hell as he tries to situate himself on the couch. I can't help but laugh into my wine, the sound echoing.

"I'm so happy I amuse you."

I take a sip, then swirl the wine around the glass before looking him directly in the eyes. "You look good, Axel."

A sly grin creeps onto his face.

"And now, less so."

His face falls. He clears his throat as he straightens his shoulders, then slowly lifts a brow, his mouth rigging to the side ever so slightly. "How about now?"

Fuck. I try not to widen my eyes or swallow the knot that's suddenly formed in my throat but . . . well, I already said it. *Fuck.*

"I'll take that as a compliment," he croons, eyes glimmering.

"Nope, not fair. You don't get to just push inside the gates of my mind without giving me access to yours—"

"How do you know you don't have access?"

I pause, dumbfounded, suddenly catching his meaning. "I suppose I haven't tried."

"Too busy being angsty and stubborn." He raises his glass. "Which I'll certainly toast to, as I know all about that."

"Yes, you most certainly do," I say, clinking my glass with his. We each take a long sip, but the silence stretches on long after we've finished.

"So?" he says, breaking the streak. "Are you going to try?"

For a moment, I forget what we'd been talking about. "Oh. That." I study his face, trying not to get lost in the churning sea beneath his gaze. "If it's all right with you, I think I prefer talking to you. Like this. Like we have been."

A flicker of amusement dances across his face. "How can you know what you prefer if you haven't tried both options?"

I can feel my cheeks heat at the question, knowing full well that he's talking about something else entirely. Something I'd been thinking about the moment I'd seen him in human form. "It's just that, speaking mind-to-mind . . . that was something I did with Xero." The words come out stuttered, and I can only pray I make a swift recovery. "It kind of feels like our *thing.*"

Axel seems to consider this, which is unlike him. "I wouldn't want to encroach on that. Lines are lines, boundaries are boundaries—drawn and set for a reason."

The weight that'd been pressing on my chest eases. "Thank you." I raise my glass to my lips to buy myself a little time as I figure out what to say next. "But I still want to talk to you—*learn* from you, as you put it earlier."

He leans back into the couch, the picture of debonair perfection. "And what would you like to learn, Elara?"

Yet another question that my mind turns sexual. *Stop it,* I scold myself, feeling both guilty and rotten. I'd felt Xero's effect on me instantaneously, but this . . . this is different. Like I'd just been slapped in the face with everything I thought I hated but turned out to secretly love.

"It's a natural response, you know. What you're feeling." Axel's voice is quiet, almost pained. "I may look a little different, sound a little different, go by a different name . . . but so do you, Elara Friis." His forehead softens, as do his shoulders. "That doesn't make you any less Elara Wells. Just like me being Axel doesn't make me any less Xero. It's just a . . . different side."

It's the most he's ever said and the most explaining he's ever done. No riddles. No jokes. No sarcasm. Just blunt, honest, straightforward truth.

"But you're . . . his shadow," I say somewhat cautiously, not wanting the openness between us to cave in on itself. "And shadows are . . . well, bad—"

"Are they?" he interrupts.

"The way you spoke to me earlier. The way you pushed my buttons, irked me, wouldn't answer a single question . . . I wanted to punch you in the damn face."

Another sincere laugh. I hate to admit how much it warms my heart to see him smile. This seemingly broken, hidden away, "shameful" side of the person I love.

"I can't say his connection with you didn't help with that," he confesses. "Knowing how to push your buttons, that is."

"So you've been doing it on purpose?"

"Regardless of my intention, a trigger is just some aspect of yourself you haven't yet acknowledged."

I don't respond as I allow that to really sink in. I look down at my wine. "That was deep," I finally say before lifting my gaze again. "You're deep."

He finishes the rest of his glass before pouring himself another. "There are things you chose not to share with Xero. Would that assumption be correct?"

I stare at him, not sure I'm liking where this is going.

"But today, we did something that triggered you. Together. You answered that call and—"

"More like *was forced to*," I scoff. "You intervened every step of the way."

"I told you, it's what I'm here to do. What do you think shadows *are*, exactly?"

"Oh, believe me, I know. I have plenty of my own, let me assure you."

He leans forward then, as if I've just stumbled into an open snare. "And how often do you look at them? Listen to them? *Acknowledge* them?"

I open my mouth to respond, then close it again. He has a point. As much as I'd like to say I don't run from the hard stuff . . . I do. I ran away from my aunt after my mother disappeared. I changed my name after my father was indicted. I ended my engagement after my miscarriage. I ran to Kensie when I'd gotten fired, but withheld that "hard news" from him, just like I'd withheld my "hard past" from Xero . . .

Run, hide, suffer. Never acknowledge, face, heal.

"I knew about your father, but I didn't judge you," Axel goes on. "You may call it intervening, but I prefer to call it the gentle push you needed. Otherwise, you never would have acted."

I try to find the flaw in his thinking, but there isn't one. He's right. Utterly and undeniably so. "So what, are you expecting a thank you or something?"

A muscle flexes along his jaw. "Don't do that. Don't build that wall back up."

I swallow, feeling insanely uncomfortable, but manage to say, "You're right. That's exactly what I was about to do."

"You see, Elara, *we* can talk about the things you haven't shared with anyone. The things you hold close to your heart but tuck deep into the shadows. And that's because I'll understand them better than anyone. I'll listen without judgment. Advise only when asked. Perhaps even share my own . . ."

And that's when I feel it—the part of Xero that had felt *locked*. Inaccessible. The part of him he hadn't *known*. Every time he'd said he didn't know or needed to figure things out—*this* had been the missing link he'd been referring to.

A fully integrated shadow.

"This is why you're here now," I say quietly, the pieces falling together. "Because if I am to love Xero, I am to love *all* of him. Unconditionally."

He nods. "And do you think that's possible?"

I don't answer right away because that's the type of question that deserves deep contemplation. A question someone like Axel only knows the answer to.

When I look at him again, I recognize the hope simmering in his eyes as my own. "I don't know," I say, "but I'll be damned if I don't at least try."

41

I'M TWO GLASSES of wine in when Axel finally joins me, belly-down, on the rug. I'd pushed the coffee table out of the way and had grabbed as many pillows and blankets from the couch as my hands would allow.

"Comfortable?" he teases, fluffing one of the pillows behind him.

"Not as comfortable as you." I shoot him a sidelong glance as I reach for the open bottle of wine.

"Here, allow me." He tops off my glass before doing the same for his.

I nod in appreciation, then bring the glass to my lips. For some reason or another, I'm at a loss for words—partly because *this*—being here, with him—feels vaguely familiar and yet also brand new. I turn my head just enough so that I can study him without being too obvious.

"It's way obvious," Axel says without even looking at me.

"Then why don't you tell me why this feels familiar?"

"Haven't you already confirmed this? With Xero?"

There's a sharp pang in my chest at the mention of his name. "Yes," I counter, somewhat defiantly, "but that felt different. *This* feels different."

He arches a brow. "How?"

Shadows darken his gaze and, with the expression he's wearing, it's almost as if I've stumbled onto something I'm not supposed to know—or perhaps it's something I'm not supposed to figure out just yet. In either case, it's unnerving.

It almost reminds me of . . .

"Tell me about him."

The bluntness of his statement catches me off guard.

"About whom?"

He swirls the wine around in his glass. "About the love of your life *before* Xero."

The way he phrases it has my chest tightening, throat closing. I blow out a long breath before saying, "There isn't much to know."

His eyes flicker in the dim light. "Isn't there?"

"We didn't work out. That's all there is to it."

"But you wanted it to." My gaze tracks to his, wanting to talk about anything *but* this. "So why didn't it?"

"People grow apart. They change." I shrug, hoping that by acting nonchalant, it'll shift the topic of conversation. *Highly unlikely.* "I was never the girl who dreamed of weddings and marriage and kids." I toy with the stem of my glass, surprised at how easily the words tumble from my lips. "We just didn't fit. I felt like I was always doing everything. Taking care of everything. Cleaning up everything. Being the responsible one." I heave a sigh. "The thought of continuing that trajectory made my skin crawl. In fact, it still does."

Axel nods in understanding, slightly rocking against the back of the couch. "Did you tell him? How you felt?"

"I tried. Things would change for a couple of days, a week if I was lucky, and then it'd be back to the same old thing."

"So you gave up on him."

I recoil so fast, I nearly spill my wine. "No. I left a situation that wasn't what I wanted."

"But it was at one point."

I look at him, puzzled.

"What you wanted," he clarifies.

"Well, yes, I thought . . ." I can't finish my sentence because the look of regret that flashes across his face is undeniable. "What was that?"

He averts his gaze. "Emotion, I suppose. This human form is quite—"

"Atrocious?"

He angles his head. "You really think that?"

"It can be. And the more frequent the emotions, the harder it is to work through them. It almost becomes an automatic response, completely subconscious."

"Like your need for absolute independence." His mouth rigs to the side. "What's that in response to?"

I narrow my eyes, then smile. "Dare I even say when you already know the answer?"

"Your family . . . they were emotionally unavailable."

"I suppose you could put it that way."

"How would you put it?"

"Nonexistent." As soon as I say it, I know it's something that's needed to be spoken for a long, long time. I shudder at the memories. "It's like I was forced to grow up before I was ready. Without anyone to hold space for me, I had to learn how to hold space for myself. And in that space, I taught myself that if I only ever depended on myself, I wouldn't be disappointed."

A long silence stretches between us.

"Has that been true?" he asks softly.

I lower my head, a single tear falling. "No."

"Did your ex know?"

"About my family history?" I nod. "He did. What I told him, at least."

"Did you tell him all of it?"

I shake my head. "It's hard for people to grasp something they've never been through themselves."

"What if he'd been through the same thing?"

"That's not the impression I got."

"Perhaps that's because he did exactly what you did."

It's an epiphany of a statement, although I'm not sure he realizes it. I meet his gaze, suddenly feeling the urge to move closer to him. He extends his arm along the back of the couch. *An invitation.* I hesitate, then recall what he just said about my need for absolute independence. I inch closer to him, immediately feeling vulnerable and foolish, but before I can change my mind, he tightens his arm around my shoulders.

"It's going to feel uncomfortable," he says as he leans his temple against mine. "But if we want to experience something different, we have to do something different—and see it all the way through."

"Like this," I whisper. "Is this . . . holding space?"

I feel him nod against me before pressing a gentle kiss to my head. The way we're sitting reminds me so much of how I used to sit with my ex before things had turned sour. The nights we'd just sprawl out on the floor and laugh and play and kiss. Those had been happier times—times I'd nearly forgotten about in my bitterness and rage.

He shifts against me then, and it's almost as if he's just as uncomfortable as I am. "It feels like a weakness, doesn't it? Allowing someone to be there for you?"

I nod. "Because when they're gone . . ."

He squeezes me even tighter. "It takes two people to hold space. The giver and the receiver. Although, in your case, it wasn't an even exchange. Ever. And for that, I'm sorry."

I lean into him, on the verge of tears hearing the apology I'd never received. Even if it's not coming from the person who caused me so much heartache, it's still nice to be acknowledged. Understood. Seen.

"Thank you," I murmur, still blinking back tears.

"If you'll let me, I'd like to give that to you—all the space you never received, that is."

I bite my trembling lip before whispering, "I don't know if I can." I'm shaking now, just from being held—and that right there is more than enough reason to do this, no matter how uncomfortable it feels.

"What we resist persists. Do, feel, and be whatever it is you need to do, feel, and be. I'm right here, Elara."

With those words echoing in my mind, the dam finally wriggles loose. And, for once in my life, I don't try to stop it.

42

MUCH LIKE XERO and I had, Axel and I end up talking into the wee hours of the morning. We've only just realized that the sun is coming up, our teeth stained a deep plum after all the wine we've shared.

"You must be exhausted."

I reach for my glass of water. "And why would you say that?"

"Because not many people can recount a lifetime of trauma in one evening and still be coherent enough afterward to tell the tale."

"I suppose I'm just different," I say, popping a cracker into my mouth.

Axel smiles. "That you are." He clears his throat before running a hand through his ebony hair, the movement smoother than ever. The ease with which he does it almost makes me forget that this isn't his natural form. For some reason, my heart sinks at that.

"Feeling better?" he asks.

"Much," I answer. "I feel like I could run a marathon—all uphill, at that."

"Easy there, tiger. Let's walk before we run."

The remark sobers me almost immediately. Xero had said the exact same thing to me about our telepathic connection. I can feel my cheeks warm at the memory, but it's quickly doused with ice water. "You really are him and he really is you, huh?" Soft spoken, the words are barely audible.

His eyes glint in the rising dawn, flecks of amber dotting the usual gray. "Have we not spent the entire evening confirming this?"

"Not when I've been doing most of the talking."

"I told you, I'm a great listener."

There's that dashing smile again.

"But really, if you're going to try opening that safe again, best do it with a clear head."

I pout. "Is that your way of sending me to bed?"

"I'll clean this up," he answers, hopping to his feet.

He extends a hand to me and I take it. I'm about to turn to head up the stairs when I suddenly feel the urge to hug him. "Thank you," I say, wrapping him in a tight embrace. "I can't even begin to tell you how much better I feel. And how happy I am to have met you."

I feel his arms fold around my waist. "The pleasure is all mine, Elara." He presses a gentle kiss to the top of my head, then releases me. "Now go get some rest before I intervene and *make* you." He smirks, then stalks off to the kitchen.

Damn him. That remark leaves my body flushed the entire way up the stairs, all the way to the bedroom, until I pull the covers over my head. I know I shouldn't be thinking about the potential insinuations of that statement *or* the possibility of them occurring, but I can't help it. Eventually, my eyes close and I drift into a deep sleep, the thought of Axel lying next to me just within reach.

I wake around noon to the aroma of freshly baked goods and a pot of dark roast coffee. I don't bother looking into a mirror as I glide down the stairs and into the kitchen, the scent as enticing as ever.

"There she is," Axel says, bright-eyed and cheery. "I made muffins. Breakfast for lunch seemed appropriate."

"I can see that," I say. "And smell it."

When he turns around, I can't help but laugh a little at the ridiculous yellow apron he's wearing. Complete with oven mitts and a sparkling pan of treats, he could be the next Martha Stewart.

"What, a man can't bake?"

I take a big bite of the plump blueberry muffin as he pours me a cup of coffee. "Oh no, you most certainly can, judging by the taste of *this*." I nearly drool as I take another bite, then realize something. "Xero never baked for me. Well, I take that back. He did once, made me breakfast in bed, but I never actually *saw* him make anything. Unlike this," I laugh again, gesturing to Axel's ensemble.

"Just another shadow," he says nonchalantly. "So many men think baking is 'too feminine'."

"Well, I'm happy you don't. Because these are delicious. Seriously. We'll have to get you a job at the café. Kensie would love—"

I notice his smile falter.

I pause. "What? Did I say something?"

And then I remember. Other people can't see him. Only me. To other people, he's merely a ghost, a wraith, a figment of long-lost tales—of innocent bedtime stories that evolve into nightmares. "I'm sorry."

"Don't be," he says pulling the apron over his head. "Never apologize for the truth."

"But what if the truth sucks?"

"What if it only sucks because you think it sucks?"

I narrow my eyes at him before taking another delectable bite. "Touché."

"So," he says, moving the empty baking pan to the sink, "will today mark round two of lockpicking the family safe?"

"Is it really lockpicking when you have the codes?"

He turns just to raise a brow and say, "Touché."

"Uh huh, I see what you did there." I hop off the stool and swipe my mug of coffee from the counter before waltzing over to the giant windows that overlook the mountains. I glance to the east, reminded of when Xero and I had climbed to the cavern. I bet Axel would like it there.

I raise the mug to my lips when I hear a low, husky sigh from behind me. I turn to see Axel leaning on both elbows against the countertop, sans the apron. He looks exactly the same as he had last night . . . but *better*. And in this morning light? It hits him in all the right ways, highlighting all the right angles. Not surprisingly, his gaze draws me in, enrapturing me.

"You're trouble," I say, clicking my tongue against the roof of my mouth. "*Trrr*ouble."

"No more than you are."

I remain rooted in place, only angling my body so I'm no longer craning my neck to look at him. "You can't just sigh like that and lean like that and not act on your impulses—"

He tilts his head ever so slightly, the golden flecks in his eyes gleaming. "*My* impulses?"

I clamp my mouth shut. *Had I really just said that?*

"And what impulses might those be?"

It's a taunting sort of question—almost like he's challenging me. And I know exactly what I want to do about it. I refuse to break his gaze as I set the mug down on the end table and stalk over to him. My breath hitches in my chest as I get closer, but I don't dare show even a hint of trepidation. I seamlessly move his leg with my knee and ease into the small space I've just made before gently placing one arm over his shoulder, then the other. I glance at his mouth, making sure to take my time roving back up to his eyes.

Finally, I say, "Why don't *you* tell me?"

It's the closest we've been, physically speaking, but he doesn't so much as flinch. In fact, he almost seems *comfortable*, especially when he pushes off the counter with one elbow and takes me by the hips. My heart is thundering in my chest while he's the flawless embodiment of calm, cool, and collected.

It dawns on me then that I'd only just rolled out of bed and hadn't even bothered to look in the mirror. Feeling slightly self-conscious, I'm about to back away when he says, "Don't." There's a sort of pleading in his tone. "Stay." And then, "You are painstakingly beautiful."

I can't help but feel surprised at the unexpected sob that nearly breaks free from my chest—not because of the compliment or even the words themselves, but because, emotionally speaking, this is the person I'd bared my *soul* to last night. This is the person I'd shared my deepest fears with. My insecurities. My shame. My trauma. My unspeakable regrets. This is the person I'd willingly shown my scars, my wounds . . . all the places I'm most vulnerable. This is the person who had listened. Who hadn't judged, or laughed, or fled. This is the person who had accepted them as if they were his own.

And so that word, *beautiful*, isn't some ploy just to get in my pants. When *he* says it, I know he means it as encompassing *all* of me.

Even my sharpest edges.

Even my darkest corners.

Even my most reprehensible shadows.

All of it . . . painstakingly beautiful.

It's enough to leave me breathless, at a complete loss for words.

As if he can sense what's stirring within me, he gently moves his hands from my hips to my waist and brings me in closer. I wrap my arms around his neck and bury my face in his shoulder . . . letting him just *hold* me again.

For I don't know how long.

For a length of time I never want to end.

For as long as it takes for me to come up for air.

"It's okay," he whispers into my ear. "You're okay."

I slowly pull back from him, resting my palms on his shoulders. "I don't know how many more times I can say it without you getting tired of it, but . . . thank you."

He grins. "I hate to break it to you, but that was all you."

I give a defiant shake of my head. "You prompted me, encouraged me . . . dare I say, *intervened* just right."

"I—"

"—aim to please," I say, finishing his thought. "And that you do."

He brushes a soft kiss to my cheek before sliding out from under me to head back into the kitchen to finish cleaning. It's weird how exposed I feel without his presence when that was the first time we've ever even touched like that. My thoughts scatter as he reminds me about cracking the code to the safe. I feign enthusiasm, not wanting him to know that that's the last thing on my mind at the moment.

Despondently, I leave him to cleaning and head upstairs to shower and collect myself, more or less, but after what's just happened? Even I know that's a long shot. The entire time the water is pouring down on me, all I can think about is the feel of Axel's hands on my hips, my waist. The way he'd tugged at my shirt to pull me in closer. The way his breath had felt on my cheek, my neck. The way he'd just held me. Unwavering. Protective. Reassuring. The way those words had tumbled from his lips. *Painstakingly beautiful.*

I'm in the middle of washing my hair when I hear the steps being climbed, then a soft knock at the bathroom door. I intentionally hadn't locked it. I take a deep breath before closing my eyes. *You can come in,* I say silently, not knowing if I'll get through.

There's a brief pause, but then I hear the knob turn, ever so slowly. I can see his silhouette appear from behind the shower curtain. And then, like warm drizzled honey, his voice floats across my mind. *I realized I never answered your question.*

I turn to face the curtain, but don't pull it back. *And what question is that?*

The one about impulses. His silhouette moves then, his shirt dropping to the floor, followed by his pants.

Even though I can only see his shadow, the sight of him undressing has me tensing in all the right places.

I'd like to try again, if that's all right with you?

Well . . . you can't just not act on your impulses.

Just like it had before, his head tilts to the side. And just like before, he says, *My impulses? And what impulses might those be?*

Even though I'm not physically speaking, my throat goes dry. *Why don't you tell me?*

I watch as he slowly inches the shower curtain back, little by little. *Better yet, why don't I show you?*

It takes everything in me not to rip the damn thing down, but I patiently wait as he joins me in the water. I almost expect his eyes to rove my body, and mine his, but they don't. Instead, he holds my gaze—which is *way* more attractive. I realize that he's already seen me and I've seen him . . . since, *technically,* he's Xero. But there's something a little less primal about Axel—

a kind of rawness that's rare to come by. He lifts his hands and caresses the length of my arms, from my shoulders to my fingertips, then interlocks my fingers with his.

I don't think I've ever held eye contact with someone for this long, certainly not whilst naked and in the shower. We step closer to one another in a synchronized fashion, our movements mirroring the other. He breaks our grip only to gather my hair in his hands and carefully move it behind my glistening shoulders. His touch causes me to shudder. A knowing smirk pulls at the side of his mouth.

I didn't mean to interrupt your shower. He reaches behind me and grabs the conditioner, then lathers it into my hair. I can feel myself starting to melt under his heated gaze as he expertly massages my scalp. His hands fall to the nape of my neck, just behind my ears, giving me full body shivers. He's close enough now to where I can feel the length of him harden against my thigh, his chest rising and falling a bit more rapidly.

Now rinse.

He grips my lower back for support, his hands firm and callused against my skin. It's only when I'm leaning my head back into the shower that I break the epic stare-off between us. Eyes closed, the water trickles down my face, neck, and shoulders, and it's then I feel a sensation that most certainly *isn't* water.

I gasp, grabbing the marble-tiled ledge for support as Axel's mouth trails down the front of my neck, past my collarbone, right in between my breasts. He drags his lips to the right, pulling at my nipple with his mouth, his tongue flicking the sensitive area. Everything in me heightens as he moves to the other side and repeats the motion, his teeth grazing my skin as he tracks back up the way he came. I arch into his grip on my lower back, and he's at my neck within seconds, devouring me, pushing me into the ever-growing length of him.

I let out a moan as I reach down between us, needing to feel him, to make him feel as good as he's making me feel. I begin to stroke him, slow at first, stopping at the head to make a tighter circle with my thumb and index finger. His breath is hot against my ear as he releases a guttural groan, and then his hand is running down my stomach, past my navel, right between the apex of my thighs. The pads of his index and middle fingers press against my center, moving in slow, lazy circles with just the right amount of pressure. It's enough to make me tighten every muscle in my body, falling deeper into him, feeling him harden even more.

Ravenous, his mouth moves to mine, his fingers drawing faster circles, my hand pumping harder, faster. He nearly growls into my mouth and I take his tongue between my lips, gently sucking on it to indicate *exactly* what I'm thinking about. He smiles against me and, in response, grazes his teeth against my bottom lip, pulling it just enough to have me wishing his mouth was doing all the work instead of his hand.

I begin to move him closer to me, inching the length of him up higher, *needing* him, but that's when he stops. Eyes alight with pure desire, he takes my face in his hands. "Not here."

I search his expression, questioning. Confused.

His gaze darkens. "I don't want to feel the water. I want to feel *you*. Just you."

If I didn't know any better, I'd think my skin had caught fire. "I'm all yours."

He moves with such ferocity that, suddenly, the water's no longer beating down on us, my bottom half is wrapped in a towel, and I'm straddling him as he carries me into the bedroom. He lays me onto the bed, his hair no longer slicked back, but shaggy and curled out at the edges, the amber flecks in his eyes highlighting the fire that's raging between us. Small droplets of water land on my chest as he moves the towel down to wipe any excess water from my body. It's such a sensual act, for some reason or another, and it's probably because I've never been sprawled out like I am now, open and waiting—unabashedly so. Without looking away from me, he towels himself off, and I catch myself staring at every glorious inch of him. Blood boiling, I open my legs a bit wider in invitation. A feral grin graces his face before he kneels beside the bed and dips his head in response.

His tongue finds me and he's doing everything he'd done with his hand, and then some. My back arches skyward, hands gripping the sheets beneath me. Sucking, pulling, tugging, ever so gently, those circles growing faster and more refined. *Fuck, you taste good.*

Hearing him in my head is nearly my undoing. "Out loud," I manage through ragged breaths. "Say it out loud."

I glance down at him in between my legs, chest heaving, as his eyes lift to mine. His mouth curls into a smirk as he says, "Fuck, you taste good, Elara."

My toes curl at the way he adds my name afterward. In one deft movement, I sit up and pull him to me, needing him to fill me in a way only he can. He starts to climb over me, hair damp and still dripping. I begin to guide him toward me when he growls and flips me over so fast, it takes me a moment to realize it.

"Let's do it exactly how you like it," he purrs into my ear from behind me, pulling me up so that I'm on my hands and knees.

A chill races down my spine. Of course he knows what I like, not just what I'll tolerate. Of course he won't accept anything but. It's such a liberating feeling that I nearly climax as he dips two fingers inside of me, using my wetness to prep himself. He positions himself behind me, taking me by the hips, but before he presses into me, he grabs a fistful of my hair. I know exactly where this is headed. "Please," I pant, as I feel him get closer, his tip nudging at my entrance.

He does exactly as I ask and slams into me. Stars explode in my vision as he fills me, claims me, tugging at my hair with every other powerful thrust. I moan, arching my back as he goes deeper and deeper, as deep as he can go. His hand shifts to the front of my throat, creating even more tension in the arch.

I want to feel you moan.

His fingers pressed against my neck, even I can feel the vibrations from the sounds I'm making. He presses firmer, tighter, pulling me back just enough so that he's hitting exactly where he needs to—my most sensitive spot. He releases my neck and dips his hands to my center, the feeling of him touching me *and* filling me simultaneously causing me to circle him and ride him harder than I ever have before.

Let me feel all of you, he repeats. *Drench me.*

The slight change in wording has my head spinning, heart pumping as I move back and forth in faster, shorter bursts. I'm nearly sitting up at this point, my back flush against his chest, when he pushes me back down and presses me into the bed. Hips thrusting, he groans as we release in tandem. I fully coat him before he allows himself to fill me, quivering with each small jerk of his body.

I slide off of him and turn to face him, our faces flushed from the activity.

"Now I understand the preference for this form," he says cheekily. "That was—"

"—just the beginning," I say as I crawl over to him and gently suck the remnants of us off of him. When I finish, I make eye contact with him as I wipe the corners of my mouth.

A shadow flickers in his gaze as I sit back up. "Seems I'm not the only one who knows what I like."

"Now if you'll excuse me," I say, gliding across the bed, "I need to continue the shower that was so rudely interrupted." I flash him a devious smile before darting out of the bedroom.

As I hoped he would, he laughs and chases me down the hall.

After taking yet another nap, Axel and I are sitting on the cabin's balcony underneath a string of soft lights, sparkling apple cider in hand. After last night (and this afternoon), I'd needed a bit of a respite from the usual cabernet. The sun's just starting to go down, a hawk soaring overhead as it circles the perimeter of the property. Axel's still in his human form, pulling me close as we curl up on the outdoor couch. He throws a blanket over us, then wraps his arms over my chest. I lean into him, nuzzling the space right between his neck and shoulder.

"Eventful day," I say, somewhat absentmindedly.

"That it was."

There's no mistaking the edge to his voice—enough so that it has me sitting up and turning around to face him. "Is everything okay?"

There's a hint of disappointment in his eyes as he says, "Yes. And no. I can't stop thinking about our conversation last night."

Funny, because I can't stop thinking about what we'd shared this afternoon . . .

"About what happened with your ex."

I lower my gaze to my hands. "What about it?"

He hesitates, and it's the first time I've seen him do so. He almost looks . . . *nervous*. Finally, after a long silence, he says, "How I possess every single quality he did. How you didn't want to have a future with him." His voice drops, "Or make one with him."

There's something else in his expression, something I can't quite read.

"It just makes me wonder, if things were different, if I weren't what I am—"

"But I love what you are." The words come rushing out of me so suddenly I'm convinced that not even the strongest dam could keep them at bay. "I love *all* of what you are."

"And I you," he whispers. "That's what makes this so hard."

It's barely a murmur, but there's no mistaking what he's trying to say. We could never have a future together, because in *this* reality, Axel doesn't exist. He's a wraith. A phantom presence. A . . . shadow. The knowledge of this, something I've been aware of all along but never thought mattered, hits me square in the chest.

"I wish I knew what to say."

He sighs. "Me too."

"Do you regret it? Taking human form?" I don't know why I ask it, but I know he'll tell me the truth. Because that's what shadows are: the undeniable truth.

"No. I don't regret it." His mouth quirks to the side, the sight of it easing the tension in my chest. "Knowing what it's done for you," his throat bobs, "again, that's what I'm here for."

I gather that I might be missing something in what he's just said, but I let it slide. "I didn't take you for the brooding type," I tease in an effort to lighten the mood.

"It shouldn't surprise you, given that you've seen all sides of me."

I tilt my head to the side, swirling the cider around the glass. "And I look forward to seeing them *all* again."

A sad smile. "Come here," he says, helping me turn around and lean into him again. "Let me hold you a little while longer."

I do as he says, my stomach knotting at the thought of not being able to touch or feel him, only *see* him. Piece by piece, I can feel my heart starting to shatter. I lace my fingers in his, squeezing them gently against my chest, right over my heart. I don't mention the safe, and he doesn't ask. I haven't attempted to open it today, and I won't be attempting it tonight. Because something tells me that when I do, it'll be the end of our *little while longer* . . .

43

THE NEXT MORNING, Axel's not in the bed beside me when I wake up. He isn't in the kitchen. He isn't outside on the patio or the balcony. I feel a swell of panic rise in my chest at the thought of him being gone. Of not getting to say goodbye.

Like I hadn't gotten to say goodbye to Xero.

I exhale a heavy sigh when I find him in the very last place I check: the study. He's hovering over the safe, black wisps swallowing the corner of the room, back in wraith form. "I thought you'd left," I say, wanting to give him a hug and quickly realizing that I can't.

"I thought this was more appropriate, seeing as it's Halloween and all." A flash of guilt sweeps across his eyes. "Happy Halloween, by the way."

I don't smile. Or laugh. Or return the sentiment. "What are you doing in here?"

He gives me a knowing look. "I think you already know the answer to that."

I glance at the safe, then back at him. "We can give it a go tomorrow."

"Elara." His tone is unyielding. "You need to open the safe."

The way he says it reminds me of when I'd first met him and couldn't stand being anywhere near him. Harsh. Cynical. Condescending. But I don't hear those things. I just hear Axel. "Why?"

"Just call it another part of my intervening."

"Bullshit." I call him out, desperately trying to get a grip on my rising anger.

He blanches. "Please, Elara. Just open the safe."

I study him, trying to bite back the quake building in my throat, one that threatens to rattle the very bones in my chest. "What happens if I open it?"

"You know I can't tell you that," he whispers, "but, as I'm sure you've gathered, it's what comes next."

I close my eyes and squeeze them shut. "If you're going to leave, just do it already."

"Open it."

My eyes open in a flash of fury. "I don't know the second half of the combination."

"*Try.*"

I glare at him as I march over to the safe and kneel before it. It takes a minute for me to remember the code my father had told me—it feels like it's been so long since then, but it's only been two fucking days. A lot can happen in forty-eight hours . . .

8-2-5-1.

I spin the first dial, then move on to the second.

I try myriads of combinations, each one resulting in a slightly more aggressive bang of my fist against the safe. "I haven't even had my morning coffee," I grumble, on the verge of giving up entirely.

"You're overthinking it."

"No shit, Sherlock." I hate how brazen my tone comes across, but I'm hurt. And lashing out feels right. Because I don't care what's in this safe—

Yes, you do. Axel's voice is a calming presence in the chaotic waters of my mind. *Stop overthinking it.*

Twice he's used that word. I know it's for a reason. Axel never says anything unintentional. So, I'm overthinking. But when am I not? I try another approach.

When am I . . . *not* thinking?

When I'm . . . sleeping.

Dreaming.

Astral traveling.

What had the voices said?

Forty-five. Seven.

But that's only three numbers. Unless . . .

Xero.

I spin the dial to four, then five, then seven, then *zero.*

Something in the safe clicks.

"Holy shit," I breathe. "We're in."

"For someone who hates riddles, you sure are good at figuring them out."

I cautiously pull at the metal door, not sure what it is I expect to find, but hoping it's along the lines of some long-awaited (and much deserved) answers.

Axel's floated over and is behind me now. I can nearly feel him breathing down my neck as I reach into the enclosed space. I glance over my shoulder at him, not wanting our last words to be bitter and spiteful. I refuse to let that be our last memory. "Might I ask why you're so curious to see what's in here? Seeing as you know all, *oh wise one.*"

He's quick on the banter, happy that I've seemed to come back around. "You're becoming quite the comedian, Elara. I like to think I bring that out in you."

"You bring out a lot of things in me." I reach further into the safe before pulling out an old school manila folder with a thick rubber band around it. After where I've been and what I've seen, especially in astral form, I can't help but feel like I'm in the twilight zone.

"Retro," Axel remarks.

He's not the only one who thinks so.

I lug the file over to the desk, then stack the newspapers from the last time I was here and move them to the far corner. I slide the rubber band off of the file and carefully open the folder. At first, I'm not entirely sure what I'm looking at, until I come across a boarding pass to Switzerland with my mother's name on it.

"What in the—?" I whisper to myself as I thumb through the rest of the file: a flight itinerary, timestamped photos of my mother *in* Switzerland, a handwritten note to my father, and a jewelry box tagged with my name on the front of it.

I lay everything out in front of me in the order I'd found it. The flight itinerary is dated for May, right before my twelfth birthday. The photos appear to have been sent with the letter, and they're all of my mother in front of iconic landmarks in Europe—Lake Geneva, The Matterhorn, Oberhofen Castle, Saint Germain Church, Chateau de Chillon, Chapel Bridge . . . and they're all timestamped between April and June of 2011.

I take the envelope that contains the letter in my hands, knowing exactly what I'm about to uncover: the truth. I'd expect nothing less with Axel by my side.

"My father had nothing to do with my mother's disappearance," I murmur.

"Read it," he urges.

I pull the letter out of the envelope and carefully unfold it, reading each and every line of my mother's beautiful calligraphy. When I finish, Axel is floating in front of the desk, studying my every move. A long silence ensues, but he doesn't push or press. Just patiently waits.

"He's had the proof," I say in disbelief. "All this time, he's had physical *proof* that he had nothing to do with my mother's disappearance—yet he's just sat there, *rotting*, in jail." I shake my head, unable to process the swarm of emotions.

"Were those the answers you were looking for?"

I consider his question. "Yes. And no. Truthfully, this just raises even more." I look around at the study. "I wonder if this was her study or if it's my father's."

Axel doesn't comment on my last remark. Instead, he's staring at the one thing I haven't yet opened: a small purple jewelry box.

I'm about to open it when I feel the outline of a strange pocket on the back of the folder. Of all the manila folders I've ever seen, I've never known one to have a pocket like this. Whatever's inside is thick, rectangular, and feels oddly familiar . . . I turn the folder upside down and shake it until the mystery item falls out. A chill runs down my spine as I pick up the white laminated badge.

My *mother's* university badge. ID #8251.

The same code my father had given me.

But what's even more chilling is the department my mother was in. One I'm all too familiar with. *Astrophysics at University of Colorado Boulder.* "My mother was a . . . professor?"

Axel frowns. "You say that as if you didn't know."

"I didn't," I say. "Or if I did, I don't remember."

But it would make sense—her disappearance, that is. She'd left for Switzerland (with no return flight, based on her itinerary), and sent my father the very evidence he'd need to prove his innocence. And yet, he hadn't used it. That's the most confusing, not to mention *frustrating*, part. Why had he chosen to reveal this *now*? To wait this long to get this information to me? To allow my hatred to grow and fester for over two decades?

There has to be a reason.

Tears prick my eyes as I open the purple box to reveal a beautiful crescent moon necklace that's outlined with tiny emeralds, no larger than my thumbnail. I unclasp it and pull both ends out of the box, admiring the craftsmanship. Just as I'm looping it around my neck, it dawns on me that Axel has been unusually quiet. I look up from the desk. His somber expression stills me.

"First you tell me to open the safe, and now you look as though you didn't want me to find any of this."

"Not at all," he replies, his tone mellow. "I'm glad you did."

"Your face says otherwise."

He doesn't try to force a smile. He doesn't try to be anything other than what he already is. "Here," he says, floating toward me, "let me help you with that."

I try to stop him, but I can't. My hand passes right through him. "What aren't you telling me? And why today?"

He sighs, taking both ends of the necklace from me. "Because the veil between worlds is at its thinnest today. It'll all make sense soon enough. I promise. You couldn't see me then how you see me now; but you'll get the chance to do for us what we've done for you. After all, that's what this lifetime is for." He's speaking faster now, and I have so many questions, but the moment the moon falls flush against my skin, I feel a rush of heat spread throughout my chest. Axel's breath is hot on my ear as he whispers, "There is light to be seen here yet. Carry that with you. Without form—"

Without regret.

That sentence, from open mic night, goes unfinished as everything begins to fade—his voice, his presence, his essence, *him.* The papers, the jewelry box, the desk, the walls, the chair. The cabin, the forest, the sky, *life.* A sensation I know all too well grips me.

Falling, falling, falling.

But there's a difference this time. I feel . . . alone. More alone than I've ever felt before. I don't feel Xero. I don't feel Axel. I don't feel *connected.* I almost feel . . .

Forgotten.

I shudder at the realization as a gray cyclone begins to form around me. Still falling, still traveling through space and time, but doing so completely unattached. No tether. No cord. No way to pull myself back through.

No, wherever I'm headed this time, it's for the long haul.

It only takes a moment, one just slightly altered compared to the last, to cease the feeling of falling. To bring me upright, as if I were sitting again. To present, in all its technicolor glory, every memory of my life, played back in real time . . . and all at the *same time.* There are no intervals of separation. No "this came before this". No superiority or inferiority. No comparison. Just a reel . . .

A reel of it *all.*

And not only are hundreds of thousands of memories playing back all at once, but I'm able to see them all. Hear them all. Witness them all. Feel them all . . . all over again.

It's a nonstop tidal wave . . .

To feel everything at once is like plunging into an icy river in the middle of winter moments after a steaming hot bath. The contrast is undeniable; the duality so profound, you wonder how it's even possible to occur simultaneously, in one single moment.

I'm on the verge of bursting when, suddenly, I'm thrust into a familiar landscape. My sense of connection returns as I emerge from a silver pool of liquid, with countless waterfalls and boulders dancing around me.

Marking me.

Protecting me.

I realize that I'm even further into the Pleiades now than I ever was before. A glance behind me tells me that much. The first time around, I'd been on the edge; but *now* I'm in the thick of it—and I'm not alone.

It isn't Axel.

It isn't Xero.

Which leaves only one person it could be. My spectral hand reaches for the pendant that's dangling at my neck. As if it were a calling card, my mother materializes out of nowhere.

I breathe a sigh of welcome relief. *Finally.*

44

"ELARA."

Hearing her say my name again is so surreal, I can only choke out the word I haven't said in what feels like a lifetime. The word I haven't spoken out loud at birthdays or holidays. The word I was never able to say whenever I felt like calling "home" while away at college. So many occasions missed. So many memories never made.

"Mom."

She's just as radiant as I remember, but even more so, seeing as we're in astral form. Her hair is still a beautiful wavy blonde, just like mine—and hasn't been touched in the slightest by age. Her eyes are a darker blue than mine, a shade of cobalt . . . ones that always seemed to hold the secrets of the night sky itself. That shade of cobalt is the exact one I'd ombréd into my hair all those years ago.

Her porcelain skin is dotted with light freckles over her nose, which accentuate her already defined cheekbones and pale pink lips. But the feature that sets her (and me) apart from most blondes? Perfectly arched, luxuriously full, chestnut eyebrows. Not once did I ever question their design. The kids at my school may have whispered and stared, especially the girls, who plucked and plucked until all that remained were mere lines—but I'd never cared.

Her eyebrows had been her favorite physical feature, and so they became mine, too. How lucky I'd felt to share something of hers that I could witness and look at every single day. After she'd disappeared, I used to spend hours just staring into the mirror—staring into my own sea of blue, framed by the very thing society told me was "too much". As I'm sure Alice would agree, I'd never wanted to lose my *muchness*. And so, I'd made it my mission not to.

Funny how life can make you forget.

My mother draws closer, her hands covering her mouth. "Look at you. I've waited what feels like eons to see you." She waves a hand in the air, as if to correct herself. "That isn't to say I haven't checked in on you from here—I most certainly have. But it's different being in your presence like this . . . in your true form."

I can feel myself beaming as her love pours into the very depths of my soul. "I can't believe I'm finally seeing you, *speaking* to you." I stop, hoping that this isn't just a lucid dream. "This is real, right?"

"Does it *feel* real?"

Tears prick my eyes as I nod. "When Xero told me he saw you . . . contacted you . . . I was so angry. Jealous. Hurt. I didn't understand why you'd choose to see him and not me."

"It was, more or less, a crash course in discernment. If I'd come to visit you in your dreams, or even on the astral plane, at *any* point in your timeline except for this one . . . well, to put it lightly, it could have changed the course of everything."

"Chaos theory."

"You remember."

"How could I not?" I laugh. "Every story you ever read to me ended in a giant question mark."

"That it did. And while those stories didn't exactly satisfy the 'fairy tale' status quo, they *did* cause you to ask questions. Lots of them."

"And for that, I thank you." I smile. "To be a student of life, for life. That's what you taught me."

"That's all you ever really needed to know." She winks. "Come. We have much to discuss."

I begin to walk—er, glide—alongside her, marveling at the beautiful platinum structures floating in our midst. "I couldn't see these when I first came here," I say. "Just the waterfalls, the streams, and the boulders."

"The Pleiades has much to offer. And seeing as it's all curated at soul-level, every individual has its own unique experience."

I stop in my tracks. "So, do you mean to say that what I'm seeing . . . *isn't* what you're seeing?"

"That's right. Seeing as it's all energy to begin with, it just takes the form of whatever and however the individual perceives it—however, I *can* tap into your consciousness on a visual level, just as you can tap into mine."

"So what are *you* seeing?"

"I'll show you."

She turns to face me, her eyes locking on mine, before slowly traveling to the space right in between my eyebrows—my third eye. I watch as her gaze softens and her face relaxes, all tension leaving her body. She almost looks frozen in time, like an idyllic watercolor painting that's somehow managed to capture the undeniable serenity and stillness of a moment undisturbed. A small pulse begins to build in and around my third eye, climbing up my forehead and around my skull, until the very top of my head is tingling. It feels natural to close my eyes, so I do.

When I open them, I'm utterly convinced that I'm not in the same place I started. I *cannot* be. Instead of being surrounded by metallics and silvers, waterfalls and floating boulders, I'm in . . . a garden. But it's not just any garden. It's as if every nature setting ever recorded—myth, legend, or otherwise—decided to take its best pieces and join together into one stunning landscape. Avalon, Lemuria, Atlantis, The Garden of Eden, Shangri-La, The Elysian Fields . . . all merged together into one harmonious entity. I can feel its heartbeat, its pulse—a glowing reminder of the life within it and around it.

"This . . . this is what you see?"

"Astounding, isn't it?"

"I never thought so many pieces of so many different cultures, of so many different *times*, could come together to create something as beautiful as this."

"Well, that's just it. They all exist, right here, right now. As one."

"Time is but an illusion." I murmur the exact phrase Xero had used. *If that were true, why does it feel like a lifetime since I've seen him? Felt him? Him and Axel?* My shoulders sag at the thought.

My mother glides in front of me, starting on the seemingly infinite path ahead.

"Where does it lead?"

Even though I can't see it, I can feel her smile. "All the places you've been. And all the places you have yet to go."

Speaking in riddles. She's much like Xero and Axel in that way. I know that, technically, they're only one entity, but I can't help but distinguish between the two. My heart bangs against my chest, like metal on metal. *Stop torturing yourself. Stop ruining the one moment you've hoped for your entire life.*

"I sense your struggle." She turns and lowers her eyes at me. "It's okay. Very human of you. We can't possibly understand what we haven't been through ourselves." The last sentence lingers on her lips. "I felt the same way about your father."

All thought of Xero and Axel vanishes as I realize where the conversation is headed. We're deep into the garden now, and I'm not sure how we got this far, seeing as we'd stopped all movement during our conversation. I try to find a rational explanation, but logic won't serve me here. That I already know intrinsically.

"I knew when I was presented with the choice what I'd ultimately choose," my mother continues, a small smile gracing her lips. "I'd already chosen *long* before that moment. But remembering? Well, that can take a lifetime."

"What choice?"

There's a glint in her eyes as she answers, "The one your professors made. The one you're about to make right now."

There's something about the way she says it that causes my breath to catch in my throat. I look down at my astral body, then at her. I speak the first thought that comes to mind. "Did I . . . die? Am I *dead?*"

She angles her head. "To them, it may feel that way; but for those who *know,* we're never really gone—"

"Am I no longer alive in my human form?" I clarify.

"That's a difficult question to answer, Elara. We are always alive, although we may choose to leave the form we've taken. But our very essence always remains."

I'm pretty sure that's confirmation of "being dead" in human speak.

"My dear girl, you've entered The Rift, much like I did when you were just eleven years old. And, if I had known, if I had *remembered* the path to which I'd been ascribed, I would have held you so much tighter, would have read you so many more stories, would have told you, over and over again, just how much I love you . . ."

Her words hit me hard as the meaning sinks in. "You *chose* to leave?"

"A choice made long before you called me mother and I called you daughter. A choice older than the stars themselves."

The truth begins to stir within me, like a storm just outside a cracked window. It begins to seep in, little by little, filling the dark spots . . . the light spots, too. She left my father. She left me. She left our family. To come *here*. "To do *what*?" I ask, suddenly feeling very unsteady.

"To help guide those who struggle to guide themselves. To lift those who have fallen. To help them remember, just as I have. Just as *you* now are."

Her words drift around me like falling snow. "I'm . . ."

"More than just human, yes."

"But how much more?"

She considers this, searching for the words I'll best understand. "You're an Ascension Guide, so to speak."

"The Pleiades," I say. "This place . . . is my home?"

She nods. "One of many. But it's where you were ascribed this particular soul mission, for this particular realm—for this . . . *version* of Earth."

I want what she's saying to make sense, but it doesn't. To me, an Ascension Guide sounds like someone who has their shit together. Someone who made a massive difference in the world—like someone who cured deadly diseases, accomplished world peace, or solved world hunger. Big picture stuff. Not someone who broke off her engagement with her fiancé, endured a miscarriage, lost her ex-fiancé to a car crash (*and hardly grieved either*), consistently struggled to make ends meet, got fired from multiple jobs, excommunicated her father for years for something he didn't do, and blamed everyone and everything but herself for the way her life turned out—a.k.a. *me*.

"How could anyone possibly want *me* as their guide?"

I don't realize I've spoken the words out loud until my mother counters with, "How could they not?"

And with those four words, I feel myself break—or perhaps piece myself back together, I'm not sure which.

"You've nearly completed your karmic cycle, Elara, which is all any soul can hope to do. To not repeat that which they've already been through. It was all for a reason. It's all *always* for a reason."

Tears slide down my cheeks. The pain, the trauma. The guilt, the shame, the suffering. The emotional torture of the human experience at times . . . was all designed.

Was all something *I* chose.

Was all something Axel had helped me recognize.

"You chose love, Elara. Over and over and over again. Even when it didn't always feel like it. You chose love when you unbound yourself from a commitment you couldn't see through."

My ex-fiancé.

"You chose love when you guided yourself through the birth experience in a dimension beyond your own."

My miscarriage.

"You chose love when you answered the one call you swore you'd never take."

My father's.

"You chose love, even when it felt like you shouldn't. Even when it felt like those you loved betrayed you and abandoned you."

Xero.

"You chose love when you acknowledged the darkest shadows of the one you held so dear."

Axel.

"You chose that which you truly are, at your core, over and over again, without fail."

Love.

"That *is* the lesson. The only one that matters across all lifetimes, across all realms, across all dimensions." She pauses, sensing the recognition in me. The flicker of deep knowing in my eyes. "You remember."

I don't bother wiping the freefall of tears that are currently streaming down my face. I don't hold in my sob, nor do I hide or cower. I don't feel embarrassment or shame or guilt. I just *feel*—and it is the most liberating thing I've ever experienced.

My mother wraps her arms around me before pressing a gentle kiss atop my head. "Welcome home."

45

THE RIFT IS unlike anything I ever could have imagined or dreamed of. I'd deem it wholly impossible if I weren't here *experiencing it* for myself.

The way my mother's explained it to me, The Rift is a sort of meeting point, a middle ground. What humans have twisted as "limbo" is actually the most peaceful and serene pocket of space and time to ever exist. It's more of a "checkpoint" than a "judgment", a *how're you doing?* versus a *here's where you're going*.

I like it here. I'd prefer not to leave. I've spent what feels like years with my mother, catching up and making up for lost "time". If I had known an opportunity like this existed, I probably wouldn't have spent so many of my former years angry, depressed, and cynical. If I had held space for *this possibility*—seeing as that's what all things really are anyway—perhaps I would have experienced things differently. But I'm not going to dwell. That would defeat the purpose.

I'm resting atop one of the boulders, listening to the metallic stream sing, when I feel her approaching. I look to my left. My mother gives me a warm smile as she takes her place next to me.

"I could feel you pulsing from across the cosmic bay."

Which is Pleiadian speak for, I can tell you have a lot on your mind.

"I suppose I do." I know I'm about to walk the next part of my path. I know I can't stay here forever. I know that this has been but a brief moment in time—a mere blip in the ever-expanding universal timeline. And I know that questions are the livelihood of that expansion. I didn't expect to have them all answered at once . . . or at all, actually. But I still feel like I'm missing something.

"Before I embark on this path of *Ascension Guide*," I start, the words feeling only slightly less foreign on my tongue, "is there a chance I could . . . go back?"

"Back where?"

I at once catch the confusion lining my question. *Because time is but an illusion.* "To Earth," I clarify. "How much, uh, *time* has passed there?"

"Well, I'm not speaking in exact terms, but mere minutes. Why? Why do you want to go back?"

"For a lot of reasons. Namely because my father does not deserve to be behind bars. Because I want to tell him that I was wrong and that he was right. That I forgive him." I choke on my words. "That I love him."

"He knows," my mother whispers. Her tone is so confident, so reassuring, that it immediately puts me at ease. "And believe it or not, *he* chose that path."

The words break from my chest in a half laugh, half sob. "I have a hard time believing that."

"It was his karmic cycle. His soul contract. To give *time* for *love*." Starlight dances in her eyes. "Who are we to intervene?"

"Who indeed." I manage to laugh. "Although . . . *I* had someone intervene." It takes everything in me to say his name without shattering. "Axel. Xero. I don't know which name to call him by."

She chuckles. "That's because 'intervening' doesn't apply to your Ascension Guide."

I don't know how it's *just now* that I'm finally putting two and two together. Here I am, thinking that my mother was the one to fill that role when, all along, it'd been him.

Which makes me wonder . . .

"Is he here, too?" I can hear the excitement in my voice, the buildup of energy given the slightest possibility.

"I'm here by design. He, I'm afraid, is not."

"So, I'll probably never see him again." What a ruthless realization. To never again see the person who'd taught me how to love. *What kind of shitty karma is that?*

My mother just smiles. And therein lies the answer.

"Although," I say, decoding her grin, "I never thought I'd see *you* again—yet here we are."

She nods. "The Universe is full of surprises, Elara. But in order to experience them fully, we must trust in our choices."

"Like the choice that brought you here."

"And the one that brought you here," she echoes.

"I'm not going to remember this, will I?"

"Not in the way you'd expect. But you will . . . in *other* ways. It'll be a feeling."

"A feeling," I whisper.

What is life but not a culmination of feelings?

46

MY EYES ONLY close for a moment, but when they open, I'm no longer surrounded by beautiful waterfalls and my mother's soothing presence. Instead, I'm shrouded in darkness. Not *scary* darkness. But a void. A microchasm. A tear in the fabric of space and time.

My eyes close again but, this time, they open to a giant platform that spans the length of an entire planet. It's brighter here, but it's as if a net has been cast over my vision. Soft. Hazy. A bit scattered.

I make my way onto the platform ahead of me, immediately feeling drawn to the raised pit in the center. Whenever I used to think of a pit, I used to think of something concave, like a crater, but this is nothing like that. It appears stationary at first, but as I draw closer, I can see the ever fluid, ever changing motion going on inside of it. It's as if everyone on planet Earth had boarded the same train at the same time, then exited at different intervals. Some decide to get back on, some change their minds, and some leave with the knowledge that this *is* their final stop.

When I reach the edge, it feels like I'm peering into a house of mirrors. Light bending, images reverting, sounds echoing. It's all around me. I haven't even stepped into the pit and yet, here I am. It's more like the pit's stepped into me.

Time whizzes by me in a flash, as do the memories of every experience every recorded. The creation of the stars, the planets, the galaxies; the seeding of life, light, and love; the terror, the war, the destruction as darkness reigns; the Annunaki and the Lyrans, the Lemurians and the Atlanteans, the first civilizations; Gaia in all her realities, with all her dimensions, all her inhabitants: the dinosaurs, Neanderthals, Babylonians, Egyptians, Shang Dynasty, Greeks, Romans, Vikings, Mayans, Olmecs, Incans, Aztecs, and beyond . . .

I know exactly what this is. The Akashic Records.

The library of souls.

An archive of every event, every timeline, every reality—and every soul that ever has been and ever will be. To Akasha, I am not Elara Friis. I am not Elara Wells. I am not the daughter of Seth Wells and Adeline Richards. I am not blonde or Caucasian or American or an "adult". I'm not rich or poor, smart or dumb, healthy or ill, funny or boring. For these are all just expressions. False identities. A byproduct of something a flawed society cultivated, nurtured, and valued.

To Akasha, I am love. An expression of the most powerful energy in this Universe. And as love is a choice, it is always free to choose. We are so free, in fact, that many use their freedom to choose bondage.

It's in this very moment that I understand *why* I changed my last name. Why I chose Friis, pronounced *free*. It was only another hint, another clue, of this pure expression. A fragment of a brighter light whose only purpose was to guide me home. To right here. To this very moment.

To *remember.*

Akasha whirls around me, enveloping me in the most magnificent display of white light. I am completely immersed in the library of souls, witnessing everything and nothing as it all occurs in real time.

In *the now.*

My senses heighten as it begins to slow, then stops altogether, although it hasn't *really* stopped. Expansion waits for no entity, no soul, no being. But it seems to have paused, just for me, in this exact moment.

And it's then I *see* it, *feel* it—the next soul journey I'm walking into. It feels familiar, yet foreign. Close, yet far. Exciting, yet equally terrifying.

I prepare to close my eyes, sending my sincere thanks to Akasha, knowing that the next time I open them, I won't be *here,* but somewhere else entirely . . .

47

AT FIRST, WHEN I come to, I think I must be dreaming. That Akasha must have spit me out back where I'd started. But that recognition right there—of Akasha—tells me that I hadn't been dreaming. That this is real. And that I'm exactly where I'm meant to be.

Which just so happens to be in the study at the cabin—my *family's* cabin—although it does look a bit different. The papers from the manila folder aren't on the desk, which is how I'd left them. The safe is still there, but it's not propped open, as I'd left it. The desk is made of pure wood instead of glass and plastic and whatever unnatural manufacturing products humankind uses. And the walls seem wider, the ceiling taller, everything *softer*.

I look to the mirror that's hanging on the wall just by the door and nearly jump out of my skin—if I *had* any, that is. I can't see myself. I'm completely invisible. I don't know how that's possible when I can see and hear and *feel* the smooth coolness of the very glass that sits beneath my palm . . . but I am wholly concealed. Entirely hidden from this world, wherever and *whatever* it is.

I start down the hallway, stopping at a room that feels familiar, but I can't place how or why. The door creaks as I push it open. The lights are off. The bed is made. The skylight above is covered by an even darker shade of glass, obscuring the view. And there's a thick layer of dust on the nightstand, the dresser, the inside handle of the door.

I lower my head and close it, trying to place *why* it has this kind of effect on me. Why it makes me feel so . . . *sad*. A strange longing overtakes me, but I decide to keep moving, to figure out what I'm doing here and exactly where I am. And then . . .

Laughter erupts from downstairs.

I don't know why I wasn't expecting anyone to be here—but I wasn't. I walk along the hallway to the landing of the stairs before peeking over the railing. The back of a golden head of hair faces me as a child claps his hands. He's no more than six or seven. "Again! Tell it again!" he squeals.

I step farther down the stairs, nearly tumbling down the rest when I get a look at who's sitting across from the boy. Shaggy russet hair. Storm-gray eyes. A soft gaze with that accentuated jawline that only highlights his knowing smile. It's Xero, fully integrated with his shadow, Axel.

The dam bursts open as the memories come flooding in, surrounding me with all things Xero, with all things Axel. Xero's compassion, his kindness, his sweet, yet sensual nature; the embodiment of all things light. Axel's rawness, his vulnerability, his complete and utter acceptance; the transmutation of all things dark. The very essence of duality, all rolled into one. *Into love.*

My hands fly over my mouth as I try to hold in a guttural sob. Tears line my eyes, my cheeks, my chin, as I take in the sight of him. As every feeling I've ever felt washes over me.

I'm watching the interaction between him and this young boy when the questions come flying in. *Can he see me? Can they see me? Does he remember? Where are we?*

I catch a glimpse out the window, my mouth dropping at the view. It's Earth-like, but there are some major differences. For one, the pine trees outside are thicker, *fuller*, with pinecones the size of my head. The sky is the most surreal shade of blue, unmarred by pollution, waste, or toxins. And the sounds . . . no machinery, no *external* noise besides nature's coalescing soundtrack.

Out of the corner of my eye, I catch something that *looks* like a solar panel in the window, but I can tell it does much more than just power this cabin—it harnesses energy for the entire block, the entire state. This *is* Earth, but it certainly isn't the Earth I'd experienced.

I grip the wooden banister as I continue my descent, trying to figure out whether or not Xero can see me. When his eyes don't move as I move, I'm more than disheartened. I walk to the side of the table where they're both sitting. While I could see Xero from the staircase, I couldn't see the boy—only the back of his head.

I sit in the empty chair between them, first looking at Xero. It feels like it's been so long since I've been this close to him, and now that I know what I know, I want to memorize every line, every inch, every feature—but the boy's voice draws me away as he says, "Please, Dad? Just one more time?"

Dad.

My gaze finally settles on the boy. The first thing I notice are his eyes. One is hazel, rimmed with a deep gray. And the other . . . is a liquid amber.

Like molten copper.

I suck in a breath as the memory takes me over.

In the doctor's office.

Engaged, pregnant, and alone.

Waiting. For the results of that ultrasound.

No heartbeat. *There's no heartbeat,* he says.

A miscarriage. 1 in 8 women . . .

And then, nine months later, in the bathtub.

The contractions. The short bursts. The pain.

The accelerated breathing.

The impossible realization of going into labor.

That almighty, unmistakable push.

This boy . . . is my son.

And the soul of my father . . . inhabits my son.

"Dad?" he says again.

I turn to look at Xero. His *father.*

Which would mean my ex . . . had been Xero?

No . . .

It had been *Axel.*

Axel, who could *choose* his human form.

Axel, who had shown trepidation around cars because he'd *died* in a crash, in said form.

Axel, who I'd bared my shadows to in a different relationship entirely.

Axel, who had held space for me—*all* of me.

Axel, who had been Xero's missing link to full integration.

And my missing link as well.

I recall the last thing he'd said to me before clasping that pendant around my neck. *You couldn't see me then how you see me now; but you'll get the chance to do for us what we've done for you.*

But where am I? I'm here. I'm here. *I'm here!*

I'm caught somewhere between utter despair and absolute joy as I'm taken back to that night in the bathtub. I *knew* I'd given birth. I'd *felt* it happen, even if it hadn't been on *my* Earth, in *my* reality. I knew it'd happened somewhere else. It'd happened here, in this new Earth, this alternate reality. This parallel version of life.

The life I only could have *wished* to have.

But where am I?

This is my son. Xero is his father.

I must be the mother. *I must be.*

I scan the area behind me, catching holograms of still shots—also known as "photographs" back in my day.

I can't help but notice that there's one image that doesn't disappear like the others. I get up to examine it further . . . the image I never expected to see, not in this lifetime or any other. Me, holding a bundle of blankets, beaming, the last image of me ever taken—and to the right, my obituary.

Cause of death? Car crash. Flipped into a ditch.

Oh, the irony.

Oh, the *karma.*

Slowly, I turn back toward the table. Back toward my *family.* I'm walking over to them when what Xero says stops me cold in my tracks.

"Seth Axel Friis, what did I tell you about begging?"

I smile through my tears at the sound of the name.

Another integration—not just two, but *three.*

"It's not begging if there's a question," the boy answers.

Such an Axel thing to say. I laugh.

"What else do you want to know about her?"

My eyes flick to Xero. *They're talking about me.*

"How you know she's here!" He squeals as he throws his hands up in the air, and that's when I see it. On his wrist.

His mark.

My mark.

Our mark.

Once again, I sit in the chair between them, watching Xero's face. Studying him and that playful expression. The way his mouth rigs to the side just before he speaks.

"Well, she visits from time to time. And when she does, you can't always see her . . . but you can *feel* her more than anything else."

The sentiment has me near tears.

I'm here, I say, trying to communicate down our line, the way he had for me. *I'm here.*

"But sometimes," Xero says, his eyes still fixed on Seth, "when I look up at the night sky, beyond the stars and shadows, I see her." He points to his wrist. "Right here."

"Cool," Seth coos.

Xero smiles. "Very cool, indeed."

The moment is so special, so heartwarming, that I want to capture it and carry it with me for the rest of eternity. More than anything, I want him to know that I'm here. So I try again. And I'll try as many times as it takes.

Because he would do it for me.

He *had* done it for me.

On my eighth attempt, Xero straightens, a flicker of recognition darting across his eyes. And in that moment, I swear, he's looking right at me. And whether he can see me or not, it doesn't matter. Because, once again, he's found a way to give me the only thing I've ever wanted.

The feeling of being wholly and irrevocably *seen.*

Just as I am.

Just as *you* are.

ACKNOWLEDGMENTS

The idea for this book was a slow-burning one, and, while it's gone through *many* revisions, its essence remains the same: our divine oneness and interconnectedness. There is so much more than meets the eye during this existence, and to bring that to life in these pages lit me up in a way words can't even begin to express. While this book is listed under the "metaphysical fiction" category, it's also nonfiction for me in so many ways. I gave many of these characters fragments of myself, my journey, and my experiences on purpose. Not only was I writing about divine oneness, but I was also sharing my own personal experiences of this universal law through the eyes of these characters. How's that for "blurring the lines"?

I've thought a lot about writing these acknowledgments and, to be honest, it's challenging. This book was born in the middle of a global pandemic. It was birthed out of complete isolation, in quarantine. I didn't talk about it with anyone . . . I just wrote. I wrote because it was the only thing that made sense to me at the time. I wrote because I *needed* to share, in some way, my own integration of my darkest shadows. I wrote because I couldn't ignore the soul whisper any longer. I wrote solely for the expression of a metaphysical concept that became so clear to me that I couldn't *not* write about it. I couldn't not *share* it. That's the origin story of *Beyond the Stars and Shadows*.

And so, my acknowledgments for this book are quite short. I'd like to thank this Universal pause for all that it has taught me. I'd like to thank the artists over at Damonza for their incredible work on this cover (still over the moon about it). I'd like to thank Denali and Lacy for being the best fur companions I could ask for. And thank you to my readers, for supporting me over the last 6 years (wow!).

Lastly, I'd like to thank Source Energy, the Universe, the Divine Spirit. Forging my spiritual path is the reason this book exists in the first place. I am in absolute awe at the guidance and synchronicities I experience every single day, and I feel so honored to be able to live, speak, and embody my truth unapologetically. Thank you.

Kristen Martin is the International Amazon Bestselling Indie Author of the YA science fiction trilogy, THE ALPHA DRIVE, the YA dark fantasy series, SHADOW CROWN, standalone novel BEYOND THE STARS AND SHADOWS, and personal development books, BE YOUR OWN #GOALS and SOULFLOW. A writing coach and creative entrepreneur, Kristen is also an avid YouTuber with hundreds of videos offering writing advice and inspiration for aspiring authors everywhere.

STAY CONNECTED:
www.kristenmartinbooks.com
www.youtube.com/authorkristenmartinbooks
www.facebook.com/authorkristenmartin
Instagram @authorkristenmartin

9 781736 158548